A SECOND CHANCE

"I love you, Charlie. What I need to know is, do you still love me?"

She wanted to tell him she did—that in fact she'd never stopped loving him, but something stopped her.

Charlie hedged, then finally said, "I care about you a lot, Devin."

Devin's lips heated the side of her face. "Now who's being evasive? Do you still love me?" He didn't give her time to answer but covered her mouth with tiny kisses.

His kisses left her unable to concentrate, much less respond. Little jolts of electricity ricocheted through her body, leaving her tingling all over. Rational thought disappeared.

When she came up for breath, she said the first thing that popped into her head. "I've never stopped caring about you, Devin."

Devin sighed his frustration. His index finger outlined her lips. "I suppose I have to accept that answer for now. I'll just have to show you how deeply you're loved."

LOOK FOR THESE ARABESQUE ROMANCES

Remembrance

Marcia King-Gamble

Pinnacle Books
Kensington Publishing Corp.
http://www.arabesquebooks.com

PINNACLE BOOKS are published by

Kensington Publishing Corp.
850 Third Avenue
New York, NY 10022

Pinnacle and the P logo Reg. U.S. Pat. & TM Off.

First Printing: April, 1998
10 9 8 7 6 5 4 3 2 1

Printed in the United States of America

Acknowledgments

This book is devoted to my own "Devin" who supported me through this process and never stopped believing in me. To my aunt, who from the very beginning recognized my love of the written word and encouraged me to fulfill my calling. Special thanks to the members of my critique group: Shirley, Marlene, Sharon and Felicia for keeping me on track. You all made my dream become reality.

One

"ARE YOU THE CHARLIE CANFIELD, MY SUITE-MATE FROM MOUNT MERRIMACK COLLEGE?"

The words screamed across Charlotte Canfield's computer, surprising her. The Internet was supposed to grant virtual anonymity. Now she'd been exposed.

Straightening the papers on her desk, Charlie bought time. She darted a furtive glance around the small office shared with coworker Ellis Greene, the popular Hot 101 radio host. Thank God, no one else was around. She'd just given in to curiosity, surfed the net, and under People Connection found Mount Merrimack, Reunion Class of '80. It had been too much to pass up.

Memories of the small liberal arts college in upstate New York flooded her mind as she clicked the mouse again, bringing up the message that had intrigued her.

"Class of '80. Join your freshman mates aboard a fun-filled Caribbean Cruise on *The Machination*. Ready to party? Contact Kimba."

She'd need to know more. She'd held on to that mouse, clicked on to Add Message, and typed in, "Give me the details."

The surprising inquiry had immediately come back. "Charlie?" So much for using the screen name, Chaz. It hadn't proved to be much of a disguise, not if this Kimba knew her.

Charlie searched her memory. Kimba would have to be Kimberly Morgan. She hadn't seen the ex-*Playboy* bunny in years, although they still kept in touch via the annual Christmas card.

Carefully Charlie typed in her response. Anyone with access to a computer would be able to read what she had written. She was a fiercely private person, and only a handful of people knew of her whereabouts: basically close friends and family. She was no longer the "Charlie," Kimberly Morgan would have remembered. She'd changed.

"Are you still in Virginia?" she typed then clicked Send.

"No, I moved to Long Branch, New Jersey."

"Are you in the book?"

"Yes, I'm listed."

"I'll call you," she added before signing off.

At that precise moment, Reginald Barker, Hot 101's production assistant, stuck his head through the door. "You're on in ten minutes," he reminded.

"Thanks, Reg."

Charlie turned her attention to the mirror. Even though it was radio, she was always conscious of her appearance. If you looked good, you sounded even better, her mentor, Agnes Wilkins, had once told her. She'd never forgotten the advice. She ran a brush through tight brown curls, framing a copper-colored face, outlined her lips in sienna, and smiled at her reflection. Not bad for thirty-seven years old.

She entered the studio and found Ellis Greene waiting. He turned his slicked back head in her direction and eyed her up and down. "Yo, lady. My, are you turned out today. New man?"

Charlie fixed him with a frosty stare. The two hosted the successful talk show, *He Said, She Said*. Outside of that they were hardly friends. Ellis, despite a wife and three kids, was a notorious womanizer. She hated men like that. She used to be married to one.

"Today's topic should be pretty hot," Charlie said smoothly, ignoring Ellis's lascivious looks. Taking the seat next to him, she quickly became absorbed in her script.

"You can say that again." Glancing at his own sheaf of papers, Ellis read out loud: " 'Is the professional black woman deserting the homies for whiter pastures?' I wonder who came up with this genius idea." He looked up. "Give this five minutes and, honey, this station's going to be cooking."

Charlie snapped on her headphones and focused her attention on Reginald's countdown.

"Five. Four. Three. Two. One. Show time," he mouthed.

Exactly on cue, Ellis's rumbling baritone opened the broadcast. "I want to welcome you to another hour of *He said . . .*"

"*She said . . .*" Charlie filled in.

"Tonight's topic is just going to blow your mind."

They were off and running. And as predicted, in less than five minutes every line lit up.

Nearing the end of the hour, Charlie felt exhausted but triumphant. The controversial topic had been her idea, and she was confident the ratings had soared.

"We've got time for one more call," she said in the voice that had earned her her share of fan mail. "Then we're going to have to wrap this show up till tomorrow. Same time, same place."

Charlie picked up the line. A familiar voice, one she hadn't heard in at least two weeks, growled, "Hey, sweet thang, you're my fantasy, my reason for living, I just love that cute—" Charlie hit the kill switch, cutting off the call. Thank God for the few seconds granted between receipt and live transmission. Her audience would not have heard the overzealous fan. She signaled frantically for Reginald to go to commercial.

Ellis arched an eyebrow. "That old beau never gives up. Isn't it about time you reported him to the police?"

Charlie reached into her pocketbook and found a tissue. She patted away the moisture on her upper lip. Sounding more confident than she felt, she responded, "What am I supposed to tell the police—that some old crank caller gets his jollies from propositioning me on the air?"

Ellis slid out of his chair. "Suit yourself. But what if the guy's dangerous? He gets more disgusting with each call. You really should be more discriminating about the men you sleep with and discard."

Charlie bit back an angry retort. Why allow Ellis to goad her? He'd said pretty much the same things to her as the pervert, except that he'd couched it differently. He was just a pig who wore crocodile shoes.

"Come on, fine thang, I'll walk you to your car."

She was tempted to decline. But truth be known, the call had shaken her up badly—and it was late. More and more she'd gotten the sneaking suspicion that the crank caller was someone she knew. But who? Even her ex-husband, Tarik Connors, wouldn't stoop that low. Charlie forced her lips to smile.

"Thanks, I'll take you up on the offer, Sir Galahad."

Charlie picked up the satchel-shaped pocketbook she always carried, and checked to make sure her cellular phone was inside. She swung the strap over her shoulder.

"Looks like you could use a little help, Ms. Canfield." Sam, the doorman, hurried to Charlie's side. Charlie clutched the small grocery bag tighter. She smiled into Sam's twinkling brown eyes. "Thanks, but I think I can handle this one. You're a love, though."

Her doorman seemed crestfallen but backed off. "Night, Ms. Canfield." He held the door wide, letting in the crisp spring air.

"Night." Charlie fluttered her fingers.

Thanks to some wonderful investments paying off, she'd

been able to move to Croton-On-Hudson, a picturesque village on the banks of the Hudson River. The town attracted an eclectic assortment of residents. Artsy folks co-existed alongside wealthy business types, and she'd been immediately made to feel at home.

Charlie's thoughts returned to her doorman. Sam had been hired shortly after she'd moved into the luxury high-rise. From the beginning he'd offered his help, even hanging her bookshelves. She'd tried to pay him a little something, but he'd been adamant about not accepting money. She'd finally baked him a cake.

Upstairs, in her tenth-floor apartment, Charlie kicked off her trademark high heels and flexed tired arches. In what had become a nightly routine, she pinched her inner arm, still not quite believing she'd moved up. Not that there was anything wrong with her hometown, Mount Vernon, with its predominantly middle- to upper-middle-class population. She'd just fancied herself on the water. Finding the deluxe high-rise with its panoramic river view had fulfilled that dream.

Deciding she could use a drink, Charlie plopped her pocketbook on the coffee table, padded to the refrigerator, and poured a generous glass of wine. She set it down on a nearby table and sprawled out on the couch.

Through half-closed lids, she focused on the room's tasteful decor. From the cream-colored damask couch to the hand-carved Nubian ladies, all had been chosen with such loving care. She sipped slowly. Hell, she was still wide awake. Was it too late to call Kim?

The long hand of the grandfather clock rested on the half hour. Eleven thirty wasn't that late. Then again she was the proverbial night owl, and so was Kim, from what she could remember. Kim, having successfully negotiated her fourth divorce, lived alone, or so she'd said in her last Christmas card.

Charlie picked up the phone and dialed. A too cheerful

operator supplied Kim's number. Charlie punched out the digits. What in the hell was Kimberly Morgan-Smith-Goldberg-Daniels-Rosellini-Morgan doing in New Jersey?

A feline voice purred into the receiver on the third ring, "Hello."

"Tell me I'm not calling too late, old friend."

"Charlie! Charlie Canfield! God, it's been ages."

"At least ten." Charlie chuckled. Same old Kim, the purr hadn't changed one bit. The last time she'd seen Kim was when she'd been the *Playboy* Pet of the Month. Had the buxom jet-skinned beauty aged?

"Say it ain't so. Time does fly."

"Tell me," Charlie interjected before Kim got going. "How did you know it was me on the web?"

This time it was Kim's turn to chuckle. "Shoot, girl, couldn't you come up with a better screen name than Chaz? I knew all the guys on campus. I didn't go out with no Charles."

Charlie had almost forgotten but not quite. Kim had sampled most of the meager male population. She'd stolen more than her share of Charlie's men. Even Devin Spencer had succumbed. Why, after all these years, did it still rankle?

"Hey, Charlie, you still there, girl?"

"I'm here." Charlie stretched out on the couch, sipped her wine, and wiggled a toe.

"So you coming to the reunion or what?"

"In case you forgot, I didn't graduate with the class."

"So?"

"So I'm not invited." Charlie smothered a smile when she heard Kim suck her teeth. Even that habit hadn't died.

"Don't gimme that nonsense, girl. The gang would love to see you. Come as my date if that's an issue."

The thought of seeing old friends was irresistible. Charlie dug into her pocketbook for a pen and uncapped it.

"All right, give me the lowdown."

Kim fired off the details. Charlie scribbled. "Who's coming?"

"Everyone and his mother. We've chartered half the ship. The travel agent's kissing my toes and counting her commission."

God, it really was tempting. She was due for vacation— needed one. Still . . . what if she ran into her ex, Tarik? She wouldn't put it past the louse to show up. Worse, what if she ran into Devin?

Kim jabbered on. "Lisa's coming. She's single again and loving every moment of it. And Onika promised to let me know tomorrow. Girl, she's a pediatrician now, never been married, but still fine—"

Charlie cut her off. "How about you? What the hell are you doing in Jersey?"

"Running a dating service."

"What!"

Kim chuckled, a low throaty sound. "It's perfectly legal, girl. No funny stuff. Haven't you heard how difficult it is for professional black women to meet professional black men? No, you wouldn't know, not with your bad self. Anyway I aim to make it that much easier. That's why I created Coffee Mates."

Kim, an entrepreneur? Who would have thought. On reflection, it wasn't that surprising. "Why Long Branch?"

"Hey, the Central Jersey shore's a happening place. Long Branch's got a big African American population. Besides, I like the beach. So tell me, you coming with us or what?"

Charlie was sorely tempted. Kim, Lisa, Onika, and her together again. The foursome had shared a three-bedroom suite in the only co-ed building on campus. Though she'd been forced to leave Mount Merrimack at the end of her freshman year, she still cherished bittersweet memories.

"Let me get back to you," Charlie said, setting her glass on the coffee table.

"Don't wait too long. Space is filling up. I've got only half a dozen cabins left. Love ya, girl."

Charlie hung up to Kim's raucous laughter. She set the receiver down and the phone rang again. A glance at her watch confirmed it was way after midnight. She usually didn't entertain calls at that hour. Still she had to pick up—what if something had happened to Kasey?

She crossed the fingers of both hands, then reached over to answer. It better be good, or she'd give the unwelcome intruder an uncensored piece of her mind.

"Hi, sweet thang."

Charlie froze. Him again! How had he gotten her unlisted number? She clenched her jaw to control her chattering teeth.

"I have dreams about you . . ." the man's gravelly voice continued. "You're lying next to me—"

Charlie slammed down the phone, covered her mouth, and raced for the bathroom.

Five minutes later she emerged, holding a damp towel to her forehead. She'd lost what little dinner she'd choked down. But the time had come to do something about the pervert. First she'd have her number changed, then she'd take that cruise. Her nerves deserved a break.

Two

"Your documents, please."

Charlie smiled at the perky, blond cruise line representative and handed over her ticket and passport.

"Is this your first time vacationing with us, Ms. Canfield?"

Charlie simply nodded. Her gaze took in the bustling activity in the Miami terminal, where groups of chattering travelers jockeyed to keep a place in line.

The agent eyed Charlie's ringless left hand and enthused, "You'll love our product. Now be sure to go to the singles parties. There's always one or two good men to be found. Have a great trip." She winked.

Charlie followed her fellow passengers through the security checkpoint. Smiling broadly, she adjusted her wide-brimmed straw hat, struck a pose, and let the photographer capture her on film. Literally thousands of people milled around. How come she didn't recognize a soul? Ignoring a group of paunchy, gaping men, she continued on.

It had been eighteen years since she'd seen any of these people. Eighteen years seemed eons ago. Naturally they were bound to change and not necessarily for the better. Look at her, for example. Freshman year she'd been the timid one, the one with metallic braces and wall-to-wall zits. As she'd gotten older, she'd grown more confident, but she'd never forgotten what it was like to get hurt.

Charlie still remembered her first day at Mount Merri-mack. She'd walked into her assigned suite and damn near died. It had been plain old Charlie Canfield's luck to be matched up with three of the best-looking women the col-lege had recruited. The first to introduce herself had been Lisa Williams, a petite coffee-skinned beauty with a wild mane of hair and the personality of bubbling brown sugar. She'd then shaken the hand of Onika Hamilton, a half-African/half-British combination of classic good looks and subtle sex appeal. Her café-au-lait complexion, cluster of freckles, and amazing brain had kept the men drooling all that year. Then she'd met Kim—Kimberly Morgan, who became her best friend and worse nightmare. Statuesque Kim, who in her stocking feet fell short of six feet by only half an inch, whose bra size was a smidgeon short of a thirty-eight D, and whom all the men desired and ulti-mately had. But that was such a long time ago.

Where was the threesome? Charlie wondered. They'd promised to meet her in the atrium, right in front of the Information Desk where she now stood. She could hardly wait to see them and catch up on the gossip. It would be like old times, all four sharing a suite again.

"Can I help you find your cabin?" A white-gloved stew-ard handed Charlie a deck plan. She accepted the map of the ship, gave it a cursory glance, then put it away. Smiling, she declined the steward's offer. "Thanks, maybe later. I'm waiting for my friends."

"Perhaps you might be more comfortable over there." One white-gloved finger pointed to a spot where a couple lounged on gray leather sofas in front of a silent TV.

"I promised I'd wait right here—"

"Charlotte! I mean, Charlie, is that you?"

Charlie's head swiveled. While time had mellowed the voice, she would recognize that clipped British accent any-where. "Onika! My God, you're every bit as beautiful as I remember." She hurried to embrace the striking woman, who still hid behind heavy horn-rimmed glasses.

Onika set down the bulging leather knapsack she'd swung over one shoulder. "Thank you. You were always very kind. But, Charlotte, pardon me for saying this, you've aged remarkably well. You're hardly the little mouse I remember. You've blossomed."

Charlie knew no slight was intended—that was just Onika's way. She smoothed down her crumpled linen walking shorts and settled the brim of her hat over one eye. "We all have to grow up some time."

"Charlie! Niki! I can't believe it." Turning, they saw Lisa Williams and an unfamiliar man hurrying toward them.

Not much about Lisa's appearance had changed. Judging by the billowy white gauze dress Lisa wore, she still shopped the flea markets and thrift shops. But today's version looked cleaner and a lot more expensive. The wild mane of hair had been twisted into a knot at the top of her head and secured with a silver implement that looked vaguely like a chopstick.

Lisa lowered harlequin sunglasses. "It's so good to see my favorite buddies. Where's Kim?" Dutifully she pecked them on the cheek then pushed her companion forward. "You remember Fred?"

Charlie didn't but smiled anyway.

Fred's eyes never left Onika's face. He ran a hand across a balding pate. "You, I remember from my biology class. How could I forget that awesome combination of brains and beauty?" The puzzled frown Fred threw in Charlie's direction indicated she wasn't the faintest memory.

Onika clasped Fred's hand. "Well, well, well. Fred Willis, isn't it? My competition. You were always top of the class, although I did try to oust you. Tell me, are you traveling alone, or is there a Mrs. Willis lurking in the distance?"

Fred looked as if he'd swallowed something unpleasant.

He smoothed his pate and supplied, "Lucky for me, there no longer is a Mrs. Willis."

"Hey, girlfriends!" The shout came from above. All four looked up and finally found the source. True to form, Kimberly Morgan-Smith-Goldberg-Daniels-Rosellini-Morgan was surrounded by men. Even now Kim's elaborately braided head peeked over the shoulder of a man so amazingly handsome, he made movie star Denzel Washington look like Godzilla. Rendered speechless, Charlie's lips formed into an *O*. Oh, God! Devin Spencer!

Time and place ceased to exist. Charlie no longer saw Kim. She'd been transported to a balmy spring day at Mount Merrimack. She'd sat next to that same man on a rolling green lawn, enjoying his kisses. Back then he was only a boy, barely nineteen and as gorgeous as ever. Plain old Charlie Canfield, zits and all, had snared Mount Merrimack's most eligible jock.

"I'm coming down. Don't move," Kim shouted.

Charlie watched Kim fly down the winding brass staircase, Devin Spencer in her wake. Was their affair still going strong after all these years?

"Uum-uum-uum, girlfriends!" Kim purred when she was only feet away. "Looks like we still got it going on." She embraced all four simultaneously and nodded to Fred.

"Damn, where are my manners?" Kim extricated herself from the girls' bear hug. "Look who I found in the terminal." She reached out a hand and tugged Devin forward.

Even after all those years, Charlie tensed up. Devin had always had that effect on her—one look into those soulful gray eyes of his, and every limb turned to rubber. How could it be happening again after all this time?

Mesmerized, she watched him turn on that brilliant Colgate smile she remembered so well, and shake his head. In a voice designed to produce shivers, he said, "Niki Hamilton, you're more beautiful than ever." He squeezed the hand Onika held out. "And Lisa. Lisa Williams, it is still

Williams?" He eyed Lisa's unadorned left hand. "Why, you haven't changed a bit. If I didn't know better, I'd swear you were just seventeen."

Charlie saw Lisa's head snap up. Her friend narrowed her eyes but seemed to enjoy the flattery. "I see you can still dish it out, Devin Spencer."

Could he ever. He'd sold her some bill of goods then walked out of her life with not even a backward glance. Before Devin could greet her, Charlie turned to Fred, still hovering, and began an animated conversation about nothing.

"Charlie Canfield!" Devin exclaimed, planting himself between them. "What a wonderful surprise. I never expected to see you here. Not after you damn near broke my heart when you ran off with my roommate." He clutched his chest and pretended to stagger.

Talk about revising history! What nerve! He'd actually made the comment with a straight face. Run off with his roommate, indeed! He'd been the one to leave her in the lurch. Tarik Connors, the rat, had only bailed her out.

Out in the open was no place to have this conversation. For the benefit of the people around her, Charlie forced herself to smile. "It's been a long time, Devin."

"Too long." He held on to the hand she offered and stared into her eyes.

Kim's voice broke the spell. "Hey, girlfriend, we better go check out that suite of ours. Guys, we'll see you at the cocktail party. Promenade Deck, six o'clock sharp. It's semiformal—hope you guys brought jackets."

Later that evening, after the ship had sailed, Charlie stood before the full-length mirror with a brush in hand. Lisa and Onika, anxious to see old classmates, had gone off to Happy Hour, leaving Charlie and Kim behind.

Kim, busy inventorying a pile of clothing on the queen-sized bed, discarded one sexy outfit for another and stood with arms akimbo.

"Yo, girlfriend, how about this one?" She held up a slinky creation that reminded Charlie of a flapper.

Charlie, who'd played fashion consultant for the last hour, forced herself to be objective. She eyed the hot red number then nodded. "Yeah, that'll do. It's not too fancy and not exactly casual. It's in between."

Kim, clad only in a scanty red bikini brief, slithered into the tight silk dress, then twirled about. Layer after layer of swaying fringe moved with her. "Well, do I look hot or what?"

"You're sizzling. Did you forget to tell me something?"

Kim feigned innocence then tossed beaded braids. "Hell, I'm the hostess. I'm the person who put this thing together. I gotta look dynamite." She pushed a braid out of the way and continued. "There's a man I'm after."

So it was still going on after all this time: Kim and Devin Spencer. Charlie felt a twinge of regret but pulled herself together. What she and Devin shared ended a long time ago. He'd hurt her badly, and she'd never quite recovered.

"Well, aren't you going to ask who I'm after?" Kim took the brush from Charlie and placed it on the dresser. "Girl, we gotta do something with you. You got any mousse?"

Charlie found a jar on the cluttered dresser top and handed it over. "I already know his identity, if that's what you're after. No need to rub it in."

Kim scooped a healthy glob of gooey stuff onto her palms, rubbed them together, and smoothed them through Charlie's curls. She set the record straight. "Chile, puh-lease. I don't want Devin Spencer. I done had him, and he wasn't that good in bed. Ooops . . ." Her voice trailed off. Sounding contrite, she continued. "You of all people should know that he don't make the earth quake."

Charlie remained silent, though she privately disagreed. Even now she could still remember Devin Spencer's lovemaking—and what lovemaking it had been. That lovemaking had gotten her pregnant.

As if reading Charlie's mind, Kim changed the topic. "I never did ask how Kasey's doing." She added another dollop of mousse to Charlie's scalp.

Trying hard to conceal her emotions, Charlie adjusted the double strand of pearls at her neck, then flicked an imaginary piece of lint off the simple black minidress. "Actually my baby's doing real well. I'm proud of her. She's a freshman at Mount Merrimack, and she made the dean's list last semester. Tarik, that lying dog, keeps telling everyone she's still in high school. He hates having an eighteen-year-old daughter, says it makes him look old."

Kim sculptured another of Charlie's curls in place, then suddenly became serious. "Tarik's on board, Charlie."

"What!"

"He was practically one of the first people to pay. I couldn't not take his money."

"Why did you wait until now to tell me?"

Kim handed Charlie a tube of sienna lipstick. " 'Cause if I did, you'd find an excuse not to come. It's the same reason I didn't tell you Devin Spencer was coming."

Fifteen minutes later Charlie and Kim entered the Mango Lounge to standing room only. They had just crossed the threshold when a waiter outfitted in crisp white jacket and gloves, bearing a silver tray, approached. "Ladies, would you care for champagne?"

Before the waiter could move on, Kim smiled her Ms. Black America smile, swiped two glasses, and handed one to Charlie. Charlie gratefully gulped down the bubbly. She was jittery as all hell and would need more than one glass to deal with Devin Spencer and Tarik Connors. One man was bad enough but together? Well . . . the ship wasn't big enough.

"Do you recognize any of these people?" Charlie whispered.

"Hell, yes. But tell you the truth, none of them look so hot. Be cool—we'll hang out for a while and see who comes by."

They didn't have long to wait. Fred sailed in like the *QE2*, in what could only be one of the ship's rented tuxedos. His hangdog expression seemed to indicate the evening was not going as planned. Running a hand over his bald spot, he scanned the room before giving Kim and Charlie a kiss. All the while his eyes roamed the distant horizon.

"Ladies, you're the hottest things on board," he said, turning to check out the rest of the lounge. "Hey, aren't you missing people? Where's the lovely Onika . . . and Lisa?"

Kim made a sweeping gesture with long red nails. "They're here somewhere. Why don't you go hunt them down and bring them over. We'll be right here."

Fred's eyes lit up. "Good idea. I'll be back in a moment."

Stifling a giggle, Charlie watched him part the crowd in search of his prize, Onika.

A woman dressed in a sequined version of a captain's outfit approached and saluted. Her shrill scream caught the attention of those in earshot. "Kimberly Morgan! Why, honey, you haven't changed a bit. You look every bit as good as you did in that *Playboy* spread."

Charlie waited for the explosion. Kim hated to be reminded of her bunny days. What's more, behind the woman's loud words was a definite putdown. The fringe shook as Kim's chest thrust forward. A tight smile emerged. She grabbed the newcomer's ample shoulders and aimed a kiss into the air. Her eyes focused on the name tag they'd all been forced to wear. "Bessie Collins," she crooned, holding her companion at arm's length. "Why, you haven't changed a bit. You still scoffing down that fried chicken and grits by the bucketful?"

Charlie moved away from the scene so that she could chuckle unobserved. As she made her way through the crowd, she bumped into Lisa deep in conversation with a man in a blue double-breasted jacket. Reluctant to interrupt, Charlie nodded a greeting and attempted to sidle by.

"Where do you think you're going?" Lisa called, tugging on the hem of Charlie's black dress.

Charlie waved her half-empty flute. "To freshen my drink."

"Wait one minute, I'd like to introduce you to Oliver." Lisa's fingers were adorned with the silver rings she'd designed and made famous. Her nails had been painted a fashionable shade of blue. They matched exactly her flowing silk caftan. She gestured to the distinguished man standing beside her.

Charlie took the hand the man offered. "Hi, I'm Charlie Canfield. Have we met before?"

"Oliver Stanton. No, I don't believe we have." He smiled warmly, his eyes caressing her face. "I would have remembered—"

Lisa quickly interrupted. "Dr. Stanton is Jennifer Stanton's brother. She took your place in our suite sophomore year. Jennifer's around someplace. I'm sure you two will eventually meet. Where's Kim?"

Charlie pointed vaguely at a spot in the crowded room. "Some place back there." Realizing from Oliver Stanton's fawnlike gaze that he was more than a little interested in her, she decided it was time to move on. He'd have his hands full with Lisa.

Charlie drained her glass and jutted her chin in the direction of the bar. "Anyone need a refill?"

"No, thanks," both said in unison.

Offer declined, Charlie excused herself. Looking neither right or left, she wove her way through the crowd in search of a drink. She would need another if she were to run into Tarik—or even worse, Devin Spencer.

She'd just pushed her ex-boyfriend's image out of mind when he materialized. Devin wore cream-colored slacks, gray blazer, and cream-and-gray-striped tie. He stood, feet slightly apart, blocking her progress. His voice was deeper than she remembered.

"Can I get you something?" He pointed to her empty glass.

Charlie called upon everything she'd learned in broadcast school to get her through. "Hi, Devin," she ground out. "Actually I was just going to get myself a drink. Would you like one?" She waved her empty glass.

Instead of answering, he took her elbow and propelled her along. Amazing, but even after all those years that slight contact made her shiver. On their way out to the covered deck, Devin lifted two glasses from a passing waiter.

Surreptitiously Charlie glanced at the man beside her. The years had made Devin's terra-cotta skin darken into a deep bronze. She would hazard a guess he no longer lived in Boston.

Outside Charlie watched couples of every age head for the early dinner seating. Devin had already found a vacant table, set down the glasses, and stood holding out a chair. When Charlie hesitated, he motioned for her to sit. Rather than make a scene, she complied.

Devin's gray eyes lingered a little too long on the black dress Charlie had labeled tasteful. His gaze moved upward to settle in the hollow of her neck, right in the place he used to kiss. He sipped his wine, cleared his throat, and drank in his fill. Lifting his glass to toast, he broke the silence. "Why, little Charlie Canfield, you've grown into one stunning woman."

Charlie wanted to say, "And you've grown into the man I'd always known you would be: drop-dead gorgeous." Instead she smiled tightly and said, "Thanks, that's nice of you to say that, but you were always a charmer."

"I've always meant every word. This isn't the first time

I've told you you were beautiful." His wide smile made two dimples appear.

Since when had he become so smooth? Charlie's stomach knotted into a double loop. She couldn't say a word if she'd wanted to.

Devin's voice brought her back to earth. "So what you been up to?"

Charlie took a long sip of champagne and bought time. Finally she answered, "A little of this and a little of that."

Devin's index finger outlined her lips. "From what I hear, a lot of this and a lot of that. You did all right for yourself, girl. Tarik tells me you're a radio talk show host."

Try as she might, she could no longer keep her face blank. "I didn't know you two were still in touch."

This time Devin's smile revealed only one dimple. "Don't tell me you didn't know we patched things up right after you divorced? It's funny how time somehow has a way of making you forget how badly you've been hurt. Though we're not exactly friends, Tarik and I are in the same business, so it's hard to remain enemies. Besides, nursing a grudge has never been my style."

At a loss for words, Charlie stared into his soft gray eyes. What she saw in their depths forced her to look away. Had time also made Devin forget the reality of the situation? It hadn't been her choice to break up—he was the one who'd dumped her. That summer they'd gone their separate ways, she to a job in her hometown, Mount Vernon, New York, and Devin, to life-guarding in Cape Cod. Of course he'd promised to call and write, but that never happened. At the end of that summer, when her pregnancy had been confirmed, she'd been left with little choice but to marry Tarik Connors.

"Ms. Canfield?"

Charlie's head snapped up. She nodded, surprised that the waiter already knew her name. Must be the name tag, she decided.

"Ms. Canfield, I've been asked to give you this." The man turned over an expensive-looking cream envelope with a burgundy seal and moved off.

Devin's slender fingers tapped the flap. "Don't tell me I already have competition?"

Despite her resolve not to let him goad her, Charlie countered, "You have to be in the game to compete. It's too late Devin—eighteen years too late."

Devin twirled the liquid in his glass then set it down. "Ouch. I guess I deserve that. Would it help any if I told you that I left you several messages that summer? Your father kept telling me you'd get back to me. When you didn't, I flooded the post office with letters. Girl, I must have written you at least fifty. And even after those same letters came back with a big old red stamp, 'Address Unknown,' I figured we'd patch things up when we got back to school. But you never came back. By then you'd married Tarik."

Charlie didn't want to believe him. It was all a lie, an outrageous fabrication. Face to face, what else could he say? She ripped open the envelope and made a great production of unfolding the paper. Little red hearts descended like confetti, covering her short black dress and sticking to her hose. The majority had been cut in two. Charlie's lips moved, silently echoing the words on the paper.

"Sweet thang, you better not make me jealous. I've waited a long time to have you. Don't go give it to someone else, or Daddy's going to get real mad."

"Oh, God, *no!* He's followed me." The words slipped out before Charlie could stop them. She threw the crumpled note as far away from her as she could, then tossed down the remaining liquid in her glass. Never had she imagined the pervert would be on board this ship.

Three

"Who, Charlie? Who's followed you?"

Devin's words finally penetrated the haze. He scooted his chair alongside hers, claimed her hand and squeezed, imploring her to answer.

"It's a long story. I hardly know where to start."

"Try starting from the beginning. I have all the time in the world."

Charlie knew Devin would not give up until she'd told him the whole sordid tale. Her hands shook as she toyed with the stem of her glass and finally came to a decision. Why not tell Devin? It had been six months and five days since the pervert had entered her life. With the exception of her co-host, Ellis Greene, no one else knew of his existence.

Devin's hands kneaded her shoulders. "This isn't a good place to talk. Let's go to my stateroom. I'll order a couple of glasses of wine, and you can tell me about this man who's after you." He made it sound as if the pervert was an ardent admirer.

"I wish it was that simple."

"Love . . . lust, whatever you want to call it, never is. You can tell me the whole story"—he glanced at his watch—"in exactly fifteen minutes. That should give us enough time to place a call to room service."

Devin's fingers circled the nape of Charlie's neck. She

wanted to close her eyes and erase all that had gone bad between them. She longed to tell him that they'd had a girl, a beautiful teenager who resembled him. If only it were that easy. God, she'd missed his touch—missed wanting him so badly it created a physical ache. He'd always made her feel safe. That had been the problem. She'd trusted him.

Moving out of the public eye wasn't such a bad idea. She knew there was no underlying motive to Devin's invitation—deviousness had never been his style. Charlie drained the contents of her glass and took the hand Devin offered.

Devin's suite was one deck above Charlie's. When she hesitated at the door, he shooed her in. "You're perfectly safe with me, Charlie Canfield," he said, holding open the door. Safe? Why did her heart say otherwise? She entered a poshly appointed suite, crossed over to the sitting area, and perched on the edge of the striped couch. Devin was already on the phone.

After Devin hung up, he came to sit beside Charlie. He stretched long legs, loosened his tie, and threw an arm around the back of the sofa. "Good, that's done. Our wine should be here in a few minutes."

Charlie was painfully conscious of the man sitting beside her. Disconcerted, she looked around for evidence of a roommate. There were no visible signs of excess luggage, not even the odd pair of shoes peeking from under a chair.

"I booked a single," Devin said, answering the unspoken question. "I've never done well with roommates. You can speak freely."

Charlie thought about the one hundred and fifty percent surcharge the cruise line tacked on for the privilege of being alone. How could Devin afford it? She certainly couldn't. "You must be doing awfully well," she said. "I'm sharing a suite with Lisa, Kim, and Niki, and it still wasn't cheap."

Devin's two dimples emerged. He ran long fingers through cropped curls at the base of his neck. Choosing his words carefully, he answered, "I've got a lot to be thankful for. After years of hard work, I finally have my own advertising firm. There were some lean times, but thank God we held on to our major accounts. Now business keeps getting better and better. God willing"—he crossed his fingers—"I should be able to retire by age forty-five."

That had always been Devin's dream, and he was only seven years away from his goal. She wondered if he still planned on devoting time to inner-city kids with learning disabilities. He'd told her at least a hundred times that if he ever made enough money, a large portion of it would go to underprivileged kids with a true desire to learn. Either way it was nice to know that his fantasy would soon become a reality. But who was "we"? Did "we" mean that there was a Mrs. Spencer somewhere in the picture? She'd once heard something about him getting married.

Devin continued. "Harry Campbell, my partner and best friend, is ten years older and incredibly brilliant. He's become the brother I never had. That man's seen me through some rough years: the death of my mother, the collapse of my marriage. If it hadn't been for good old Harry, I would be in a nuthouse by now."

Charlie doubted that. The Devin she remembered had been a together person, far more emotionally stable than most. That could have changed, but she didn't think so. Even at nineteen he'd been levelheaded and a far cry from the stereotypical dumb jock. Devin had been a straight-A student, and according to Tarik, had gone on to get his Master's in business.

"Tell me, Charlie, who is this man you can't seem to shake?" Devin's question brought her back to the present.

Charlie's fingers drummed her kneecap. "It's not what you think. The guy's sick."

Devin smiled indulgently, "So the guy has a crush on you. Aren't you being a wee bit harsh?"

"Not at all. By sick, I mean he's perverted. He started calling the radio station about six months ago. At first he seemed harmless; he'd just ask me out on a date. But over the months he's grown bolder. Now he calls and says the most disgusting things. One of the reasons I came on this cruise was to get away from him. I can't believe he's followed me here—" There was a catch in Charlie's voice when she broke off.

Devin's fingers stroked her shoulders. "Have you reported him to the police? He could be dangerous."

"It wasn't as if he was threatening my life or anything. But after tonight . . . well . . . you saw those hearts falling out of the envelope. They were snipped in two, Devin. What kind of animal would want to ruin my vacation?"

His stroking fingers increased their intensity. "Is that what that was? I wondered about it. You're right—he's not playing with a full deck. We'll have to do something about him."

A knock at the door ended the conversation.

"Who is it?" Devin yelled.

"Room service."

"I'll be with you in a minute."

Before rising, he cupped Charlie's chin in the hollow of his palm. Gray eyes, so much like their daughter, Kasey's, locked with golden-brown. Devin smiled reassuringly. "Together we'll get to the bottom of this mess, Charlie Canfield. You'll see. We'll uncover the slime."

Kim's raised voice echoed through the crowded dining room when Charlie entered on Devin's arm. "Hey, girl-friend, I been looking all over for you. See, even saved you a seat." Kim patted the seat next to her and winked. "I guess you won't be needing it."

Heads swiveled in the direction of the newcomers, speculative glances thrown their way. Out of the corner of her eye, Charlie spotted Tarik. Deliberately she looked away.

Devin's fingers traced a pattern over Charlie's hand. He flashed the Mount Merrimack crowd a perfect Colgate smile and hissed, "From the way your ex is gaping, I'd say he fancies you as the entree. Let me handle this. I'll slip the maître d' a little something, and have him locate a table for two."

"Thanks. That would be great. I'm really not up to dealing with Tarik right now."

Devin squeezed the tips of Charlie's fingers. "Not to worry. I wouldn't even let him get close. I know he can be a regular charmer when he wants to be, but more often than not he's a pain in the butt. He's already called my room half a dozen times and left at least two dozen messages at the Information Desk."

"What do you think he wants?" Charlie asked. "He must want something." In college Tarik had wanted whatever Devin possessed. He'd always been envious of him.

"I'm in the process of negotiating with one of the larger cruise lines. It's a huge piece of business. That's what brought me to Florida in the first place. If I know Tarik, he got wind of it and wants a piece of the action, if not the whole."

"That's typical."

The conversation ceased. They'd come to the maître d's podium. Charlie wondered how different her life would have been had she married Devin. Wishful thinking. What's done was done. Luckily her marriage to Tarik had been mercifully brief. It had served one purpose—her child had been given a name. Love had never been a part of the equation. Even from the beginning he'd cheated, and she'd been quite glad to be rid of him.

Charlie watched Devin and the maître d' shake hands. To the casual observer it would appear just a friendly greeting. Charlie knew better.

There was bounce to the little man's step as Devin and Charlie followed him to a remote section of the dining room. A smile, brighter than any Christmas tree, lit up his face as he gestured toward a table only large enough to accommodate two. Pushing the fronds of an oversized potted palm aside, he waited for Devin's nod of approval. "Will this do?"

"It'll do perfectly, George." Again the two shook hands.

This must be costing Devin a fortune, Charlie thought. The maître d' moved on. Charlie eased into the chair Devin held and allowed him to scoot her closer to the table.

"The payoff was worth it. We've got the best seat in the house," Devin whispered. He sank into the chair across from her and opened his menu.

Nodding, Charlie agreed. The location of their table was perfect, affording them some semblance of privacy, and at the same time allowing them the opportunity to observe their fellow diners unobtrusively.

"Have you run into anyone you remember?" Charlie asked, after giving the menu a quick glance.

"As a matter of fact I haven't. Except for you girls and a handful of guys I played football with, there aren't many people I recognize." Devin signaled to the sommelier hovering in the background.

"What made you decide to come?"

The wine steward's appearance halted the conversation. He stood with pad and pen poised ready to take their order.

Devin's eyes glittered. His two dimples were prominent. Lowering his head, he scrutinized the wine list then said,

"I'll answer the question in a minute. It's been eighteen years since we've had dinner together. How about we celebrate with something special: Perrier Jouet?"

Charlie's lower jaw fell. Apparently a lot had changed with Devin. Perrier Jouet was a far cry from Boones Farm. During the time they'd been together, it was the only wine they could afford. Way back then the drinking age in New York State had been eighteen. It seemed a lifetime ago.

"An excellent choice," the sommelier confirmed, breaking into Charlie's musings. Before she could protest, he departed to fill Devin's order.

With the wine steward out of sight, Devin picked up the conversation where it left off. He reached across the table and captured Charlie's hand. "Now to answer your question."

"What question?"

"You asked me why I'd come."

For something to do, Charlie sipped on her water. "Oh, yes. Why did you come?"

Devin crumbled a bread stick between slender fingers and seemed to think about it. "Curiosity, I guess, plus my business trip just happened to coincide with the cruise. As you get older and wiser, staying in touch with friends becomes more important. It probably has to do with the mortality thing. Hell, I'm growing all philosophical on you, talking around the issue. The truth is, I hoped you'd be here."

Devin's admission came as a shock. Most likely he was just feeding her a line; still she was flattered. Charlie fingered the double strand of pearls she wore like worry beads. What could she say? Devin obviously expected some kind of response.

"Sir, madam, your champagne is here." The sommelier returned bearing a silver bucket with the wine and holding two glasses. He set his booty down, expertly popped the cork on the bottle, and poured a small amount of bubbly into Devin's glass. Devin sipped. Satisfied that the right noises were made, the steward departed.

"Well, Charlie, why did you come?" Devin filled Charlie's glass.

She couldn't avoid the issue. Devin's direct question deserved a direct answer. Looking up, she gazed into his piercing gray eyes then looked away. Devin passed over her glass. Accidentally his fingers brushed the back of her hand. Charlie shivered.

"Are you cold?" Devin was halfway out of his jacket.

"No, I'm fine. I just didn't expect the champagne to be so chilled."

They clinked glasses and drank.

"I came," Charlie began, "because it was a great opportunity to see the girls again, because I needed a vacation, because the pervert was really getting to me . . . and because . . . well, because"—she took another sip of wine—"Mount Merrimack has a special place in my heart."

"Did I have anything to do with that?"

Charlie kept her face purposefully blank. She twirled the stem of her glass, refusing to answer.

Devin continued, his voice a little above a whisper. "Charlie, you're not the only person with fond memories of the college. Mount Merrimack is a place I'll never forget. We fell in love there, remember? If there's a chance—"

"What are you having?" Charlie interrupted, setting her glass aside and feigning interest in the menu. Had she heard right? Did Devin really expect them to pick up where they'd left off? If so, he really had a set.

"Please don't change the topic."

"Devin . . ."

"So this is where the two of you been hiding."

Looking up, Charlie didn't even try to hide her disdain. Tarik had obviously had one two many drinks. She could tell by his swagger. "What do you want, Tarik?" she spat. "You're disturbing my dinner."

Tarik's chocolate-colored face wore the look of a man used to getting his own way. "You, sweet thang. It's always been you."

Charlie froze. *Sweet thang?* Since when had Tarik taken to calling her that? Years ago it had been sweet face, despite the fact she'd told him she hated the endearment. She struggled to keep her voice even. "What could I possibly have to offer you now? Why would you want me after all these years?"

"Don't be like that. Hey, can I sit down?" The last part of the sentence was aimed in Devin's direction.

Devin smiled amiably. "If there was another seat, sure you could. But, brother, this table barely holds two people. And Charlie just doesn't seem to want to share."

Surrendering, Tarik threw both palms in the air and backed off. "Then I guess I'll have to wait until the beach party tomorrow in St. Martin. There ain't no tables for two there. See ya tomorrow, sweet thang."

After he'd left, Charlie accepted the handkerchief Devin offered. With a shaky hand she patted the moisture on her upper lip then quickly drained her glass. Tarik Connors was scum, but she'd never considered he might go to such extremes as disguising his voice. She'd never suspected him.

Four

"St. Mar-tin. Here we come!" Kim picked up the rattan tote bag she'd set down. Twirling around, she announced, "Girls, we ready to rock and roll?"

"In a minute." Onika scanned the room and found the book she'd been reading. "Now I'm ready." She stuffed the novel into her backpack and followed Lisa and Charlie.

Bypassing the elevators the foursome walked down to the Sunshine Lounge, where a crowd had gathered.

Devin waited at the entrance. Charlie focused on his long muscular legs and slowly worked her way upward. Her breath caught in her throat as she took in his casual attire.

Khaki walking shorts did justice to bronze athletic legs. A beige linen shirt stretched across his broad expanse of chest and remained unbuttoned at the neck, where a slender gold chain nestled.

He'd been dressed in almost the same manner the very first day she'd met him. It had been an unusually warm fall day in late September. She'd been sitting under a shady oak tree, studying for an English literature test. He'd come up to her, flashed that killer smile of his, and politely asked if it was okay to join her. She'd stammered something nonsensical, whipped off her glasses, and quickly buried her nose in her book. But despite her less than enthusiastic

welcome, he'd joined her anyway. She'd never quite figured out what it was he'd seen in her.

Devin touched her arm, returning her to the present.
"Hi, Charlie."

"Hi, Devin." She sensed interested glances thrown their
way; obviously any of a number of women would gladly
trade places with her. For some unexplainable reason
Charlie wanted to throttle these women. Instead she focused on the hint of dark hair that ran from Devin's neck
to . . . and blushed, remembering.

Theirs had been considered an unlikely romance. Devin
Spencer, superjock and intellect extraordinaire, dating
skinny Charlie Canfield, the bookworm? Charlie had been
a too tall girl with a spotty complexion. He'd been the guy
all the women panted over. Yet despite their differences
he'd made her feel like a princess. She in turn had learned
his secret—learned how insecure a young man with dyslexia
could be.

"You look fabulous," Devin whispered. He bent over to
peck her cheek, his wide smile welcoming Kim, Niki, and
Lisa. "Hi, ladies, ready for a day on the beach?"

Kim's bright orange sarong billowed as she stepped forward. "Hey, share some of that sweetness."

Dutifully Devin kissed each girl's cheek then returned to
Charlie's side. "So where is this beach? French or Dutch
side?"

Lisa Williams swept a handful of hair from her face while
fanning her neck with a wide-brimmed straw hat. "The
French side," she supplied. "At least that's what the flier
says. I take it you've been to St. Martin before. Tell me,
are there art galleries worth seeing?"

Devin nodded. "Some are quite exceptional, and for
the most part, the art is unique and typically Caribbean.
Over the years I've acquired several wonderful pieces."

"Gee, I hope we get to see something of Phillipsburg,"

Onika said wistfully. "The shopping's supposed to be wonderful. I'd like to buy some perfume."

Kim's eyes lit up. "I've got a bar at home that needs replenishing. Stick with me, child. We're going to find a duty-free store and shop to our hearts' content."

"Mount Merrimack, Class of '80, can I have your attention?" a voice boomed from inside the lounge.

"Shall we?" Devin offered Charlie his arm. He made a sweeping gesture toward the door.

As they were escorted to vacant seats by the friendly cruise staff, Charlie wondered if the pervert was looking. For some inexplicable reason she felt safe knowing that Devin would claim the adjacent chair. In the past he'd always protected her. He hadn't even allowed her to walk back to the dorm alone.

The plan was for the Class of '80 to spend the day scuba diving and swimming on a private island. Onstage the social host gave the bus and water taxi schedules. Charlie listened to the woman ramble on with half an ear. Devin's proximity was much too distracting. The citrus smell of his expensive cologne assaulted her senses. She could even feel the heat radiating from his skin. And she'd convinced herself she was over him?

The social host introduced the group leader, Kim. Kim, being Kim, welcomed everyone with a hearty, "Now hear this. Today we're going to party." In a matter of minutes, she had the Class of '80 laughing. Then another announcement advised the ship had been cleared by Customs officials. In unison the Class of '80 surged to the front of the room.

Devin's hand cupped the small of Charlie's back. "You smell great," he whispered. They followed the crush of people through huge double doors. But despite Devin's reassuring presence, goose bumps rose on Charlie's arms. She found herself scanning the crowd. Was the pervert among them?

* * *

His ship had finally come in.

Devin winced, reacting to the lousy play on words. Who would have thought after eighteen years of separation, he'd be escorting Charlie Canfield, the love of his life, to a beach party?

He'd adored Charlie with all the passion that a boy of nineteen could summon. He would have done anything for her—even given up college, if only she had asked. He'd trusted her. She'd been the only person on campus who knew about his dyslexia. He'd shown her his vulnerable self—the side of him that the other students never knew existed. Charlie'd been the one who'd held his hand through that first challenging year, staying up till dawn to help with his studies. They'd connected mentally and physically. He'd never forgotten her.

It had been Charlie's coaching that had helped him maintain a straight 4.0 average that year. His parents had been so proud. He'd shown them that years of support and hard work had been worth it. The expensive prep school, specializing in learning disabilities, hadn't been a waste of their hard-earned money after all.

In return he'd given Charlie his heart. Why then had she turned around and married his ex-best friend, Tarik? He would never understand that.

Devin knew Charlie and Tarik had a child together. By rights that child should have been his. But Charlie had given birth to Tarik's baby. A beautiful baby girl, from what he could remember. Years ago Tarik had produced a picture of a sunny-faced toddler with skin the color of warm cinnamon and a smile that lit up the world, just like her mother's. What Devin still couldn't figure out was when Tarik and Charlie had hooked up.

Charlie slanted a smile his way. Devin longed to kiss the soft lips that he knew unfurled like rose petals under pressure. His fingers itched to caress Charlie's bare back where her halter top tied into a bow. He shook his head and struggled to clear the erotic vision of a naked Charlie. His eyes roamed the length of her long, long legs, liking the way the navy walking shorts hugged her hips and clung to her shapely behind. He had to get himself in check. It was too early in their tentative reunion to scare her off. He'd already made one blunder in the dining room. He couldn't afford another. Lucky for him she hadn't bolted.

"Stay cool, man," Devin muttered.

"What was that?" Charlie shot him a look of puzzlement.

"Nothing. Just talking to the guy behind me. I hate all the pushing and shoving. We'll get where we're going eventually, whether we act like Neanderthals or not. Besides, Kim wouldn't let the buses leave without us."

Charlie's laughter tinkled like crystal clinking. "My, you're cranky today."

"Did I just hear my name?" Kim planted herself between Devin and Charlie. She threw both arms around their shoulders. "Share the joke. I could use a good laugh. That Bessie Collins just made me so mad. She's got this idea we should go banana boating, and she wouldn't let it drop. Got a whole group stirred up. Now can you picture Bessie on a banana boat?" Kim guffawed.

Indeed it was hard to visualize a woman of Bessie's size on the inflatable yellow floats shaped like bananas.

"I'm sure you were diplomatic," Devin added, though his lips twitched. Kim wasn't one to be diplomatic if her life depended on it.

Kim chortled. "Hell, no. I told her like it is. I said, 'Bessie, be thankful we don't have any of those fancy joyrides available, or we'd be calling the Coast Guard for you.'"

"You didn't!" Even Charlie was shocked. Kim was usually never that unkind, unless provoked.

"She did, too," Fred interjected, arriving unexpectedly

with Onika in tow. Today a bright red cap covered his bald spot. He smiled warmly at his companion.

"Yup, Fred's my witness." Kim linked an arm through Fred's. Her bobbing chin encouraged him to elaborate.

Self-consciously Fred fingered the bill of his cap and reluctantly told the story. His eyes never left Onika's. "Well, the truth is, Bessie started the whole thing. First she told everyone in earshot that Kim had more husbands than Liz Taylor. That's before she launched into the banana boat thing. I, for one, thought she deserved to be dissed. Doesn't she look beautiful?" he added, referring to Onika.

"You're great for my ego, Fred," Niki responded, settling her prescription sunglasses firmly in place and blushing like crazy.

Charlie barely had time to wonder if the elusive Onika was finally succumbing to Fred's charm. Devin tugged her hand, propelling her forward. "Time to go, love."

She had just enough time to wave goodbye before they were swallowed up by the crowd.

Outdoors big white buses with the tour operator's name emblazoned on the side waited. It appeared that masses of people had turned out to welcome them. Natives with chocolate faces creased into smiles held huge signs welcoming the Class of '80 to the island of St. Martin.

"Shall we find a spot at the back of the bus?" Devin asked, tightening his grip on Charlie's hand.

Nodding, Charlie followed him into the air-conditioned interior.

In a matter of seconds, the bus filled up. Charlie saw Lisa, Niki, and Fred board another bus, Tarik on their heels. She exhaled with relief. At least the bus ride would be relatively peaceful.

The slow journey through downtown Phillipsburg was a blur of crowded sidewalks. Their tour guide explained that time would be allotted for shopping on the return. After

clambering off the bus, they boarded small water taxis.
Devin kept his arm around Charlie's shoulders. While she
felt he was moving too quickly, his presence made her feel
secure.

They found a shady spot on Pinel Island, where Charlie
set down her straw bag. Devin soon loped off to find them
drinks and returned carrying huge coconut husks adorned
with the requisite flower.

"What have we here?" Charlie asked, accepting the exotic concoction and sipping thirstily. "Mmmm. This is
good."

"Dem tell me is rum punch," Devin quipped, affecting
a West Indian accent.

"You do that quite well." Charlie took another sip of
the heady drink then sank onto the towels Devin spread
out.

"Well, what's it to be? Scuba? Snorkeling? Or shall we
just lie here like beached whales and catch up?"

Charlie contemplated the options Devin presented. Anything water-related would mean she'd have to wear a bath-
ing suit. The high-cut red number she'd brought didn't
leave much to the imagination. Wet, it would be even more
revealing. On the other hand, she was dying to see if Devin
still wore those tight little gym shorts that flattered him.
Did he still have the washboard stomach you could bounce
a quarter off? Charlie sighed, envisioning the muscular
physique of the nineteen-year-old Devin.

"Charlie?" Devin's smoky eyes registered amusement.
"You're a million miles away."

"Sorry. I've never been scuba diving, so that's out. And
I'm not up to snorkeling, at least not right now—maybe
after lunch. Why don't we just sit here and talk for a while."

"I'd hoped you'd say that." He smiled at her over his
own exotic flower, then removed the hibiscus and tucked
it behind her ear.

A woman looking vaguely familiar wandered by in an

itsy-bitsy bikini. She held the hand of an overweight man and waved in their direction.

"Ever thought of doing commercials?" Devin asked after acknowledging the couple.

"Can't say I have."

"Remember the Un-Cola man?"

Charlie chortled, envisioning the commercials featuring a large West Indian man, with a distinctive accent and an oversized straw hat. "You're aging yourself," she joked.

"I think of you as the Un-Cola woman," Devin said in a pseudo West Indian accent, sounding more like James Earl Jones than choreographer Geoffrey Holder, the man who'd actually played the part. "You are peddling an exotic fruit juice." He snapped his fingers, getting into it. "Even better, rum. That red suit peeking out of the top of your bag must complement the copper of your skin perfectly. You'd look great in an ad."

Charlie sifted a handful of crystal sand through slender fingers and debated tossing it at him. What a flatterer he was! Ultrasmooth. She doubted he was sincere.

"Don't," Devin said, anticipating her actions.

A second too late he rolled out of the way.

"Now you've done it." He set down his drink, dusted himself off, and slowly shrugged out of his shirt.

In the midst of taking a sip of the potent punch, Charlie paused. She didn't remember Devin's chest being that wide, the muscles of his arms that defined. She sipped on her drink and gazed at him through lowered lids. The smell of coconut oil and ocean was suddenly overpowering. The sun way too hot.

When Devin slipped out of his khaki walking shorts, Charlie took deep breaths. It must be the drink—she was even beginning to sweat. Eyes never leaving his body, she watched him strip down to olive gym shorts. One thing about Devin hadn't changed: his tight little butt.

"Your turn," Devin said, yanking Charlie to her feet and pointing her toward the changing rooms.

Glad to have an excuse to put distance between them, Charlie retrieved the straw bag she'd set down and quickly got lost in the crowd.

When she returned, someone had erected a volleyball net and an enthusiastic game was under way. Lisa and Onika were on opposite teams. Fred of course remained with Niki. Devin sat on the sidelines, deep in conversation with cantankerous Bessie Collins. When he spotted Charlie, his long low whistle made her blush. The old Devin would never have been that bold. The new one she wasn't sure about. He patted the striped towel next to him and beckoned her over. She folded her arms across her breasts, wishing she'd brought a wrap, and quickly walked toward him.

"Hot suit," Devin whispered, drawing her into the circle of his arms. "I like." He planted a kiss on one bare shoulder. Charlie shuddered. Damn! Why was she letting him do that to her?

Bessie's enormous breasts thrust forward. She seemed none too pleased to be upstaged. The fluorescent green one-piece swimsuit she'd squeezed her size twenty-six body into showed symptoms of splitting.

"Hello, Charlotte," she said, her voice dripping with displeasure at the interruption.

Charlie forced herself to smile at the plump little woman. Bessie glared back. Surely she didn't have designs on Devin? And what if she did? A little voice reminded, You don't have dibs on Devin. He's single and free to pursue his own interests. Besides, you're letting lust get in the way. You don't even trust him.

"So I hear you did well for yourself," obnoxious Bessie continued.

Charlie didn't acknowledge the backhanded compliment. She simply smiled and waited for Bessie to go on.

"My brother phoned me yesterday. He tells me you have a successful radio show."

Brother? She barely remembered Bessie Collins, much less a brother.

"Some would say that. Is your brother in the New York area?" Charlie kept her voice even. She waited for the put-down to come. Why couldn't the woman just go away?

"He lives in Hartsdale."

"Ah, that explains why he's familiar with *He Said, She Said.*"

Bessie's eyebrows arched. "I suppose so. God knows, I've never heard of it. Still, he's your biggest fan—gives you all the credit for the show's success."

"That's very kind of him."

Bessie lowered lime green sunglasses and fumbled through the canvas bag she clutched to her middle. "As a matter of fact, just in case you never got his note, he asked me to give you this." She withdrew a cream-colored envelope with a burgundy seal.

Charlie froze.

Devin retrieved the envelope from Bessie's hand and squeezed Charlie's shoulders. To cover the awkward moment, he added, "You're not going to read fan mail from another man while I'm standing here, Charlie." He tucked the expensive envelope into a backpack he'd stowed next to Charlie's bag and returned to claim her hand. Then drawing her close to his side, he said smoothly, "You'll have to excuse us, Bessie. Charlie and I have a date with the snorkel instructor."

As they wandered off, an annoyed Bessie shot them a look that could freeze water.

* * *

"All right, Charlie. Take it easy. Deep breaths . . . yes, like that . . . breathe."

Under a shady almond tree away from the rest of the crowd, Devin rubbed Charlie's back.

When she was reasonably calm, she turned to Devin. "What I don't understand, Devin, is why Bessie's brother would be so cruel."

Devin stroked the inside of Charlie's arm. "You're jumping to conclusions, Charlie. The ship provides that stationery. Last evening I found the same cream-colored envelopes with the burgundy seal in my dresser drawer. Why don't you read the note Bessie gave you?"

Charlie accepted the drink Devin proffered. She took a long sip and set down the coconut husk. "I can't say I've found any in my suite, but knowing that certainly makes me feel better. I'm just relieved that Bessie's not doing her brother's dirty work. Still, it doesn't solve the mystery of who's responsible for yesterday's little surprise. Either way I'd rather not ruin the remainder of my cruise. To be safe I'll open my fan mail when I get home."

"Spoken like the woman I fell in love with." Devin cupped Charlie's chin and forced her to look at him. His voice grew huskier. "Surely you must know as long as I'm here, I wouldn't let anyone harm you, Charlotte Canfield?"

He looked at her with such intensity and such longing, she almost believed him. Was it really possible that he still loved her? If so, then why had he abandoned her?

Out of the corner of her eye, she spotted Tarik with the irrepressible Bessie in tow. "Here's your opportunity to come to my rescue, Sir Galahad," she said, taking Devin's arm.

"At your service, m'am. Let's go check out the food."

Devin directed her toward a bright red canopy, where a line had already formed. As they drew closer, the smell of barbecued chicken and burgers grew stronger.

"Wait up, you two."

Charlie wanted to ignore Tarik but knew that he would only get louder. She sent Devin a silent SOS before turning to acknowledge Tarik's summons. Noting her ex-husband's flushed face, she realized he'd been sampling the rum punch. Though it was the last thing she wanted to do, she pasted on a bright smile. When he and Bessie stopped, she actually greeted them with a cheery, "Hello."

"Mind if we join you?" Though Bessie had a grip on his arm designed to leave skid marks, Tarik's eyes lingered on the high-cut red suit then zeroed in on Charlie's cleavage. He took a drag on his cigarette, gawked at her, and fell in step.

Devin quickly whipped an arm around Charlie's shoulders. "We've already eaten," he lied, "and we've still got that date with the snorkel instructor." He tossed an apologetic look in the couple's direction and hurried off, shouting over his shoulder, "Catch you tonight at the captain's cocktail party."

"Thank God, I wasn't really hungry." Charlie said when they were out of earshot. "What do we do now?"

"We take a walk up the beach. Listen to some of that awesome reggae music the band's playing and chill out."

"Good idea."

After a five-minute walk, they found an isolated spot of beach. Devin spread his towel and motioned for Charlie to sit. In the background the band's Rastafarian lead singer sang a heart-wrenching version of "Red Red Wine."

"Wheeew! That was a close call," Devin said, stretching long legs before him.

"Do you think they bought our story?"

"Who cares. The important thing is we got rid of them." The tips of his fingers caressed her cheek. "Charlie?"

"Yes, Devin." He fingered her earlobe, tugging gently.

"I've always wondered. No, never mind."

"Wondered what?"

His lips nuzzled her neck, making her lose her train of thought. "Nothing."

Oh, God! He was warming her up for the kiss. And as irrational as it seemed, she was dying to taste his lips again. Would the magic still be there?

"Charlie?" Devin's lips brushed hers ever so gently.

"Hmmm."

"I've missed you."

The muted sounds of conversation broke the mood. Charlie tore out of his arms, scrambled upright, and brushed herself off. She attempted to make light of what had just happened. "Time to head back. Looks like our territory's about to be invaded."

"Rain check, then?"

She pretended she didn't hear him.

Back on the ship Devin shrugged into the jacket of a midnight blue tuxedo. He checked the mirror to see if the satin bow-tie and matching cummerbund needed adjustment. Then whistling softly, he ran a hand over cropped curls, finally satisfied with his appearance.

All in all it had been a good day. Charlie had actually let down her guard but not entirely. She'd let him kiss her. Nothing too sensual: a peck on the lips actually. Still, one kiss was better than no kiss at all. Tonight he'd try to get a little more of that sweetness if she'd let him.

Devin acknowledged that she'd probably felt just a touch grateful to him for getting rid of Tarik. His old roommate would have made a pest of himself if he'd let him. And it wasn't as if they'd lied. Eventually he and Charlie had gone snorkeling.

The phone rang.

Frowning, Devin glanced at his watch. He wasn't late getting Charlie, he even had a few minutes to play with.

Picking up the receiver, his voice held a tentative note. "Hello."

The crackle of a bad connection assaulted his ears. Devin waited for it to settle. "Hello."

The static grew louder. Over the noise a man's muffled tones were barely discernible.

"Harry?" Only his partner and secretary knew he was on a cruise.

The connection cleared up perceptibly. "Spencer?"

"Yes?"

The voice wasn't Harry's or his secretary's.

"Thought it was you. Now that I've taken care of business, I'll be expecting my check."

Before Devin could answer, the man hung up.

Five

Charlie had been anticipating Devin's arrival. Just the same, she jumped when he knocked. One perfectly manicured hand was pressed against her chest as she willed her thundering heart to stop thumping. "I'll only be a moment," she shouted.

"Take your time, darling."

Darling? Where did that come from? One kiss and already he'd taken a lot for granted. Charlie straightened the skirt of the shimmering gold sheath she'd chosen for that evening. It was formal night, and she'd decided to pull out all the stops. It wasn't often she got to dress up.

Earlier Kim, Lisa, and Niki had left for the captain's cocktail party. Charlie had used precious moments of solitude to add the final touch to her makeup. Now she checked the mirror and decided that the additional minutes spent on her eyes and lips had been worth it. The dangling gold and topaz earrings framed her face and matched the slender tennis bracelet that encircled her wrist. Even her eyes sparkled.

Remembering the tiny shopping bag Devin had handed her after they'd left one of the duty-free stores, she retrieved it from the dresser drawer. She removed turquoise and fuchsia tissue paper and withdrew a sheer silk scarf with flecks of gold. Looping the gossamer material around her neck, she posed in front of the full-length mirror, admiring the effect. Why, the little sneak had obviously heard her say that the scarf would match her evening dress perfectly. Was he trying to buy her?

Charlie threw the door open, prepared to read Devin the riot act. What few words she could remember lodged in her throat. She couldn't think, couldn't even formulate a greeting. Devin in a tuxedo was devastating. Awesome! Easily the handsomest man she'd ever seen.

"Well, hello, there," Devin greeted.

Although his tone seemed bright enough, and the gleam in his eye warmed her, something about his expression didn't seem right.

"Hello," Charlie said, finally finding her voice. The tips of her fingers lingered against his silken sleeve.

Devin took the hand she'd placed on his arm and slowly brought the open palm to his lips. Against her flesh he whispered, "Why, Charlie . . . Charlie Canfield, you've never looked more ravishing. I especially like the scarf."

Charlie inhaled the poignant smell of citrus. In the past she would have hurled herself into his arms, lost herself in the safety of his embrace. But it was too late for that now, too much had gone sour between them. It had been a mistake letting him kiss her earlier. Obviously she'd sent him the wrong message.

Stilling her wayward thoughts, she teased, "Thanks. The person who gave it to me has wonderful taste."

"In women, too, I've been told."

Charlie didn't like the way the conversation was heading. She needed to nip it now before Devin got any further ideas. She'd allowed him to be her escort because she felt more secure having him at her side. Not that she'd ever enjoyed playing the role of the poor helpless female, nor had she ever felt the need to validate her existence through a man. Plain and simple, Devin's presence had so far kept the pervert away. While the maniac had made covert attempts to contact her, she hadn't been forced to listen to that eerie voice talk dirty. And as grateful as she was to Devin, she didn't want him to get the wrong impression, to assume that he now had permission to take up where he'd left off.

"Shall we head upstairs then?" Charlie asked, closing the door behind her.

Devin held out a midnight blue arm, "Lady, your wish is my command."

Elegant white-suited men guarded the entrance to the Sunshine Lounge. Devin and Charlie moved through the reception line and stopped briefly to have their picture taken with the captain.

"You've got a beautiful ship," Devin said, shaking Captain Santorini's hand.

The debonair silver-haired commandant flashed a capped-toothed smile. Eyeing Charlie, he gushed, "Thank you, my friend, but she is nothing in comparison to your beautiful lady. Bella, bella."

Charlie barely had time to thank him before Devin whisked her away.

Inside the lounge waiters held out their trays for inspection, calling, "Wine, champagne?"

Another server tempted, "How about coconut shrimp or a taste of salmon?"

Devin said yes to both offers, retrieved two champagne glasses, handed one to Charlie, and took the plate of hors d'oeuvres. He set the dish down on a nearby table and turned to toast her. "To the best-looking woman in the room. Even the captain thinks so."

Charlie sipped her drink and regarded him steadily. When had the suave, sophisticated gentleman who knew all the right things to say, replaced the naive boy? She missed that boy.

"The captain was just being kind," Charlie said, quickly taking a sip from her glass.

Lisa floated across the room, wearing an antique black taffeta dress and more of her jewelry. Fred Willis trailed her. The twosome stopped to exchange greetings then moved on.

In the background a trio played a haunting ballad. For the first time Charlie noticed the cleared space on the dais where several couples swayed, Niki and Oliver Stanton among them.

Devin's voice grew lower and huskier. "I disagree. The man's a connoisseur of beautiful women and so am I. But why stand here discussing the captain when we could be dancing?"

She gaped at Devin, not quite comprehending his question. From what she could remember, Devin had two left feet for anything but disco. Slow dancing had never been his thing, and this wasn't exactly a Donna Summer tune. How could she gracefully say no without being rude or admit that his proximity made her nervous? Now she'd waited too long to answer. It was too late to say no. Devin pulled her into his arms.

When he twirled her about, she giggled. Then abruptly the music changed and the band struck up the most ridiculous melody. Eighteen years ago the tune hadn't seemed absurd. In fact it had been one of the most requested romantic ballads. Now Charlie found herself humming along to the syrupy lyrics and joining in when Devin's voice echoed the singer's words. Niki and Oliver Stanton had somehow maneuvered a spot next to them. Charlie looked up in time to see Niki wink, settle herself more comfortably in Stanton's arms, and dance away.

Charlie closed her eyes tightly and just floated, giggling at Devin's slightly off-key version of the song. When his hands tightened around her waist, bringing her closer, she opened her eyes, drawn by two smoky magnets. Surely he wasn't planning on kissing her again? Not now. Not out in the open.

"Will I see you again?" Devin paraphrased a line of the song, his tone incredibly serious.

Charlie couldn't answer, could hardly breathe. She inhaled his cologne. Citrus. So clean, so fresh, so Devin. Ignoring her accelerated heartbeat, she gazed into his eyes and missed a step. "Sorry." The music receded into the background as again she followed his expert lead.

Rudely an announcement blasted over the intercom: "Charlotte Canfield. Please come to the Purser's Information Desk for a message."

"Charlie, sweetheart. That's you," Devin crooned against her hair. "I hope nothing's wrong."

"Mmm." Charlie gazed into troubled gray eyes. Devin had stopped dancing, though his arms remained around her waist.

"Baby, you've just been paged. I think you need to find out what that's about. I'm coming with you to the Information Desk."

Lost in her memories, Charlie threw him a perplexed look, not really comprehending. "You don't need to go with me. I'll meet you back here in five minutes. It's probably Kim or one of the girls leaving me a message. I've hardly spent a moment with them. I've monopolized all of your time."

"Like I mind." Devin's arm remained around her waist as he led her off the dance floor. They made a path through the crowded lounge, stopping to acknowledge their classmates' greetings.

Near the exit Charlie spotted a vacant table. "Hey, we're in luck. Why don't you grab that seat, and I'll meet you here in a few minutes."

Through the gossamer material of her gown, Devin's fingers traced her hips. "Not to worry. You're not getting rid of me that easily. I don't plan on sitting when we get

back, so don't you even think of stopping me from coming
with you, Charlie Canfield. There's an animal at large, and
I couldn't live with myself if something happened."

"You don't think . . ." Charlie let the sentence dangle.
She hadn't thought about her stalker for at least the last
few hours. She'd been much too wrapped up in Devin.

"Nah. I don't think. Like you said, it's no big deal. Probably just a message from Kim or one of the others setting
up a place to meet later."

In front of the Purser's Information Desk, Charlie interrupted a redhead busy at a computer. "Excuse me,
someone just paged Charlotte Canfield."

A freckled face looked up, struggling to make the connection. "Oh, that page. Yes, I did. Some man called looking for you. He said it was urgent, so I took a message and
told him I'd have you paged. I'll get the message for you
in one moment." Returning to her keyboard, she continued to enter data into the computer.

After half a minute Devin intervened. Splaying slender
fingers on the mahogany barrier separating them, his
tone brooked no nonsense. "Could we have that message,
now?"

The woman's face closely matched the color of her hair.
"Why, certainly." She disappeared into a back room, returning with a cream-colored envelope. "Here it is. Sorry
for the delay."

Charlie couldn't bring herself to accept the note. She
stared at the envelope with its familiar burgundy seal. What
did it hold? Was she letting her imagination get the best
of her? Noting the stricken look on her face, Devin stepped
forward to claim the envelope. "Ms . . . ," he said, glancing at the name tag dangling off the redhead's white
jacket, "Lewis. Please do me a huge favor. If you happen
to hear from this person again, have the call transferred
to my suite."

He removed a page from a notepad conveniently left

on the counter, scribbled his stateroom's number, and handed it over. Taking Charlie's hand, he led her toward glass elevators.

Inside he added, "Could be someone from your job calling. The professional that you are, you would have left the ship's number with the station."

Charlie's face brightened. "You're right. I did. Ellis Greene, my co-host, could be trying to track me down. I did tell him to call if he needed me."

Devin's fingers traced a pattern on her upper arm. "Come," he said. "No use in playing guessing games. We'll have a glass of wine and open the letter together."

When they'd reached Veranda Deck, Charlie followed him to his stateroom and waited while he unlocked the door. He led her over to the burgundy-striped sofa, reluctantly released her hand, and waited for her to sit. Plopping the envelope on the coffee table, he moved off to retrieve a bottle of wine chilling in an ice bucket. He returned to her side, picked up the note, and waved it at her. This prompted, "Would you like me to do the honors?"

"Sure . . . go ahead," Charlie croaked.

Wrapping the scarf around her index finger like thread being spooled, she watched Devin slit the burgundy seal. A single piece of cream-colored paper dangled between his slender fingers. He scanned the note briefly and held it out to her. The set of his jaw indicated it wasn't good news. Even his eyes had lost their sparkle. What did it mean?

"Read it," Devin insisted. He folded her hand around the stationery and pulled her into the crook of his arms. "Try not to panic, baby. It'll be all right. I'm here for you."

Why did she have the feeling something was terribly wrong? Devin acted as if someone had died.

"Please, God . . ." Charlie whispered. She held the note in a trembling hand, glanced at it, and in hushed tones repeated: " 'Charlie . . . Please come home. Kasey's hurt.' "

In slow motion the cream-colored paper floated toward the burgundy carpeting. "Not Kasey. Please, God, not Kasey," Charlie cried.

Reaching for the phone located on a side table, Devin held out the receiver. "Baby, why don't you call home?"

Charlie didn't ever remember a telephone being that heavy. She dialed the number and waited for the ringing to cease.

"Hello. Marilyn Canfield here." Her mother's chirp eventually broke through the fog.

She was in luck tonight—someone was actually home. More often than not, one parent or the other had a social obligation. Hopefully her luck would hold, and her mother would tell her that it was all a huge misunderstanding, someone's idea of a sick joke. Yet despite the feelings of relief that her mother's calm voice brought, she couldn't utter a single word.

"Hello, can you hear me?" Marilyn Canfield repeated.

The back of Devin's knuckles brushed Charlie's cheek. His face seemed to mirror her emotions. "It'll be all right, Charlie, you'll see," he comforted.

"Mother . . ."

"Charlotte?" Her mother's voice rose several octaves. "Charlotte, is that you?"

Stifling the lump in her throat, Charlie finally got out, "Yes, Mom. It's me."

"Oh, Charlotte. Are you having a good time? Are you relaxing? Tell me, is a cruise everything it's cracked up to be, lots of food—"

Charlie cut off her mother in midsentence. Why was she acting so normal if Kasey was hurt? "Mom, how's Kasey?"

"Fine, the last time I talked to her. Let's see, that was yesterday. You know that child, she carries on and on. Yesterday she told me all about this new boyfriend of hers, Brian somebody. I'm sure she'll fill you in on his life story."

"Mom, is Kasey hurt?"

Marilyn's voice rose another few octaves. "Why would you say that? Where did you get such a crazy idea?"

Charlie's puzzled expression made Devin mouth, "What's going on?"

Holding one hand upright like a traffic cop, she signaled to him to be patient. "Are you telling me, Kasey isn't hurt?" she repeated.

Marilyn's words rushed over each other. "Of course I haven't spoken to her in a day or so, but she sounded positively ecstatic yesterday. She was jabbering on about this new romance. You would think someone from the college would call if something was wrong. Did someone contact you?"

Relief flooded through Charlie. She squeezed the hand Devin offered and avoided the question. "You're right, Mother. I would think that someone from the college would call. Still, I won't get a moment's peace until I get that child on the phone."

She ended the call and dialed another number committed to memory. The phone rang and rang before a recorded voice repeated, "The cellular customer you are trying to reach is not available or outside . . ."

Frustrated, Charlie slammed down the phone. The fingers of her free hand drummed the mahogany table in front of her. "That child."

Devin's concerned voice penetrated the funk. "Who are you trying to reach now, love?" His grip on her hand tightened.

"Kasey. She's not answering her cell phone. Now I'm really worried."

Devin raised an eyebrow. "Your child has a cellular phone? Aren't there phones at the dorm? Why not try the college?"

Now why hadn't she thought about that? "I suppose I could. The phone's community property though. It's a pay phone located in the hallway. When Kasey chose a sleep-away college, I got her a cellular phone in the event of a flat tire or something. I flatly refused to foot the bill for two phones."

"You're a smart lady. Now call," Devin urged, handing over the receiver.

Charlie's fingers depressed the numbers. This time the phone rang for several minutes. She was tempted to hang up but consoled herself that at this late hour, this was to be expected. At last a shrill voice squeaked into the receiver.

"Elisabeth Irwin Dorm, sixth floor."

Relieved to get a living, breathing person on the line, Charlie forced her voice to sound upbeat. "Hi, Elisabeth Irwin Dorm. This is Kasey Connors's mother. Is she there?"

"Hold on, Ms. Canfield. I'll have to check."

Thump. The phone was set down.

Charlie waited for another eternity before the coed returned. "Sorry, Ms. Canfield, she's not answering her door. Can I take a message?"

"Tell me, have you seen her today?"

"Can't say I have, but I've been at class all day, and later I went to the library. I'd be glad to take a message though," the young woman offered.

This time Charlie didn't even try to hide her dejection. "Could you please ask her to call home the moment she gets in."

"Sure thing, Ms. Canfield."

After disconnecting, Charlie put down the phone and moved into Devin's waiting arms.

Six

"We've got to make a plan," Devin whispered against Charlie's hair.

Charlie's fingers massaged her pounding temples. She lifted her head to search Devin's face. "Plan? My plan's to go home, find my child, and see for myself how badly she's hurt."

"I know that, sweetheart, but what we need to figure out is how to get you home." The smell of spring filled his nostrils as his cheek rested against Charlie's hair. "Where is home nowadays, sweetheart, and shouldn't we find Tarik?"

Charlie'd totally blanked out her ex-husband's existence. With some reluctance she acknowledged Devin made sense. Common decency dictated that she notify Tarik of his daughter's predicament. Still, she resisted the idea. After the divorce Tarik had made it abundantly clear that he would not take responsibility for Kasey. He'd balked at even paying child support until her lawyer stepped in, reminding him that as Kasey's legal father (the name listed on the birth certificate), he had responsibilities. And yes, though he now made perfunctory phone calls to check up on Kasey, he still remained a miserable failure of a parent.

"Charlie! Ch-a-rlie!" Devin repeated, waving his hand in front of her face. "Where's home?"

Slowly Devin's voice penetrated Charlie's thoughts.

"Croton-On-Hudson," she croaked.

"So you never left Westchester?"

"And I most probably never will. I love the area and my job."

Actually she'd left the New York area for two agonizingly long years. The most painful years of her life, the years she'd been married. She'd followed Tarik to Chicago, his hometown, where he'd found work, gone to night school, and later accepted a job with the same advertising agency employing him as a messenger.

"What about telling Tarik?"

"What about it? I'll tell him eventually. I doubt he'll want to get off."

Devin shot her a strange look. He smoothed her hair. "What do you mean? I realize you guys are divorced, and there's bound to be some animosity, but I'm sure Tarik'd be concerned about his only child's well-being."

"Trust me, he's not."

Charlie's startling answer hung in the air. Briefly Devin's lips grazed her forehead. "I think you're wrong," he said, his arms encircling her neck. "Now we need to figure out how to get you back to New York. Unless you have a preference, I'd go with any of the tri-state airports. Wonder what time we dock tomorrow?"

"Tomorrow?" Escaping his arms, Charlie rose from the burgundy-striped couch. She paced the length of the room, winding the sparkling gold scarf around her wrist. "Oh, Devin, I can't wait until tomorrow. I've got to go home now."

Devin grabbed a glossy brochure from the coffee table, thumbed through it, then crossed the room to face her. Stroking the nape of her neck, he said, "I'm afraid you'll have to, love." Then glancing at the open book, he continued. "The ship's not scheduled to dock in St. Thomas until midafternoon. We'll need help with airline schedules, not to mention tickets."

"We? I told you Tarik's not leaving," Charlie added listlessly.

"We, as in you and me," Devin explained.

"But, Devin, you've got four more glorious days of cruising to enjoy. This is my problem. There's no need to ruin your vacation."

"Trust me, you're not ruining it. I've completed my business in Florida, and I've got several days coming to me. I haven't had an extended vacation in years. Besides, do you think that now that I've found you I'm going to allow you to walk out of my life that easily?"

"Oh, Devin," Charlie said, laying her head on his shoulder. "What would I have done if you hadn't been on board?"

When Devin tilted her chin, she gazed into his smoky eyes and refused to look away. Even when his mouth brushed hers in a teasing question, she never considered breaking the connection. His lips roamed her face, soothing, easing her pain. Around her, the world spun on a wobbly axis until the phone rang.

"Aren't you going to get that? Charlie asked, coming up for air.

Against her ear Devin mumbled, "No. Let it ring."

"What if . . ." Charlie's voice trailed off.

Devin sighed and reluctantly released her. "I suppose you're right. Could be the same man calling with more information about Kasey. By the way you chose a beautiful name for your daughter."

"Thanks." Chewing on her lower lip, Charlie watched Devin reach for the receiver.

"Spencer here," he said. Then: "I told you to wait until I got back." And finally: "You'll have your check as soon as I can arrange it." He hung up, clearly annoyed.

"What was that about?" Charlie asked the moment Devin turned to face her.

A muscle in his jaw twitched as he focused his attention

on the still unopened wine bottle. He unscrewed the cork, poured the Chardonnay, and handed over a glass. Claiming the seat he'd vacated, he draped an arm around her shoulder, and eventually said, "Nothing to worry about really. My assistant's looking for his midyear bonus. He hates to deal with Harry, thinks Harry will stiff him." Devin knocked back his drink. "Now back to business. We need to figure out how to get you home."

Charlie sensed the wheels spinning as Devin picked up the phone and depressed some numbers. Listening to the one-sided conversation, she couldn't believe his gall.

"Hi, my wife and I are getting off in St. Thomas," he said to the staff at the purser's office. "We're going to need help with airline tickets . . . yes, it's an emergency." He seemed to be pleased with the response and continued. "That's awfully kind of you. And yes, I know it's going to be expensive, but our daughter's had an accident, and we need to get home. JFK, La Guardia, or even Newark will do. Thanks so much, I'll wait to hear from you.

"Everything's under control," Devin said, hanging up. The back of his hand brushed Charlie's cheek. "You okay?"

Already she felt better knowing that he'd taken charge. But what would she say if she told him that his little white lie wasn't a lie after all, that Kasey was indeed their daughter? No sooner had the thought popped into her mind when she shrugged it off. She'd had her chance years ago—it was too late now.

Curious, Charlie asked, "You're coming to New York with me? I thought you'd just take me to the airport, then we'd go our separate ways."

Devin's breath fanned her cheek. He kissed her neck then folded her into his arms. "You thought wrong, sweetie. Didn't I tell you I was coming with you? There's nothing pressing in San Diego that Harry can't handle. Like I told you, I haven't taken a vacation outside of Cali-

fornia, except for this one, in God knows how long. I am
at your service indefinitely."

"Oh, Devin," Charlie said, leaning into his embrace. "I
don't expect you to leave the ship to baby-sit me."

"Why? Is there a man at home waiting? Will my presence
create a problem?"

Against the hardness of his chest, she shook her head.
It had been a long time since she'd allowed a man into
her life. There was no one waiting for her at home . . .
except maybe the pervert. Shuddering at the thought, she
said, "No, there's no one waiting."

Devin's arms tightened around her shoulders. "And a
good thing, too. I'd hate to have to vie for your attention,
Charlie Canfield."

Upstairs on the open deck, Charlie faced Tarik. After
searching the ship, she'd had to resort to paging him. The
fifth time around he'd surfaced, Bessie Collins in tow. It
had taken some doing to lose the zaftig woman. Charlie
had Devin to thank for stepping in and inviting Bessie for
a drink. Only then had the annoying woman relinquished
her hold on Tarik's arm.

Now Tarik stood facing Charlie, the ever present glass
of booze clutched in one hand, a cigarette in the other.

"So, baby, you've finally come round," Tarik said, lurch-
ing toward her. He took a drag on his butt then blew a
perfect smoke ring.

Automatically Charlie's hand covered her mouth and
nose. Tarik's alcohol-sodden breath could easily ignite a
fire. His drinking had always been a source of contention
between them. Apparently the habit had grown worse. She
stepped back, counted to five, and let the hand drop. Then
raising a palm to ward him off, she ground out, "Back off,
Tarik. This is serious business."

But despite her protests, he moved in closer, one hand

reaching out to cup her chin. "Baby, being with you is serious business."

Charlie flinched. "Stop it," she said, slapping his hand away. "I didn't bring you up here for you to maul me. I need to talk to you about our daughter."

Tarik's drunken laughter rang out. The few people around looked over in their direction. He flicked the cigarette overboard and slurred, "Our daughter? Now you gotta be joking. You mean *your* daughter. She's always been your daughter, Charlie. I tried to be her father. You just never let me."

How could he stand there and lie? From the very beginning Tarik had never made the effort to be a father. He hadn't even wanted to hold baby Kasey. While he'd never said the words "the baby's not mine," he'd told her at every opportunity that a mother's responsibility was to raise a child, a father's to bring home the bacon.

Charlie placed a hand on both hips and squared off. "Tarik, I'm not here to discuss bygones. I just thought you should know that someone called and left a message that Kasey was hurt. I'm leaving the ship tomorrow to see what the situation is."

Her words seemed to have a sobering effect. Tarik's diction was almost perfect now. "You're leaving the ship midcruise?"

"How could I stay and have a good time if my baby's hurt?"

Tarik knocked back his drink and set the empty glass on a nearby table. "You brought me up here to tell me this?" He pursed his lips, squinted his eyes, and waggled a finger at her. "You're not expecting me to get off with you, are you? I paid a whole lot of money for this cruise. Money's tight, sweet thang."

Rolling her eyes, Charlie threw both hands in the air. "You're pathetic, you know that. Now why would silly old me want to encroach on your good time? Heaven forbid you should lose out on a dime." Spinning around, she ran smack into Devin, who'd apparently come looking for her.

"Easy, girl." He steadied her with his hands then drew her into the circle of his arms.

The stars in the sky swam before Charlie. She laid her head on Devin's shoulder and blinked back tears of frustration. In a minute or so, she'd be all right. Replaying the conversation, she wondered just how much Devin had heard.

Devin challenged Tarik over Charlie's shoulder. "What have you done to her, man? What did you say to make her this upset?" He released Charlie and swung around to face Tarik.

Tarik shrugged tuxedo-clad shoulders and spread his palms skyward. He snickered. "How should I know? Women are temperamental creatures. I've given up figuring them out. Probably just that time of the month."

Devin's jaw worked. "You're a sexist bastard, Tarik Connors." Turning back to Charlie, he held out his hand. "Let's go back, get packed, and get some shut-eye. It's been a long day."

Tarik's words followed them. "This would be funny, Spencer, if I wasn't so damn angry. You of all people coming forward to protect Charlie's honor?" His laughter taunted, daring Devin to challenge him. "Since when are you so concerned?" He narrowed his eyes. "Maybe you've been getting a piece."

"I'm going to let that slide, Connors," Devin said, his voice deceptively low. "It's pretty obvious you're drunk. My suggestion would be to get some sleep. I'd hate for you to have an accident and maybe fall overboard."

The veiled threat hung in the air as they departed.

On a picture-perfect day, the cruise ship, *Machination*, sailed into St. Thomas. On board Charlie and Devin, sur-

rounded by an assortment of hand luggage, waited at the
Purser's Information Desk. Kim, Lisa, and Niki hovered
around doing their best to console Charlie. Kim had of
course taken over.

"Well, damn, girlfriend," Kim said, embracing Charlie.
"We never even got the chance to have a girls' night out.
You will call me the moment you find out how your daugh-
ter is?"

"I will, I promise."

Then Charlie was folded into Niki's arms. "Oh, Charlotte," Niki said, stroking Charlie's curls. "I'm praying that
everything turns out right—"

"It will," Lisa interjected, coming over to kiss Charlie's
cheek. "It's got to. Now don't forget to call us the minute
you hear something."

At that moment one of the pursers interrupted. He
touched Devin's arm. "Mr. and Mrs. Spencer, we hate to
see you leave under these circumstances. We've really enjoyed having you on board. I've been asked to tell you that
the ship's just been cleared by Customs, and you're free
to disembark at your leisure. Michael, our port agent, has
a car waiting to take you to the airport."

"Thank you," Devin said, shaking the crew member's
hand. He smiled his golden-boy smile and continued.
"The entire staff's been quite helpful, and we did have a
good time. You just might see us next year."

Devin reached down, picked up their hand luggage,
then placed his free arm around Charlie. To Lisa, Kim,
and Onika, he said, "Ladies, you've got my business card.
Please stay in touch."

Together they walked down the gangway and into the
scorching Caribbean sunshine, where a cacophony of
voices greeted. The harsh cries of vendors offering to braid
hair, provide escort to the beach, or sell conch jewelry
overwhelmed them. Despite the cloying fragrance of flowers and the sound of a steel pan playing lively calypso

tunes, Charlie remained oblivious to her surroundings. At any other time she would have stopped to browse the numerous shops that beckoned, enthralled by the designer ware, the perfumes that in the States cost twice as much. But not today.

"Mr. and Mrs. Spencer, over here." A dark-skinned man sporting a bright red cap and flashing white teeth waited at the side of the gangway. He held up a sign with SPENCER written in bold letters.

Michael, the port agent, Charlie surmised. And despite her melancholy mood, a tiny imp prompted her to acknowledge the salutation. She smiled and waved, liking the sound of "Mrs. Spencer" on his tongue. Again she was falling back on old memories, allowing Devin's presence to have that effect on her. They'd been together exactly four days, too soon to give her fragile heart to him again.

Devin pumped Michael's hand. "Thanks for coming to get us, man, especially on such short notice."

In typical Virgin Island lilt, Michael sang, "No problem, mon, it's my job to make sure you cruise folks get home safely."

"Well, you do your job very well, and we thank you."

They followed him to a white Lincoln Continental and waited while a surly porter loaded their bags into the trunk. Michael gestured toward the car's interior. "It hot, mon. You people from the States ain't used to these temperatures. Take a seat and cool off."

Charlie sank into soft leather, grateful for the air conditioning. Through the tinted rear window, she watched Devin stash their hand luggage then return to slide in beside her.

"Cyril E. King Airport, right?" Michael stuck his head through the half-opened passenger window before getting into the driver's seat.

"Whatever airport gets us to New York," Devin quipped.

"That's the one." Jangling his keys, Michael climbed into the front seat.

The port agent maneuvered the car through narrow streets, adroitly avoiding motorists going at a minimum of seventy miles an hour, or so it seemed. After driving for a few minutes, Charlie thought to ask, "Where do we get our airline tickets?"

"No problem, mon. It's taken care of. I set it up so you can get them at the American Airlines counter. The ship told me your documents were still in your maiden name." He winked at Charlie and continued. "So knowing newly-weds don't need no hassle, I told the people at American to write up the ticket Charlotte Canfield-Spencer. I hope you don't mind." Through the rearview mirror, he beamed at Charlie, proud of himself.

Playfully Devin patted Charlie's exposed thigh, at the point where the lime green minidress had hiked up. "You did a good thing," he confirmed.

Charlie did her best to suppress the chuckle bubbling at the base of her diaphragm. Devin's little white lie had served a purpose after all. By linking them as the couple whose daughter had an accident, the disembarkation process had been expedited. They'd gotten off the ship with very little hassle and would most likely get the bulk of their money back, thanks to cruise insurance. Not that it was anyone's business, but there'd been no need to explain why they'd maintained separate accommodations.

Smiling inwardly, Charlie had to admit that Charlotte Canfield-Spencer did have a nice ring to it. It sure would sound good introducing the show. In her head she practiced the opening lines: *This is Charlotte Canfield-Spencer . . . welcome to* He Said, She Said." She shook her head, trying to dispel the notion. What had gotten into her? The little voice she tried desperately to ignore, admonished, "Have you lost your ever-loving mind? How can you set yourself up for heartbreak a second time around?"

"We're here," Michael announced, parking the car in front of the small terminal.

"Let's go, sweetheart." Devin squeezed Charlie's hand. "Think positive. Everything will be just fine. I have a gut feeling that this is all a huge mistake, that Kasey's as safe and sound as can be."

Tremulously Charlie smiled into Devin's cool gray eyes. "I hope so," she said, giving his hand a reassuring squeeze.

Seven

As Charlie and Devin exited the American Airlines terminal at John F. Kennedy Airport, a grizzled dispatcher flagged them down. "Taxi?" the codger barked, pointing toward the line of yellow cabs.

Devin shook his head. "Thanks, but we won't be needing one."

"We won't?" Charlie eyed Devin curiously.

"I've rented a car."

Overhearing their exchange, the dispatcher grumbled, "Then you're in the wrong spot, buddy." Shrugging, he loped off, turning back to point a grubby finger at the adjacent sidewalk. "The rental car buses pick up over there."

Devin held Charlie's hand tightly. She hustled to keep up with his long strides. "When did you make arrangements to rent a car?" she asked.

"Ah, the benefits of modern technology, my dear. I requested one on the plane. Didn't you see me fooling around with the console above my tray table?"

Slowly comprehending, Charlie cocked her head. "Clever Devin. Real clever. So that's what you were doing with that remote control. And I thought you were playing interactive games."

Devin tweaked Charlie's cheek. He'd always enjoyed her quick wit. It was one of the things that had attracted him to her—that plus the fact she was easy to talk to. "No, sweetness, I may appear busy, but I never stop thinking of you. My goal is to get you home with minimum hassle."

Charlie's lips brushed Devin's shoulder. "Thank you for always being one step ahead."

Devin stopped in the middle of the sidewalk, forgot the porter dogging their heels, and gathered Charlie into his arms. His lips grazed the hollows of her cheekbones before moving downward to claim her mouth. Only the Hertz bus pulling into the curb prevented him from deepening the kiss. After the stevedore helped load their luggage, Devin gave him an overly generous tip and helped Charlie aboard.

At the rental car parking lot, the driver slowed up in front of a silver Lexus. "Mr. Spencer, you're in number 325," he said, handing over Devin's paperwork.

"Another benefit. The Gold Card," Devin said, helping Charlie out.

Charlie shot him a look of pure confusion. "Don't you have to show your license or credit card?"

"They've got my profile in the computer. For security purposes I just have to show my license on the way out."

For a brief moment Charlie felt foolish. What must he think of her? She rarely rented a car. When she traveled on business, the station always arranged a limousine.

Charlie changed the topic. "I'd hoped we'd go by a phone. I wanted to try Kasey again one last time."

A brisk spring wind caught her words, swirling them around her. She huddled into her trench coat. Devin, who'd worn a navy blue worsted jacket, didn't seem the least affected. The silence dragged out for so long, she thought he hadn't heard her.

"The door's open," Devin said finally, helping Charlie into the passenger seat. "Why don't you use my cellular to make your call?" Removing a flip phone from the breast pocket of his jacket, he handed it over. Charlie punched in the numbers and watched Devin stack luggage into the car's roomy trunk. Meanwhile she waited for her parents to pick up. When there was no answer, she dialed Kasey's dorm.

On the second ring a familiar chirpy voice answered, "Elisabeth Irwin, sixth floor."

Charlie went through the rhetoric. "Hi, this is Kasey Connors's mother. It's extremely important that I speak with Kasey."

"Oh, Ms. Canfield," the breathy voice gushed. "I'm the person you spoke to last evening, Renna Phillips, remember? I didn't forget. I left a note on Kasey's door, but I don't think she got it. She hasn't been back, at least not that I'm aware of. One of the girls mentioned she might be heading home."

"Home?" Charlie repeated, letting out a loud whoosh of air.

Devin, who'd just climbed into the driver's seat, squeezed her hand sympathetically. "Want me to take over?" Charlie nodded and handed over the phone. "Hi," Devin said to the coed as if they were best friends. "This is Kasey's dad. Her mom and I are really worried. Can you help us? We haven't heard from Kasey in quite some time, and we need to know who her friends are. Do you know anyone who might be able to tell us about Kasey's plans last evening?"

Dead silence on the other end.

"What's her name?" Devin mouthed, covering the receiver.

"Renna," Charlie supplied, chewing on her lower lip.

"Look, Renna," Devin said in his best Billy Dee Williams voice. "Surely you must know of someone she'd confide in."

"We-l-l, she is dating Brian Matthews," Kasey's dormmate said with some reluctance. "He lives off campus though—"

Devin cut the coed off. "And you wouldn't happen to have his number?"

"I do, but a lot of good it'll do you. The boys didn't pay their phone bill. The line's been disconnected."

Devin's colorful oath echoed through the car's plush interior. He hung up looking totally dejected. "I thought we'd just gotten lucky," he carped, putting the car in gear.

"Thanks for trying, anyway—you're a love." Charlie touched the sleeve of his coat. Instantly she regretted the endearment and hoped that he wouldn't misinterpret her gratitude. Even so, it felt good having him take charge. She stared out of the window and began babbling in earnest. "How fast can you get me to Croton?"

Devin scanned the map he'd removed from the glove compartment. Charlie's gaze lingered on his bent head. She traced their route with a shaky finger.

"Tell you what," Devin said, looking up and doing his best to smile. "With you as my copilot, we'll be there"—he looked at his watch—"in less than fifty minutes."

"Deal," Charlie said, pointing to the signs for the Van Wyck Expressway.

"Deal," Devin repeated.

True to his word they arrived in Croton-On-Hudson in under fifty minutes.

"Did I do good?" Devin asked, helping Charlie from the car.

"You did better than good. I'll have to buy you dinner."

"Now that's an offer I can't refuse. What do you want to do about the luggage? Shall we just leave it here until we get back from the college, or would you rather I brought it up now?"

"Take the suitcase and leave the tote and the other stuff here."

Devin tipped an imaginary cap. "Whatever you say, madam."

They headed for Charlie's building, Devin carrying the heavy suitcase in one hand and holding Charlie's hand in the other.

Before entering the lobby, Charlie experienced a brief moment of trepidation. She hadn't had a man in her apartment in ages. Sam, the doorman, didn't count. She wasn't quite ready for this. Not that she thought Devin would ever cross the line. Still, there was something about entering an apartment with this man she'd once been intimate with, that seemed so . . .

Don't be ridiculous! she chided. She should be grateful to Devin for putting his life on hold and coming this far with her. But she didn't want him to think this was an open invitation to move in, to worm his way back into her life. This was purely a temporary arrangement, because as sure as her name was Charlotte, he'd disappear again. For now she'd enjoy the tentative truce, take it a day at a time and see how things played out.

As if tuned into her thoughts, Devin said, "Tell you what, while you're listening to your messages and making your call, I'm going to use my cell phone to find a hotel."

Charlie sighed her relief. "There's both a Ramada and Holiday Inn in Rockland County."

"Right now I'll be happy to find a vacancy in Timbuktu. If we don't get a move on soon, I'll fall asleep at the wheel. I'm already bushed."

Feeling guilty, Charlie squeezed his hand. "There's always my spare bedroom," she offered and could have immediately bitten her tongue. What had gotten into her?

Double glass doors swung open, and Sam the doorman tipped his cap. "Evening, Ms. Canfield." Brown eyes devoid of their usual twinkle glanced hostilely at Devin. "Can I help you with that, suh?"

Amused, Charlie watched the exchange. Sam was mad about something. He was playing the subservient doorman to the hilt. She wondered what had prompted this.

Devin's white smile rivaled any actor's on TV. He dismissed Sam with a flick of his hand. "Thanks, buddy, I've got it under control."

"You sure, suh?"

"Yes, I'm sure."

Holding Charlie's hand, Devin swept through the door. Sam trailed them.

"Where you been, Ms. Canfield? I sure missed you," Sam called when they were steps away from the elevator.

Charlie turned and returned Sam's wide grin. "I've been on a cruise."

"That's great. Did you have a good time then? Was it like the show on TV, *The Love Boat?*" Sam's eyes lit up. "I always wanted to go on one of them cruises."

"You should. I'm in a rush right now, Sam. I've got to get up to the apartment." Charlie's fingers brushed her doorman's sleeve. "If you have some time, stop by this week. I'll show you my pictures."

Sam's eyes literally danced. "Thanks, Ms. Canfield. I'll do that soon as I get the chance—"

"Come on, Charlie," Devin interrupted. "I'd like to get to Poughkeepsie before it gets dark." He punched the elevator button.

She peeked at her watch—4:30 P.M.—they'd better get moving. Out of the corner of her eye, she saw the two men square off like boxers psyching each other out. Charlie hid a smile and stepped between them, quickly making introductions. "Devin, this is Sam. . . ." She struggled to remember the doorman's last name.

"Davis," Sam unhappily supplied.

Devin nodded his acknowledgment and stepped into the open elevator. "Nice to meet you," he shouted back. "Love to stay and chat, but you caught us at a bad time."

Once the door closed, Charlie asked, "Why were you so brusque with Sam? He's really a very nice man."

Devin squeezed the tips of her fingers. "I can't really explain it. Something about the man irked me. Maybe it's the way he was fawning over you."

Perplexed by Devin's uncharacteristic surliness, Charlie

shook her head. "Fawning over me? He was just being nice. What's gotten into you? You never used to be judgmental." She pushed the button for ten, and promptly forgot about the two warring men. Eyes closed, mumbling under her breath, she recited a prayer: "Please, let me hear my daughter's voice on that answering machine. Let this whole thing be a huge mistake."

Devin's words intruded. "Kasey's fine. I'm sure of it."

On the tenth floor Devin followed Charlie down a plushly carpeted hallway, to a front door of carved oak and polished brass numbers. He watched her grope in her pocketbook, find keys, and insert them in the lock.

"Can I help you with that?" Devin asked, setting down Charlie's suitcase.

But Charlie already had the door open. She stood aside, waiting for Devin to enter.

Walking into the apartment, Devin noticed broken shards of glass on the emerald rug. "Careful," he warned, pointing to her stocking feet then back at the splinters.

Charlie frowned. "That's strange, I know there wasn't any glass here when I left." Gingerly she crossed the room and headed for the kitchen. Devin followed.

"Could you have broken a glass?"

"I would have remembered."

"Wasn't the door locked?"

"It appeared to be."

Though her voice remained even, her expression clearly indicated she was frightened. "Want to make yourself a drink while I figure out what's going on? Glasses are in that cupboard, hard liquor in the cabinets." She pointed to the refrigerator adding, "Wine and soda in there. Help yourself. I'm going to check the answering machine."

As the designated driver, Devin opted for a can of coke. He reached into the cupboard to find a glass.

"Damn," he muttered, withdrawing his hand and staring at the bead of blood forming on the tip of his finger.

Curious, he opened the cupboard door wider and peered inside. Jagged bits of broken glass greeted him. "Charlie," Devin shouted. "Why are all your glasses broken?"

No answer from the direction in which she'd disappeared. Devin grabbed a checkered towel off the tile counters, wrapped it around his wounded hand, and went in search of Charlie.

Doors on either side of the hallway lay partially open. He knocked on the first door to his right then stuck his head in the crack. Still no sign of Charlie. An old-fashioned four-poster bed, complete with lace canopy, got his attention. That, and row after row of picture frames assembled on the dresser. Unable to stifle his curiosity, he entered the room and headed for the photos.

He picked up the closest gilt frame, peered closely at the photo, and rubbed his eyes. Strange, but the face had been cut out. A round hole now existed where the features had been. He held the picture away from him. Why would someone take scissors to the print then haphazardly stuff it back into the frame? Picking up the next picture, he squinted again. The photo had received the same treatment. And so had the next, and the next, and the next. Only the last frame remained empty.

Stunned, Devin peered at the entire line-up closely. Each picture had been decapitated then replaced in its frame. First broken glasses in the cupboard. Now this! Could Charlie's stalker have done this?

Piercing screams made Devin send the gruesome pile clattering. "Charlie?" Devin yelled, forgetting his hurt finger and racing toward the bone-chilling sounds. "Charlie, where are you?" Following her shrieks, he bounded into a room at the very end of the hall.

In the center Charlie stood like a zombie. She held the receiver in one hand and clutched a bunch of brightly colored items in the other.

Taking deep breaths to still his pounding heart, his

words tumbled over each other. "What's wrong, honey? What made you scream?" He crossed the room to join her.

Charlie's shoulders shook. Her face registered pure anguish. Even her teeth chattered. Devin felt sympathy pangs. At that moment he was certain of one thing: he would kill anyone who dared hurt her.

"What's wrong?" Devin repeated, grabbing Charlie's shoulders and drawing her to his chest.

Charlie dropped the phone and held out the brightly colored bundle.

Silently Devin took the items. He examined them closely, fingering the silken textures, surprised to find they were Charlie's underthings. What was she trying to say to him? Why didn't anything seem to make sense anymore? Speechless, he stared at the collection of camisoles, the bright red teddy with a hint of black lace, then back at Charlie.

Tears trickled down her cheeks and settled in the brackets at her mouth. Finding her tongue, she insisted, "I didn't leave my underwear on the bed, Devin. Before taking the cruise I hand washed a bunch of stuff and packed them away in my dresser drawer."

Piece by piece Devin examined the lingerie in his fist. Nothing unusual there—they seemed to be in good condition. "Are you sure you didn't leave them out? Packing for a trip gets hectic."

"I'm sure."

"Are you saying someone was in here?" Devin asked.

"Of course someone was in here," Charlie snapped. "What do you think, that I'm some hysterical female who gets her jollies screaming? See," she said, pointing to a five-by-seven picture. "The animal cut off Kasey's head."

"And whoever it was, broke your glasses . . . and destroyed the other . . ." Devin muttered. "We're dealing with a very dangerous man here. It's time to call in the pros."

* * *

A half dozen times, Charlie tried calling Kasey again. No answer. The cops' arrival provided a momentary reprieve. After taking her and Devin's statement, they left promising to be in touch.

On the cream damask couch, Charlie nestled close to Devin, drawing strength from his warmth.

"It'll be alright, baby. I'm here. I promise I won't let anyone hurt you." His cool lips pressed against her warm forehead.

Charlie stiffened. Was he planning on spending the evening?

Sensing her withdrawal, Devin put her gently away from him. "Do you feel better for getting it off your chest and telling the police the whole story?"

She shook her head to clear it. She was probably being paranoid—he hadn't even asked. "Not really. I just want the cops to catch the guy so he'll leave me alone."

"Me, too. I'd like first dibs at him though. There'd be nothing left for the police to arrest."

"I never knew you to be violent," Charlie quipped.

The tip of Devin's finger prodded Charlie's chin upward. "I've grown up, Charlie. There's a lot you don't know."

"Like what?" Charlie challenged.

Devin stalled for time. Charlie had her own problems—she didn't need to hear his. He wiggled his eyebrows and joked, "Like I've become an even better lover than you remember. Someday maybe you'll let me show you my stuff."

"Oh, quit fooling." Charlie slapped his arm. "You really are incorrigible." She could feel the heat in her face and jumped up, suddenly remembering. "Damn! I never did check the answering machine."

"You have messages," Devin confirmed, focusing on the blinking red light.

Charlie nibbled her lower lip, a habit he'd grown used to. "I can't, Devin . . . I just can't. Would you mind getting it?"

"I'll be glad to." Devin unfurled long limbs, depressed the rewind button, his eyes still on Charlie. When a man's rumbling baritone came over loud and clear, Devin winced.

"I've missed you, baby," the male voice crooned. "I'd hoped you were back by now. You and I need to talk, sweetheart. Call me the minute you get in."

Devin's eyebrows shot to his hairline. He pushed the button, stopping the tape. "I thought you told me you weren't involved with anyone?"

"I'm not," Charlie said quickly, feeling the need to explain. "That's Ellis Greene, my co-host and Hot 101's self-appointed Casanova. The man has a wife and three kids at home. He's hardly available."

Devin refrained from comment. Turning away, he pushed the play button and idly registered the number of sales calls beginning with, "I'm calling for the lady of the house." He fast forwarded and heard Charlie's mother's voice, high-pitched with worry, leave an anguished message. He'd almost forgotten how much they sounded alike. At the very end of the tape, a young woman's tearful voice urged her mother to pick up. That must be Kasey.

"Mom? Mom? Are you there? I got this strange note saying you were hurt . . . that I needed to come home right away. I couldn't reach Grandma. Mom, you will call me if you're okay? If I don't hear from you within . . . say, twenty-four hours, Brian's going to drive me home."

Charlie stared at Devin. Though Kasey sounded petrified, knowing she wasn't hurt would have been worth the $9.50 per minute the cruise line charged for a satellite call. Why hadn't she just bitten the bullet and checked her messages from the ship? Slowly her mind replayed Kasey's words. Her daughter sounded frantic but otherwise okay. But who was Brian? That's right—the new boyfriend.

"Unbelievable," Charlie muttered. "I've been had." Anger slowly surfaced as reality sank in. All because of a nasty hoax, her daughter had been terrified, and she'd been forced to cut short her and Devin's vacation. Then the scary thought surfaced, What if the break-in was in some way related? It seemed obvious someone wanted her home.

Just then the phone rang.

"Shall I get it?" Devin mouthed.

Charlie nodded, rage rendering her immobile. What had she ever done to deserve this? Why would someone deliberately set out to make her life hell?"

"Hello," Devin said.

"Hello," he repeated. "Anyone there?"

"It's for you," he said finally, holding out the receiver.

Eight

"Oh, Mom, t-t-hank God you're there," Kasey stuttered. Charlie clutched the receiver and concentrated on taking long slow breaths.

"Mom?" Kasey's voice wavered. "A-are you all right?"

"I'm fine, honey."

"Then why did I get a note saying you weren't . . . ?" Her voice trailed off. "And who was that man who answered?"

One step away from blurting, "Your father," Charlie caught herself just in time. Now how to explain Devin? Thinking quickly she said, "A friend."

Without missing a beat, Kasey came back with, "Are you dating him? Oh, Mom, that's so cool."

"I wouldn't call it that."

"Now, Mom, you're being coy. Be that way if you must, but tell me, did something happen to you? The message I got scared the living daylights out of me. And I'm smack in the middle of finals. Mom, I haven't been able to eat a thing, much less concentrate. Even Brian, who likes his women thin, claims I'm liable to waste away. Now, Mom, you are telling me the truth? You really are okay?"

Convinced by her daughter's ramblings that she was as healthy as ever, Charlie choked back the tears. She listened to Kasey ramble on in the unique way she had of running her sentences together. She waited for a pause before plunging in. "Yes, I'm fine, dear, and you?"

"Stressed. But, Mom, back to the subject. Why would someone send me a note telling me you were hurt? What would be their purpose?"

Good question. And what purpose had it served to tell *her* that Kasey'd been hurt? No sooner had the thought popped into Charlie's head than the answer came. That alarming message had been meant to get her off that cruise. It had been a less than subtle warning to let her know someone meant business. Struggling to keep her voice even and not upset Kasey, Charlie answered. "It was someone's idea of a prank, baby. A pretty nasty prank, I'll admit, but a prank, no less."

"Well, I'm just glad you're okay. I love you, Mom, and I don't know what I'd do if something happened to you. Now I've got to go. I'm meeting Brian for dinner."

"Tell me about this Brian, honey . . . Kasey! Kasey?"

Charlie never got an answer. A resounding click and the hum of the dial tone filled her ear.

Devin's warm fingers circled the base of Charlie's neck. He took the receiver and hung up. "Feeling better?"

Turning toward him, Charlie's smile said it all. "Lots better. You have no idea what it's like to hear that your child's been hurt."

"Oh, but I do."

"You do?" Puzzled, Charlie bit down on her lower lip. "How could you?"

Devin's voice filled with compassion. "Your eyes were a sure giveaway, love. Every time I looked at you, your pain was so real, I felt it." What he didn't say was that her face had reflected the same anguish he'd seen eighteen years ago. It was the time he'd broken his nose in a football game. Charlie'd been the first person out on that field. She'd even outrun the paramedics. She'd stayed to hold his hand through the entire painful ordeal, and insisted on accompanying him to the hospital. At that moment he'd realized he loved her.

Devin took Charlie's wrist and slowly pulled her toward him. When she lay against his chest, he dipped his head, claimed her lips, nipping them gently. Then nuzzling her cheek, he whispered, "Charlie, there was a time when you hurt, I hurt. Don't you remember?"

Then why did you disappear out of my life without so much as a word? she wanted to say but didn't. Still, the trusting side of her wanted to believe his story, wanted to believe that he'd made a sincere effort to reach her that summer.

"Oh, Devin," Charlie sighed, burying her face in the front of his shirt. "That was such a long time ago."

Every curve of Charlie's shapely body beckoned him to touch, to let loose, and devour her. The smell of her perfume lingered in his nostrils, conjuring up wicked thoughts. He massaged Charlie's back then cupped her buttocks. It took everything he had not to pull the skimpy dress over her head and lie her down on the emerald carpet.

"Uuumm," Charlie gasped, feeling his erection against her abdomen. "Devin—uh, Devin?"

"What is it?"

"Now that we don't have to drive up to Mount Merrimack, shouldn't we do something about—sleeping arrangements?"

"That must mean you want me to find a hotel." Devin's hot breath fanned her face. His fingers ruffled the curls at the nape of her neck.

Yes and no. She was so confused. She'd like nothing more than to have him stay. The trouble was, she didn't trust herself alone with him.

"Then just say the word, and I'm out of here," Devin said, releasing her. His smoky gaze probed her face. "But we should do something about calling a locksmith and getting you an alarm system." He glanced at his watch. "Tell you what, how about first thing tomorrow? A few hours' delay isn't going to make much of a difference, especially if it's an inside job as the police suspect."

Even though the cops had ruled out forced entry, Charlie had deliberately stored that piece of information in the back of her mind. She'd refused to acknowledge the possibility that one of her neighbors would harm her. She wanted to think that she'd forgotten to lock the door, though that had never happened before. Either way her space had been violated: an unsettling thought. "I'd feel better if you stayed over," she admitted.

"Are you sure?"

Charlie nodded. "Yes, I'm sure."

Devin's palm cupped her chin. "Are you asking me because you're afraid of being alone?"

Charlie contemplated the question while Devin debated taking her in his arms, and kissing away the little worry lines formed between both brows.

"Charlie?" he said, drawing her to him, unable to resist the feel of her body next to his.

She looked up at him with eyes the color of rich brandy. "Yes, Devin?"

"Are you scared? Is that why you're asking me to stay? You know I'd never let anyone harm you."

Charlie nodded. "I know that. I asked you to stay because I want you here with me. And yes, I am terrified. And yes, I could ask my parents to come stay with me, or I could go to their place. But the truth is, I'd rather have you with me. You make me feel safe."

Devin's heart jumped. He'd made inroads at last. Even Charlie's halfhearted declaration of . . . what? Trust? No . . . confidence, reassured. He supposed it was too soon to hope for more.

Still, in the short time they'd spent together, she'd chipped away at barriers he'd painstakingly erected over the years. It had been like old times talking to her, being with her. For the last eighteen years he'd learned the language of cool, played the game of self-preservation. He'd gotten comfortable hiding behind a mask of smooth sophistication. Though it was merely a defense mechanism, aimed at protecting a heart that had been shattered, he hadn't allowed another soul in. He'd vowed never again to fall in love. Up to now he'd kept that promise.

His separation from Charlie had been one of the most painful events in his young life. In retrospect he couldn't hold her totally to blame for what had happened. He should have demanded answers, gone after her that summer, hitchhiked to Mount Vernon if that's what it took, and pitched a tent on her parents' lawn. But even then would she still have married Tarik?

"I promised you dinner," Charlie said, reaching for his hands and tugging him back to the present. "And I know the perfect place."

Twenty minutes later they pulled up in front of an old country inn with flagstone facade and peaked roof draped in ivy. Devin helped Charlie from the passenger seat, commenting, "Now this is an interesting little place. A little off the beaten track though. How did you find it?"

"Ellis and I stumbled onto it one day. It's actually a bed-and-breakfast spot but has the best home cooking I've ever tasted. People travel for miles to sample the cuisine. And we're in luck this evening, no line."

"Good. I'm famished." Devin felt another stab of jealousy pierce his chest. Charlie had come here with Ellis. But hadn't she assured him the relationship was strictly professional? Holding Charlie's hand, he followed the tulip and daffodil strewn path leading to a vine-covered doorway. Bringing her palm to his lips, he kissed it lightly. His voice didn't betray his thoughts when he said, "We've had a difficult day. I'd say a bottle of wine is definitely in order."

"What! No Perrier Jouet?" Charlie teased.

"Will you settle for a decent Pinot Noir?"

"As long as it's not beer." She hated the stuff.

Devin chuckled softly and held the door open. He followed her into a deserted cobblestoned courtyard with pots of tulips artfully placed. The setting sun wove golden patterns on the canvas umbrellas shading rustic wooden tables.

A high-pitched voice behind them called, "Why, Charlie, how nice to see you again. Will you be joining us for dinner?"

Charlie turned to greet the fiftyish owner, Ross Liljenquist. "Ross, I didn't know you were back from Boca." She covered the space between them and bent over to kiss the gaunt cheek.

"Got back two weeks ago," Ross confirmed, missing her cheek altogether and smooching the air. "Evan's flying in Friday. He'll be glad you came by."

Evan was Ross's lover. They'd purchased the rundown old chapel five years ago and quickly turned it into the now prosperous B&B. Their winters, the slow season, were spent in Florida; the spring and summer in their upstate New York haven.

"Please be sure to give Evan my love, and let him know I'll be by to utter the same sentiments in person." Charlie's hand lingered on the sleeve of Ross's jacket.

Ross openly gaped at Devin. "And who do we have here?" he asked. One hand remained on his hip, the other adjusted huge horn-rimmed glasses.

Remembering the two men had yet to be introduced, Charlie quickly stepped in. "Ross Liljenquist, this is my friend, Devin Spencer."

She watched Devin's large hand cover Ross's frail one. The two men stood for a moment, sizing each other up. Charlie released the breath she'd been holding when Ross returned Devin's smile and began yapping in earnest. "So you're Charlie's young man. I'm so glad she's found someone. I've always despised Ellis Green, knew she could do better."

To cover the fact that she was blushing, Charlie quickly inserted, "Ellis and I were never an item, Ross." She wanted to strangle him. How had he come to the conclusion Devin was her young man?

Ross tssked loudly. His head swiveled from side to side. "Now even the visually challenged would have that one figured out. But you're hardly obtuse, though you must admit the man has the hots for you. He'd spend more time ogling you than the food on his plate."

"Ellis is married," Charlie reminded Ross, not for the first time.

Ross sniffed. "These days that's an institution subject to change. Now come"—he beckoned—"you must be famished."

Inside Ross seated them at a raised booth, partitioned off by lace curtains. Huge cabbage roses were stenciled into the ceiling. The subtle smell of potpourri mingled with the spices used for cooking.

Devin's eyes never left Charlie's. He raised the glass the waitress had set down and ran through the options. "Now what shall we drink to? My health, your safety, or just being together?"

"All of the above," Charlie said, clinking her glass against his. "Thanks for being such a good sport and staying with me."

"Sportsmanship had nothing to do with it." He winked at her. "I was glad that you suggested it, saved me from inviting myself." He sipped his wine and set the goblet down. "Charlie?"

"Yes, Devin."

"Tell me, who would want to do this to you? Is there someone you suspect?"

Twirling the stem of her glass, Charlie thought about it.

No one came to mind. "Haven't got a clue," she answered, glancing at the menu.

"When did you say this whole thing started?"

Charlie thought about it for a moment. "Probably about six months ago. I didn't think much about it then. He was just some guy with a weird voice calling the show and complimenting me on my broadcast. When he started asking me out, I treated it like a joke and laughed him off." Charlie's voice caught.

Devin reached across the table and squeezed her hand. "When did you start getting worried?"

Remembering, Charlie practically inhaled what was left of her glass. Devin refilled it with wine and quickly handed it over. "When he started talking dirty."

"Why didn't you call the police?" Devin probed.

Charlie nibbled on her lower lip. Sheepishly she said, "I guess I felt silly. If you're in the public eye, you get used to some pretty blatant come-ons from fans. Sometimes it's flattering to think you're some guy's dream."

"I can well understand that." Devin captured both hands. His thumb circled her knuckles, making brushlike strokes. Striving to keep things light, he continued. "Speaking of dreams, you've always been mine."

Charlie kept her attention on the menu. "Have you decided what you're having?" she asked, not looking up.

"I did a long time ago."

Face aflame she made her choice. "I think I'm going to have the shrimp." She stabbed the menu with one finger.

Just then their waitress, a pert blonde in a micro-miniskirt returned. She set down a steaming platter of clams casino before them. "Compliments of the house," she said matter-of-factly. "Ross says you're to eat every last morsel, or I'm not to return."

"Oh, we're confident you'll be back." Devin was already digging in. True to his word the clams disappeared in record time.

* * *

Entrees devoured and dessert declined, they sipped on cappuccino.

After awhile Devin said somewhat reluctantly, "I suppose we'd better get going." He reached for the check.

Charlie slapped his hand. "Oh, no, you don't. This is my treat."

But Devin already had his wallet out. "Sorry. When you're out with me, I pay."

"Fine. If that's what makes you happy. But only on the condition I get to cook you dinner tomorrow night."

"Now there's an invitation I couldn't possibly turn down. Ready?" He laid a handful of crisp bills on the table.

"Don't you need change?"

"No. Tip's included." He took her elbow, helping her up.

On the way out they ran into Ross.

"Again you've outdone yourself." Charlie patted her full stomach. "The meal was superb."

They said their goodbyes, Devin echoing her sentiments. Ross's beaming smile lit up the small vestibule. He called after them, "Does that mean you'll be back tomorrow?"

Charlie tossed the words over her shoulder. "Not tomorrow but maybe next week. I promised this man some home cooking, and I aim to please."

Devin kissed her cheek, putting an end to further conversation.

Nine

Somewhere between sleep and wakefulness, Devin smelled the aroma of freshly brewed coffee. The tangy scent of hazelnut tickled his nostrils and forced his eyes open. Disoriented, he shook the fog from his brain and searched his memory for answers. Staring up at the vaulted ceiling didn't give him a clue. Neither did the cream-colored room with its stenciled ivy vines rimming the perimeters. Finally his vision cleared, settling on an antique mahogany dresser where an earthen pitcher sat. At last the pieces fell into place.

Just then Charlie stuck her head around the door and said, "How about some breakfast, sleepyhead?"

"That sounds good." Lazily his eyes traveled the length of her body. A smile broke.

She entered the room in a short pink kimono. This time he felt a distinct tug in his groin. His eyes followed those long, long legs until they came to a full stop. He watched her throw open the blinds in one fluid motion. The early morning sun rushed in, turning her kimono transparent. Now he could even see through the flimsy teddy she wore underneath. His eyes focused on the curve of her breasts, the shapely buttocks outlined against silk. The tug in his loins became a distinct ache.

Devin sat up, letting the bedclothes slide to his waist.

He crooked a finger. "Come over and say good morning properly," he urged, patted the spot next to him.

Eyebrows arched, Charlie threw him a skeptical look. She crossed the room, fidgeted with the belt of her kimono self-consciously, then perched on the edge of the bed. "Yes?"

"How about moving a little closer?" Devin's fingers drummed the mattress.

He was too close for comfort. His half-naked body beckoned enticingly. Smiling, Charlie complied. And although there was no one to overhear them, she kept her voice low. "What is it you wanted to talk to me about?"

Devin's arms reached out, pulling her closer. "I just wanted to say good morning properly." He claimed her lips and covered her throat with tiny kisses.

Up against the hardness of him, she had difficulty breathing. Through the lightweight kimono and sheer teddy, the coarse hairs of his chest caressed her nipples. She felt the tips hardening, welding themselves into taunt twin peaks. She breathed in the masculine scent that only Devin exuded. He smelled of sleep and last evening's cologne. When his lips brushed her throat and moved upward to claim her open mouth, she thought she would faint. His tongue found hers, circled the roof of her mouth, and dipped in again. With each calculated exit and entry, her control lessened. When his hands slipped beneath the kimono and under her teddy, she whimpered out loud.

"Charlie," Devin groaned, "should I stop?"

She realized it was her call, he was leaving it totally up to her. But how could she end things now, when every heightened sense whirled out of control? She could hardly think, much less talk. The word "no" and Devin didn't go together.

"Charlie, there's nothing I'd like more than to love

you." The tips of Devin's fingers caressed her aching nipples.

"Love me, Devin."

"Is that a yes, Charlie?" Devin's labored breathing invaded her ear. He sounded as if he'd just jogged uphill.

"What about protection?" she had the presence of mind to ask. Every nerve in her body shuddered as she realized she'd come to a decision. Still, carried away or not, she wasn't about to take chances. A man as good-looking as Devin hadn't been residing in a monastery these past eighteen years.

"I think I can arrange something." He gave her a parting kiss and reluctantly released her to cross the room.

Charlie followed his movements, enjoying the way his black briefs hugged his tight muscular buns—the way his thigh muscles rippled when he bent over to withdraw the small foil package from his wallet—the sizeable bulge at the front of his shorts.

"I've had this awhile. I'm sure it's still serviceable," he said, flashing her a smile and retracing his path. God, how could one man be so unbelievably good-looking? Would the physical package live up to her memories?

"Was I gone too long, darling?" Devin peeled away the kimono. One hand cupped her buttocks, and the other unsnapped the crotch of the teddy. She groaned when his fingers found her throbbing core, stroked her softness, and explored the hidden recesses. "I'd say not," he chuckled. He slid the straps of the teddy from her shoulders and feasted on her with his eyes. "Oh, Charlie, you are every bit as lovely as I remember." He bent his head, capturing a toffee-colored nipple in his mouth, biting down gently. Her whole body tingled, even her ears rang.

The ringing phone was an unwelcome intrusion. Groaning, Charlie struggled to an upright position. "I suppose I'd better get that."

"Ignore it."

"Can't, might be work."

Devin sighed. "You're still on vacation. Let the machine pick up."

"I'd feel compelled to return the call. Besides, my vacation ended yesterday, right after I told the station I was back in town."

Devin's muttered expletive resounded. He rolled onto his side, hefted the receiver, and handed it over.

Charlie's eyes pleaded for understanding. Yes, the phone call had come at a bad time. But this was her bread and butter he was talking about, and she had promised the station to remain available. Only yesterday she'd learned the ratings had nosedived in her absence. After hosting just one show with Ellis, her stand-in, Karen Hardy, had thrown in the towel and walked out. The buzz around the radio station confirmed that Ellis had made Karen's life a living hell.

Charlie cradled the phone between chin and collarbone and gasped, "Hello."

The seconds ticked by with no answer. All the while Devin's fingers played sweet music across her skin. He stroked her body like a delicate instrument, his fingers plucking her nipples, and moving downward to settle between her thighs, drumming against her womanhood. In his wake he left a path of bittersweet agony. Every nerve throbbed.

"Hello," Charlie moaned into the phone.

"Hang up, Charlie," Devin urged, his voice heavy with longing.

"You slut," the voice on the other end shouted. "How could you do this to me? I've waited this long just to have you betray me!"

Gasping loudly, Charlie dropped the receiver. Tears, unchecked, flowed freely down her cheeks. What had she ever done to anyone to deserve this abuse? She clutched her head in both hands.

Devin grabbed the receiver. "You cowardly bastard," he shouted, interrupting the tirade. "Don't ever call here again, or I'll hunt you down and cut out your filthy tongue." Devin slammed down the phone and pulled Charlie into his arms.

Crooning into her ear, he added, "He can't hurt you, baby. Not if I'm around." His hands smoothed her hair. He rocked her until the tears subsided. At last the heaving stopped and he whispered, "Now how about I get us some of that wonderful-smelling coffee? Then we'll call the police, the telephone company, and the locksmith."

Determined to gain control, Charlie sniffed. "I'll make you breakfast. You must be starving."

"No, I'll make you breakfast." Devin catapulted out of bed, grabbed one of the bath towels she'd left him last evening, and draped it over his arm. Affecting a French accent, he asked, "Madam, what will it be?"

Despite the jolting pain in her stomach, the tightening at the back of her throat, a giggle escaped. "Not bad, Pierre. Tell you what, I'm going to forget about watching my figure today. I want pancakes. Lots of them. A whole dripping stack, laden with butter and syrup."

"You've got it. And about that figure—I'll be glad to watch it for you, girl." Taking her hand, Devin pulled her up to join him. "Now dry your eyes. Breakfast will be ready in fifteen minutes."

Fifteen minutes later Charlie entered her once immaculate kitchen, inhaling the mouthwatering smell of cinnamon pancakes and sizzling bacon. She ignored the drippings on her once pristine white tile counter and the jumbled contents of her refrigerator covering every inch. Devin pulled out a stool and motioned for her to sit. In her absence he'd thrown on a pair of sweatpants and a T-shirt.

"Breakfast will be up in two minutes." He cleared a spot, set down two mugs, and reached for the coffeepot. After filling both cups, he opened the refrigerator. "Do you take cream?"

"Yes. Should be in the refrigerator, unless it's out here." She made a sweeping motion in the direction of the cluttered counter.

"So that's what's in the pitcher. No wonder the liquid seemed thick."

"You didn't . . . no, don't bother telling me. I'm not going to feel guilty. I'm just going to gobble down those delicious hotcakes and pretend they're low-calorie wafers or something."

Devin cleared another path to set down dishes and cutlery. He turned back to the stove. Every movement made his muscles ripple. And although still shaken by the call, Charlie was even more angry at the pervert's timing.

"What are you thinking about?" Devin asked, flipping pancakes and bacon onto her plate.

If only he knew. "I really should stop by the station sometime today," she lied.

"No. You really should take care of personal business. We should go through the phone book and find a locksmith. In fact I think I'll call one now. When you're done eating, we'll call the police and the phone company." He turned his back on her and began opening drawers. "Where's your yellow pages?"

Charlie pointed to a cupboard. "Bully," she grumbled, forking large portions of pancake into her mouth, and listening as he spoke. "Mmm. Heaven. Where did you learn to cook like this?"

After he hung up, he returned to her side. Using his napkin, he wiped a trickle of syrup from her lips. "In answer to your question, I've been a bachelor for a long, long time, hon. You either haunt the fast-food chains, con someone into cooking, or take lessons."

Charlie knew with certainty that he'd wouldn't need to con anyone into cooking. She shifted uneasily on her stool, refusing to acknowledge that she just might be jealous. Over the years women most probably had tripped over their heels to make Devin breakfast. She'd bet her life that he'd had more than his share of female chefs. And just that thought left her with a sinking feeling at the base of her gut. While the outer trappings might have changed, she was in many ways still the insecure girl he'd dated.

"So I took lessons," Devin continued. "Twice a week. And far from being tedious, I found that I enjoyed it. Cooking was something I did well, plus it helped me relax."

Charlie bit into another delicious pancake, enjoying hearing him reminisce. An hour and a half later, they were still talking when the buzzer rang.

"Want me to get that?" Devin swiped at his mouth with his napkin.

Nodding, Charlie used her fork to point out the location of the intercom. She watched Devin depress the button on the far right and shout, "Who is it?"

Static greeted. "Who's there?" Devin shouted over the buzz.

This time a man's voice came over loud and clear. "Sorry, must have the wrong apartment."

"Who are you looking for?"

"Canfield, 10G."

Devin's gaze met Charlie's.

"It's Sam, my doorman," Charlie mouthed.

"How can I help you, Sam?"

Another brief pause, then finally, "Do I have the right apartment?"

"Yes, Sam," Charlie stepped in front of Devin. "What's up?"

"There's a man here, says you called him to do some work for you."

"The locksmith," Devin whispered.

"All right. Send him up."

While Devin let the locksmith in, Charlie retired to her

bedroom to call the phone company. After speaking with a supervisor at New York Bell, she was promised a new and unlisted number by the end of the day.

"You've really helped make this process easier," Charlie complimented the woman. "Thank you."

"You're very welcome." The operator's clipped tones held just a hint of New England. "These days so many people are opting for unlisted numbers that we aim to make the switch as painless as possible. Seems you can't be too careful."

By the time Charlie hung up, the locksmith had completed his business. He stood chatting with Devin waiting to be paid. Charlie wrote him a check and walked him to the door.

No sooner had the door closed behind him than Devin started in. "Did you get a chance to call the cops?"

"Not yet. I haven't had a moment to spare. I'll do it right after I call my mother. She'll need to know what's going on." She walked away.

"I'd feel better if you called the police now, Charlie," Devin said, following her. He handed her the remote phone and watched until she'd punched in the numbers. She waited an interminable amount of minutes for someone to pick up and even more minutes to be connected with the right department. It took even longer to locate Officer Phillips, one of the duo assigned to her case.

Just as she was about to hang up, Officer Phillips barked, "Ms. Canfield, I'm surprised to hear from you this early. Has something happened?"

She told him about the pervert's call, then asked, "I know it's probably way too soon, but have you made any headway with my case?"

The officer cleared his throat, stalling. "Well, Ms. Canfield, it's much too soon to tell, but we're following several leads. We've focused on men with a propensity for stalking single women. As a matter of fact, I wonder if you'd have the time to stop by the station today. I've got some pictures I'd like you to go over. Possibly you might recognize someone you've run into recently."

Charlie hesitated before committing. She'd promised to drop by the radio station. Not that she'd planned on making a day of it, but there was always the possibility that she'd be roped into doing the show with Ellis. "Sure thing," she said after a second or two had elapsed. "I might be able to fit it into my schedule."

"Good. I'll see you shortly then."

The hum of the dial tone reverberated in her ear. Devin came up behind her, placed an arm around her waist and asked, "How did it go?"

Charlie put the phone back in its cradle and leaned into him. He was as solid as an oak. "Officer Phillips wants me to come down to the station."

Devin spun her around to face him. His warm palm stroked her cheek. "Is there some new development?"

"No, I don't think so. He just wants me to look at some pictures."

"Would you like company?"

"Love it."

His lips grazed her neck. "It'll take me only a few minutes to shower and get dressed. I'll clean up the kitchen if you want to get ready."

A half hour later, they emerged from the elevator and crossed the building's sumptuous lobby. Heavy velvet drapes had been pushed back to let in the morning sun, now reflecting off highly polished floors. Devin held Charlie's hand as she minced across the marble surface in her trademark too-high heels. Sam's noticeable absence produced a huge sigh of relief. Today she was in no mood to make small talk with her doorman or referee two hostile men.

Outside a balmy spring breeze greeted them. Charlie's

steps faltered. She stopped short under the striped green canopy providing shelter from the elements.

"You okay?" Devin asked, noting her grimace.

"I think so." She wriggled her right ankle, hoping to dislodge whatever had caused the discomfort.

"No, you're not."

"I'm fine." She tugged him along. "Must be something in my shoe."

They'd reached the parking lot, on the side of the building, when Devin released her hand. He folded his arms and glared down at her. "Woman, I'm not taking another step until you remove that shoe and check."

"Bully," she said, inching off the taupe Kenneth Cole sling-back.

A slight movement from an overhead balcony caught Devin's eye. Acting more out of instinct than anything else, he hurled himself in front of Charlie and swept her into his arms. Together they toppled to the ground.

A mere second later a terra-cotta flowerpot ricocheted off the roof of a canary yellow Corvette, leaving behind a dent in the hood. The clay pot hit the asphalt, rolled several feet, then collided with the wheels of a silver Porsche. The pot had been reduced to shards. Its contents—a cluster of bloodred tulips and soil—lay strewn across the parking lot.

"Honey, are you all right?" Devin asked, when he was finally able to catch his breath. He cradled Charlie against him, ignoring the pain in his shins, the grit embedded in burning palms.

Charlie lay prostrate in his arms, not making a sound, not even a whimper. Eyes closed, her breath came in little gasps.

"Charlie?" Devin said, giving her a firm shake. "Answer me."

Like a broken doll her head lolled to one side, the pulse at her neck barely perceptible. Devin shook her again—

this time panic forcing him to be far less gentle. "Talk to me, Charlie. Talk to me."

It was her silence that scared him most.

Ten

Devin spoke louder and faster. "Charlie, come on, girl, say something." He clutched her shoulders and shook her roughly. "Come on, girl," he repeated. "Talk to me."

Charlie's eyelashes fluttered. She had to have the longest lashes he'd ever seen. He used to call them curled bits of chocolate. He saw the whites of her eyes just before the lids closed. Memories of Charlie had haunted his dreams for almost two decades. He couldn't lose her now. He concentrated on the pulse at the hollow of her neck, willing her to open her eyes and say something—anything. Why had he allowed this to happen?

"Charlie!" The words spilled out. "Speak to me." He cradled the back of her neck with one hand then swiped his forehead with the other. "Charlie! Snap out of it. Come on, honey."

Charlie's lids fluttered open. He could see the whites of her eyes, the dilated pupils. "Devin," she moaned, her hand reaching up to brush his cheek. "You saved my life."

"No, I simply reacted." He hugged her to him. "Baby, you scared the hell out of me." Covering her face with kisses, he added, "I love you Charlie. I always have."

Charlie's breath caught in her chest. Had she heard him correctly? Before she could respond, Sam came rushing out of the building. She shelved the conversation, determined to pick it up later.

"Ms. Canfield, are you okay?" Sam skidded to a stop. He focused his attention on Devin. "Is Ms. Canfield okay, or will she need an ambulance?"

"I'm fine, Sam." Though she was still shaken up, Charlie shrugged out of Devin's arms. Kneeling, she brushed the gravel from her trousers.

"No, you're not." Devin pointed to the place where her cream-colored slacks were torn, and a deep circle of crimson grew bigger by the moment.

She moved out of his reach, feigning a calm she did not feel, and flicked the soil from the ruined trousers. "I'll be perfectly fine once I spray on Bactine and change clothes. Shall we go back to the apartment?"

Sam hovered. "You sure you don't need me to call a doctor, Ms. Canfield?" He stood cap in hand, looking totally bewildered.

Devin interjected. "I don't think she does, Sam." Then more kindly, "It's nice of you to be so concerned, but there's really no need to worry. I'll take Charlie to a doctor if she needs one." He glanced in the direction of the building, where a small group gathered. "Better get back to your post, or you're going to have all sorts of strangers entering the building."

Sam, looking as if he would much rather stay with Charlie, crouched over her one last time. "You sure you'll be fine, Ms. Canfield? How about I get you some water?"

"Thanks, Sam, but that won't be necessary. You go take care of business, and Devin will handle things."

Upstairs in the tenth floor apartment, after Devin had tended her scrapes and bruises and put salve on his own, Charlie went to change into one of the sweat suits she favored. When she returned, Devin handed her the phone.

Chewing on her lower lip, she threw him a puzzled look. "What's that for?"

"To call Officer Phillips. I imagine he's expecting you."

Charlie's eyes narrowed. There were times when Devin

could be such a nudge. Softening the look with a smile, she punched in the numbers, waited an interminable number of minutes for someone to pick up, then said, "Can you put me through to Officer Phillips?"

An unidentified person asked, "Who may I say is calling?"

"Charlotte Canfield."

This time she didn't have long to wait. Officer Phillips, in his James Earl Jones voice, growled into her ear, "Phillips here."

"Officer Phillips . . ."

"Ms. Canfield, I've been expecting you."

"Sorry, I've been detained. I met with a little accident."

Phillips's pause was almost palpable. "What kind of accident?"

She told him, her eyes following Devin, who'd managed to open the patio door and walk out.

"I don't like what I'm hearing," Phillips growled. "This pot just fell off a patio as you walked by? It might very well be coincidence, Ms. Canfield, but I'd like to check it out. I'll stop by with my partner, O'Reilly. Can you stay put until we get there?"

"Yes. But how soon will that be? I promised to stop by the radio station later today."

"I'll be there"—Charlie imagined him scanning his watch—"in twenty minutes."

As she hung up, Devin called to her from the outdoors.

"Charlie."

"What is it, Devin?"

"I didn't know you were into plants."

"I'm a wannabe botanist," she shouted. "Gardening relaxes me."

"Why don't you come on out here and tell me what Phillips had to say, then you can tell me about your horticultural ventures."

Gardening was a hobby she'd only just taken up recently.

On a whim she'd purchased some seeds and loved watching them grow. As it grew warmer, she'd bought bulbs from the local nursery and gotten off on seeing them blossom. Now every square inch of the large patio held huge terra-cotta pots of flowering greenery. She couldn't wait to really go wild this summer.

Charlie stepped onto the wraparound patio. Still jittery from her fall, her expression softened when she saw Devin seated on her white wicker chair, his feet propped on the coffee table. Around him, colorful tulips and yellow daffodils swayed in the spring breeze.

Sensing her presence, Devin looked up. "Well?"

She told him about the conversation she'd had with Phillips, concluding, "He's coming over."

"Good. What are those?" Devin changed the subject and pointed to a terra-cotta pot of tiny purple, yellow, and white flowers.

"Crocuses."

She bent over, plucked one of the fragile blooms, tucked it behind his ear, and joked, "You look simply mah-velous, darling." Bending over again, she reached for a glint of gold partially hidden behind another enormous pot. Her fingers curved around the sparkling object before it slipped from her grasp. She tried again, this time managing to pick up the bracelet and examine it closely. It was the kind that usually had a man's initials engraved in diamonds on the plate—the type she'd seen macho men with lots of chest hair wearing. Rising, she waved the thick-link bracelet at Devin. "Did you lose something?"

One of Devin's eyebrows shot skyward. "Come now. Though I've been known to wear a chain upon occasion, I'm hardly the gold bracelet type. Did you do any entertaining prior to the cruise?" His voice held a teasing note, but his eyes looked worried.

Charlie held the bracelet up high. The sun glinted off the gold. She turned it back and forth, squinting to see if there were initials she'd missed. "Do you think . . . ," she muttered, her voice quaking.

Devin silenced her with a finger to her lips. "Let's not even think it."

"The person who owns this bracelet entered my apartment and . . ."

"Shhhhh. You're letting your imagination run wild. It probably belongs to a friend." Abruptly Devin changed the subject. "So tell me, did it take long to get this garden up and running?" He gestured at the profusion of budding greenery.

Charlie's hips rested on the wrought-iron railing enclosing the terrace. She shook her head. "Not really. I just plopped seeds and cuttings into pots, and presto! they grew. I think I must have a green thumb."

Inhaling the crisp morning air, she admired her handiwork. The effect was breathtaking, and it had taken only minimal effort to transform the terrace into a spring wonderland. Her brows knotted into a frown when she spotted a sparse area in the abundance of greenery. "I could swear," she mumbled, "there was another pot of tulips right over there." She pointed to the right of an oversized urn filled with swaying daffodils, refusing to give voice to the possibility that an unknown someone had been out there.

Devin swung himself out of the wicker chair. His arms enclosed her on either side of the railing. "Where?" He raised one hand to brush the nail of his thumb against her lower lip.

"I'm not joking, Devin. In fact I'm certain there was a pot of tulips right there." Again she pointed. "I remember because they'd bloomed a day or so ago and were a peculiar shade of red. Bloodred I called them."

Devin's face welded itself into a careful blank. "Are you sure?"

When he released his hold on the railing and took her

hand, she wondered if he was thinking what she was thinking. "Come," he urged, tugging her along. "Show me the exact spot."

She led him through a maze of pots and urns filled to overflowing with spring flowers then stopped next to the pot of daffodils. "There," she said, pointing to an empty space.

Devin's eyes followed her finger. Only a circular ring of dirt indicated that a flowerpot had once been there. "Could you have moved it?" he asked.

"No."

His grim expression didn't offer the reassurance she sought, though his fingers squeezed hers. Charlie dismissed the sinking feeling in the pit of her stomach. She couldn't believe that someone had deliberately set out to hurt her.

The doorbell rang, and for a brief moment their eyes locked.

Devin reluctantly severed the connection. "Shall I get it?"

"Sure. If you want to."

He released Charlie and took a tentative step toward the door. Charlie's gaze followed him as he retraced his path through wide French doors. In seconds she heard rumbling voices and concluded that Phillips and O'Reilly had arrived. Still, she remained frozen, unable to move, to put one foot in front of the other and go inside.

"Charlie," Devin called. "Officers Phillips and O'Reilly are here. Would you like me to bring them out?"

In a voice that sounded nothing like her own, she answered, "No, I'll be right in."

The two officers sat on the cream-colored damask couch, looking strangely out of place. Undercover cops masquerading as home boys, they'd dressed in the uniform of the inner city: low-slung jeans, oversized sweatshirts, and caps jammed on backward. Only O'Reilly's prominent freckles and bright curly red mop confirmed his ancestry.

"Hello, Ms. Canfield," they greeted in unison, awkwardly shuffling to their feet. Officer Phillips tossed a manila envelope on the coffee table and stuck out a hand. "Nice to see you again. Sorry it's under such circumstances." He beat O'Reilly only by seconds.

"How are you, Ms. Canfield?" O'Reilly added, clasping Charlie's hand in a firm grip.

Charlie's gaze shifted to the envelope then back at the cops. "I'm a little shaken, but I'll be fine once I catch my breath. May I get you gentlemen a cool drink, some coffee maybe?"

"No thanks. We're on a tight schedule."

She motioned to the couch, waited for them to sit, then perched on the love seat next to Devin.

Pen poised, O'Reilly removed a pad from his hip pocket and began to scribble. "So tell us what happened, Ms. Canfield." Charlie repeated what she'd told them earlier on the phone then added, "That's all I can remember. Devin can probably fill you in from that point on."

And Devin did. When he was done, Phillips said with a smirk, "Uh-huh. So who was on Ms. Canfield's terrace and shoved the pot off?"

The police couldn't suspect Devin, Charlie thought. He'd been with her when the pot came tumbling down. He'd saved her life. "Why don't we go outside," she hastily interjected. "Come, I'll take you."

Charlie and the cops departed for the outdoors, leaving Devin pacing the room. He took short breaths, determined to get his temper under control before facing the officers again.

By the time Charlie returned with both cops, he'd forced himself to smile.

"Well?" Devin greeted. "Have you solved our mystery?"

O'Reilly tugged at a bright red tuft escaping his cap.

"We'll have to do some nosing around, talk to the neighbors and such. Ms. Canfield just told me you'd recently changed locks but hadn't had a chance to install the alarm. Makes you wonder how someone could get onto your balcony."

"Rooftop." Phillips supplied, pointing upward. "This is the top floor."

Phillips's sarcasm seemed lost on O'Reilly—the redhead went back to scribbling in his book while Phillips resumed the seat he'd vacated. "Anything else?"

"Yes, I found this outside." Charlie withdrew the gold link bracelet from the pocket of her slacks.

"It's not yours?" Phillips eyed Devin speculatively.

Devin's smile came through clenched teeth. "Sorry, but I'm not the gold bracelet type."

"Just thought I'd ask."

O'Reilly took the bracelet from Charlie while Phillips reached for the manila envelope he'd placed on the table earlier. He withdrew a fistful of black-and-white photos, fanned them out like a deck of cards, and tossed out the question: "Recognize any of these people?"

Charlie crouched beside the table, carefully working her way through the collection. At the very end she held up a photo of a man in a red, black, and green knitted cap, squinted at it, then hurriedly put it back. The suspect looked like Ellis—a ridiculous thought. She picked up the snapshot again, this time examining it at eye level. He was the spitting image of Ellis: a dated version perhaps, but Ellis nonetheless.

She threw the question at Phillips: "How old is this photo?"

Phillips kept his eyes on her, pausing longer than it should have taken to answer. "Why? Do you recognize the man?"

Charlie hesitated and continued to flip through pictures. What if she was way off base? Was it fair to implicate

Ellis on a whim? "No. At least I don't think so," she lied, "though he looks a little like someone I might have gone to school with."

"Who?"

"I don't remember his name." Hastily she put the pictures back in order.

Skeptical, Phillips slid off the couch, gathered the photos, and gestured to his partner. "If memory returns, Ms. Canfield, please give us a call. We'll keep the surrounding areas under surveillance and have the neighborhood patrolled more frequently. We'll be in touch shortly."

"Whoosh," Charlie said the moment the door closed behind both officers. "I feel like I've been put through the ringer." She sank onto the couch.

"You have, baby. You have." Devin's supple fingers kneaded Charlie's back, easing the tension.

"Oh, that feels good. Take it a little higher. Perfect."

The phone rang. Devin's fingers stopped. "Shall I get it?"

"No, I'll get it." Charlie's tone brooked no argument. Catching Devin's quizzical glance, she hastened to reassure. "It's probably just my mom. She's the only person with the new number."

"What about Kasey?"

"I plan on calling her later. I'll give it to her then."

Charlie picked up the phone, prepared for the cross-examination. Earlier she'd told her mother that the cops were coming over. Now she'd have to repeat the conversation verbatim.

"Hello, sweet face," a familiar voice greeted.

Charlie sucked in her breath. Just how in the hell had he gotten her new number?" Her hand trembled as she positioned the phone under her chin and waited for him to go on.

"Charlie?"

"What?"

"You don't sound at all happy to hear from me."

"I'm not. How did you get my unlisted number?" She chewed on her lower lip and glanced in Devin's direction. She knew he'd be following the one-sided conversation.

"Is everything okay?" Devin mouthed.

Covering the receiver, she whispered, "This shouldn't take but a minute." She spoke into the phone again. "Well, Tarik?"

Tarik's voice oozed charm as he told her, "Your mother gave me your number, Charlie. I'm forced to call you from across the street because your pitbull of a doorman refuses to let me up."

Eleven

"I b-beg y-y-your pardon, what did you say?"

Tarik spoke slowly, dragging out each word as if speaking to a child. "I'm across the street, Charlie."

A dull throb surfaced at her temples, signaling a tension headache on the horizon. She didn't need this aggravation right now. Not a face-to-face confrontation with her ex.

"What are you doing in my neighborhood, Tarik?" Charlie practically shrieked when his words finally registered. She glanced over to see Devin still following the conversation.

Tarik's voice crackled through the receiver. "Let me up, and I'll tell you."

"No."

Charlie wondered what had brought him to her little town. She would be fooling herself to think it had anything to do with Kasey. It must have something to do with him, she decided. Tarik was too self-centered to cut his cruise short for any other reason.

"Come on."

She took a deep breath and counted to ten before answering, "I've got company, Tarik. Now isn't a good time."

"It's the only time I've got, babe," he wheedled. "I drove all the way here to talk to you. Can't you be a little more accommodating?"

Charlie rolled her eyes and sighed. She supposed there

was no harm in hearing him out. She just hoped he was sober. Her tone was pure business when she responded, "You haven't given me much choice. When you get to the lobby, please have Sam buzz me."

She replaced the receiver and turned around to find Devin looming over her. "What did that jerk want?"

Charlie chewed on her lower lip, debating how to break the news. She decided to just go for it. "Honestly I haven't a clue. But he's across the street and claims to have something urgent to discuss."

"You plan on leaving him there, I hope." Devin's arms encircled her shoulders as he drew her close. "Please, Charlie, don't tell me you've agreed to let him up?"

She wanted to tell him she'd been tempted to send Tarik away, that she'd struggled with the decision. But decency had, as always, prevailed.

Charlie's voice broke as she continued. "I don't have much of a choice. If I don't have him up, he'll only get loud and create a scene, and then the entire neighborhood will be in my business. Besides, Devin," she quickly added, "He is the father of my child, and I feel somewhat obligated."

The buzzer went off, jolting her back to the present. She shrugged out of Devin's arms, reached for the button on the intercom, and quickly depressed it. "Yes, Sam?"

"You've got a visitor, Ms. Canfield. There's a Mr. Connors here to see you."

"Send him up."

For a very long moment, the silence was broken only by Devin's grumbling. "So what I am supposed to do while this clown monopolizes your time—hide in the bedroom?"

She reached for his hand and tugged him down to sit beside her. "No, you're going to remain right here and act as my protector." Her lips grazed his cheek, and she whispered against his ear, "I'll get rid of him quickly, I promise."

The doorbell chimed.

"That must be him." Charlie rose and headed for the door.

She steeled herself for the confrontation to come. Tarik would not be pleased to find Devin in her apartment. Naturally he'd expect an explanation.

She watched Tarik sail through the open door, his Burberry coat flapping behind him. She suppressed a smile as he scanned the room, striking a pose, enviable of any *Gentlemen's Quarterly* model.

"Hey, girlfriend, you've done some redecorating since the last time I was here. Now let's see, when was that?"

"Two months ago. And no, you were just to drunk to notice."

Tarik ignored her jab. He pointed to the Nubian statuettes Charlie'd bought on vacation in Monrovia. "Yes indeed, the ladies are a nice touch." Then he spotted Devin. "That's your company?" he snarled, jerking a thumb in Devin's direction.

Charlie watched Devin rise from the damask couch and languidly cross the room to face Tarik. He seemed bent on holding his anger in check and even held out a hand, managing to sound civil. "Nice to see you, Tarik." He pasted on a smile, adding, "What made you change your plans?"

"Huh?" Tarik's icy cold hand was nowhere as frigid as his eyes. He went through the motions of shaking, still staring Devin down. "Oh, you mean me leaving the cruise. What can I say, I had second thoughts. My baby needed me, and I figured my wife could use my support. I hadn't planned on finding you here."

"Ex-wife, Tarik," Charlie was quick to insert. "Sit down if you're staying. I'll put up coffee, then you can say your piece."

"Forget the coffee. I'll take some bourbon, if you have it."

Charlie's tone was ever so contrite. "Sorry, I'm out of

booze. I can get you soda, coffee, Pellegrino, or . . . nothing." She could tell by the pungent odor of Tarik's breath that alcohol was the last thing he needed. If she fixed him a drink, he'd be parked on her couch for the rest of the afternoon. She didn't need that headache.

"Pellegrino, then," he said, his eyes sliding from Charlie to Devin.

"How about you, Devin?" Charlie's eyes pleaded with him to keep cool. Tarik without liquid fortification would be gone soon, she hoped.

Devin's answering smile was genuinely warm. He'd never been able to deny Charlie a thing. "Thanks. I'll pass, perhaps later."

Charlie left the two men sizing each other up and departed to fetch the bottled water. Once she was out of earshot, Tarik dropped any pretense of civility. "Why are you here, Spencer?"

Devin stroked his chin and seemed to contemplate the question. "Strange, but I could swear I just asked you the same thing."

Without taking his eyes off Devin, Tarik eased himself onto the love seat. He crossed one navy leg over the other, smoothed the crease on his slacks, and continued to eyeball Devin. "Like I said, I came to find out about my kid. What I can't quite figure, is your reason for being here."

Devin's dimples were prominent slashes. He flashed a frosty smile at the man calmly seated opposite him. "Don't have one. I'm Charlie's guest. I'm here to look after her."

Charlie's return ended the hostile exchange. On the coffee table she set down a coaster and Tarik's glass then perched on the couch and motioned for Devin to join her. "Well?" she said, turning her attention back to Tarik. "I'm still not quite sure why you're here."

Tarik's blue and gray argyle-clad ankle made circular motions. She focused on a rotating black shoe that must have cost a bundle.

"Do we have to talk in front of him?" Tarik's chin jutted in Devin's direction.

Reaching for Devin's hand, she linked her fingers through his and smiled benignly at Tarik. "Whatever you have to say can certainly be said in front of Devin."

A muscle in one of Tarik's cheeks twitched. He ground out, "So that's how it is, huh?"

"That's how it is."

Tarik's fingers fastened on the gold pendant peeking through the open neck of his shirt. As he twirled it back and forth, Charlie's glance shifted to the chain itself. Instinctively she knew she had seen the mate somewhere before, but memory escaped her. She released Devin's hand and stood up abruptly. "Now tell me, Tarik, why exactly *are* you here?"

Tarik's ankle continued its circular motion. He seemed to contemplate the question. "Charlie, you don't seem at all glad to see me. And to think I disrupted my vacation to be with you. How's my kid doing?"

Charlie's eyes remained fixated on the twirling pendant. Slowly the pieces were coming together. Sounding vaguely distracted, she answered, "Kasey's fine, Tarik. No thanks to you. Now if that's really the reason you're here, I'm afraid I'm going to have to cut our visit short. I have to go down to the radio station."

Tarik took his time uncrossing his legs. He stood, smoothed the creases from his trousers, then strolled over to stand beside her. Devin remained seated. Charlie didn't dare look at him.

"Actually there is one other thing." Tarik's fingers brushed a wisp of hair at Charlie's temples.

Slapping his hand away, she snapped, "I thought so."

He breezed on, apparently nonplussed. "Actually I wanted to talk to you about an investment proposal." Charlie held her breath, waiting for the bombshell. It wasn't the first time Tarik had tried to involve her in some less than up front scheme. He continued. "I'd hoped you'd front me some money just till I can get things up and running. We'd be equal partners in this venture—"

Crossing the room, Charlie tugged open the door. "Get out, Tarik." Her lips twitched as Tarik's palms flew skyward in mock surrender. What a ridiculous sight he made.

"Don't you even want to hear me out?" he wheedled.

"No, I don't want to hear another word." She held the door wide and bit back the words hot on her tongue. She was dying to tell him that he was a despicable pathetic excuse for a man, except what purpose would that serve? Right now she just wanted him out of her home.

"But, Charlie . . ."

"But, Charlie, nothing. Out." She made a sweeping motion toward the open door.

Tarik tossed her one of his puppy-dog looks. "Maybe you'll change your mind—"

"When hell freezes over. Any partnership with you is clearly out of the question." She pointed an imperious finger toward the opening. "Go home, Tarik. Sleep off whatever you're on, then call your broker. I'm sure you have some stock to fall back on."

Much to her relief he sidled by. His fingers fluttered farewell, and Charlie hastily closed the door behind him. Emitting a sigh of relief, she sank onto the couch beside Devin. She took the hand he offered and squeezed. "Can you believe the nerve of that man?"

Devin's smile didn't quite reach his eyes, though he'd enjoyed seeing Charlie stand up to Tarik. "Actually I can. He's always trying to steal business away from Harry and me. Once I'd told him in confidence that we were wooing the Harper account. Would you know that he had the nerve to contact the company directly. Lucky for us, Harper Junior and I were golfing buddies, so Tarik didn't stand a chance." Devin glanced at his watch. "Now that that's over with, shouldn't we be heading down to the station?"

Charlie's hand gripped Devin's. "In a minute. There's something I want to discuss with you first."

"What is it, sweetness?" The tip of Devin's index finger tilted Charlie's chin backward. His eyes were magnets holding hers captive.

"Remember the bracelet I found earlier? I know where I've seen it before."

For a brief moment Devin's eyes flickered. The pulse at the base of his throat fluttered. Quickly his features schooled themselves into a careful blank. "Where, Charlie?"

Wired, Charlie jumped up and circled the room. Devin followed slowly behind her. Determined to put her suspicions into words, she spun around to face him, barely missing colliding.

"Take it easy, hon," Devin soothed, steadying her, his fingers kneading the sore muscles at her shoulder blades.

She looked at him, blinked rapidly to hold the tears back, and blurted, "Heaven help me, but I think that bracelet's Tarik's. He was wearing the matching chain."

Devin exhaled a long whistling sound. "Are you absolutely, positively, sure?"

"No, I can't say that. I didn't really get to see the chain that close, but close enough to say it was a pretty good match."

Devin's fingers found the tenseness at the base of her neck. His fingers soothed, allaying her fears. She could smell the subtle scent of citrus, feel his breath hot against her cheek.

"In that case," he said softly, "you'd better call Phillips and O'Reilly."

Charlie'd done a fair job of answering all of Officer Phillips's questions. She'd had to explain that it wasn't the first time Tarik had been over to visit. She'd had to confirm that he was her ex-husband and that she'd completely forgotten about his visit a couple of months back, when he'd stopped by during Kasey's spring break. And yes, she now remembered that Tarik'd been out on the terrace, smoking the inevitable cigarette. She'd even had to explain that she and Devin were old friends.

Phillips's in-depth probing had left her feeling like a fool. She hung up believing that she might have jumped to the wrong conclusion. He'd even managed to convince her there might very well be a plausible explanation for the bracelet lying out on her terrace. Could it have been there for months?

"So what did Phillips have to say?" Devin asked, intruding on her thoughts. He draped an arm around her shoulders and pulled her against him.

Charlie laid her head against his chest, relishing his warmth and listening to the uneven beat of his heart. "Phillips didn't say a lot," she lied, not letting on that Phillips had made Devin seem the prime suspect. "He just listened and asked a bunch of probing questions but didn't offer up much."

Devin kissed the top of her head. "Perhaps there really isn't anything to be alarmed about then, other than what we both know—your ex is a jerk. Now shall we go down to the radio station and get that business over with? I'd like to show my lady off at dinner this evening."

"But, Devin . . ." Charlie protested, remembering her promise to cook for him.

"But, Devin, nothing. You've had a rough day, and you deserve a break. So right after we get back, you'll take a good long soak in the tub, get dressed in your most vampish outfit—preferably something black and slinky, something destined to seduce me. Then we'll go out and paint the town."

He was kidding, had to be. "I don't know about that. I'm already worn out."

"Come on, humor me. It'll be like old times."

In college Friday night had been their night out. First they'd head for the buffet at Tante Belle's, the local soul food joint. There they would stuff themselves with as much ribs and chicken as their stomachs would tolerate. The leftovers were wrapped in a napkin and stowed in Charlie's purse for later. Then onto Mahogany's for cheap wine and heavy-duty hustling. That year she'd learned the Latin hustle, the Brooklyn . . .

"Please, Charlie, a night out will take your mind off all this."

He had a point. Somewhat reluctantly she agreed.

They drove the short distance to the station in silence. Devin kept a firm hold on Charlie's hand, periodically bringing the palm to his lips and covering it with reassuring kisses. Earlier she'd been apprehensive about crossing the parking lot again, until Devin reminded her of Phillips and O'Reilly's promise to increase surveillance. Only then had she seemed to relax.

"We're here," Charlie announced, pointing to a two-story gray building, with neon fuchsia lips flashing off the sides. "That's Hot 101."

Devin's eyebrows wiggled. The corners of his mouth quivered. "Nice sign."

Charlie whacked him on the arm. "It's a radio station, dummy. Stop being a smart alec and pull into the parking lot."

Devin complied, slowing down for Charlie to flash her ID at a bored security guard. Recognizing Charlie, the guard snapped a smart salute and called, "Nice to have you back, Ms. Canfield." They circled the lot and finally found a spot at the rear of the building.

Charlie was already halfway out the door when she realized that Devin hadn't moved. She slid back in, nudged his shoulder, and said, "Well, don't just sit there. Aren't you going to come up?"

He looked at her, smiled that devastating smile of his, and shook his head. "Not today, hon. I need time to regroup. I've met more unpleasant people in the space of a few hours than I normally meet in a week. Besides, coming face to face with that co-host of yours, Errol whatever his name is, might be the last straw."

"Ellis Greene," Charlie corrected. She'd told Devin just enough about Ellis to have him form his own opinion. On second thought it might not be the best time to have the two meet.

She offered her lips in a silent truce then stepped out of the car. "I'll try not to be too long."

Devin called after her, "You do what you need to do. I've got my own business to tend to."

Smiling her thanks, Charlie noted that he'd already removed his cellular phone from the glove compartment where he'd put it earlier. She waved and entered the building.

No elevator today, she decided, heading for the stairs, reasoning she did need the exercise. On the second floor she acknowledged the enthusiastic greetings of the broadcast crew with another wave. They were milling around on a well-deserved coffee break.

In their midst stood Reginald Barker, Hot 101's production assistant. When he spotted Charlie, he broke from the group, and set down his coffee mug amid torn sugar wrappers and spilled powdered milk. In seconds he'd covered the short distance between them.

"Charlie," he yelled, grabbing her around the waist and hoisting her into the air. "Boy, have I missed you. You have no idea what it's been like having to deal with Ellis. He's been worse than usual." Reginald set her down, enthusiastically kissed both cheeks, then held her at arm's length. "You really are a sight for sore eyes, girl. Please tell me you're here to do the evening show?"

Reginald's exuberance made Charlie smile. She shook

her head. "Not tonight. I'm here because I've got a meeting with management. You wouldn't know what that's
about?" She rolled her eyes and continued. "While I'm
here, thought I'd pick up my mail."

Reginald groaned. "I'm glad you're back, though I
haven't a clue why you've been summoned."

Charlie patted his cheek, where a prominent red circle
was imprinted. Her production assistant held a special
place in her heart. At eighteen he'd been a gofer, running
errands and fetching coffee for the crew. Within years he'd
worked his way up to the assistant's position. Now at age
twenty-two, he knew the ins and outs of the broadcasting
business. On more than one memorable occasion, he'd
found her fast asleep in her office, minutes before the
program aired. He'd handed her a warm towel, offered
her his arm, and propped her up in front of the microphone. Then he'd brought her the strongest cups of coffee
she would ever drink.

"So fill me in on the dirt. What's been going on? Is Ellis
in there?" Charlie jerked a finger in the direction of the
office they shared.

Reginald shook his head. "No. He's running late as
usual, but he did call this time." He glanced at his watch.
"In fact he should be here any moment." Reginald made
a sweeping motion with his hand for Charlie to precede
him into the office. "Why don't I take advantage of his
absence and update you."

After Charlie was settled at her desk, Reginald gave her
the lowdown, providing a blow-by-blow description of
Karen Hardy's—her stand-in's—sudden departure.

"You're kidding me," Charlie exclaimed. "Do you really
think she'd file a sexual harassment suit?"

Reginald straddled the chair behind Ellis's desk, pushed
back his Mets cap, and scratched the front of his head.
"Wouldn't surprise me. Ellis practically stalked her."

"Anything else going on?"

Reginald pulled the cap back to its original position. "I'm starting to sound like the finger of doom, but I'd better fill you in on the other gossip. The station's buzzing about management changes—"

"Changes? How come I haven't heard?" Ellis boomed. He stood legs apart, hands deep in his trousers pocket. For once in his life, he was not the picture of cool. He looked as if he'd been jogging and forgotten to shower. "Well, go on, my man."

Charlie could only hope he hadn't overheard the previous exchange. There was nothing worse than being caught gossiping. She watched him toss an expensive-looking leather briefcase on his crowded desk before turning back to face them. "Well, don't keep us all in suspense." He waved an imperious hand in front of Reginald's nose.

Reginald's face was scarlet. He leapt up, vacating Ellis's seat, and pushed the chair toward him. "I'm s-s-sure you've heard the s-s-same rumors I have," he stuttered.

Ellis eased himself down then swung his body around to face them. "Can't say I have. Why don't you fill me in."

Charlie thought that an opportune time to depart. She interrupted smoothly. "Love to stay and chat, but I'm afraid I've got to run. I'm already late for my meeting, and I've got a friend waiting downstairs."

For the very first time, she'd captured Ellis's undivided attention. He scowled in her general direction and said, "Did I hear you right, babe? We've got a show to do later, and you're running out on me."

Charlie's smile dripped tolerance. Ellis, she reminded herself, was an overgrown kid who often stretched your patience. "I return to work tomorrow, Ellis," she explained, enunciating each word. "Not today. Tomorrow."

Ellis's eyebrows flapped up and down like birds in flight. "Says who?"

Charlie took a step toward him. "Says me. Technically I'm not supposed to be here for another four days."

Her co-host chose his words carefully. "You picked a fine time to be gone. Let's say these rumored management changes are true—I for one would want to remain visible."

Reluctantly Charlie admitted he did have a point. If there were changes to be made at the station, it paid to be around. That might even be the reason she'd been summoned today. But would the news be good or bad? Whenever management turned over, the old adage often proved true—out of sight, out of mind. Perhaps she no longer had a job.

Shaking off the morbid thought, she vowed to remain positive. Her goal was to have her own show someday—that would make all the years of putting up with Ellis worthwhile. She wasn't about to give him the satisfaction of a reaction. "Well, let's see what our trusty management team has to say," she said, wiggling her fingers in his direction and throwing over her shoulder, "See you soon, Reg. Better yet, call me tonight. Make it late though, I'm going out to dinner."

"Check out our web page?" Ellis yelled after her. "You've got some interesting messages."

Twelve

Charlie's hands shook as she fastened the diamond stud in one lobe, then paused to look at the effect. Her stomach quivered, and her breath came in erratic little bursts as she discarded yet another outfit. Over the last hour, the pile on the bed had grown, but her indecisiveness had served a purpose. She hadn't had time to think about the pervert, much less the evening ahead. Whenever her imagination had threatened to get out of hand, her suspicions outrageous, she'd taken a peek out of the window and checked for a black sedan.

Officers Phillips and O'Reilly had kept their promise. Even now surveillance men sat in the unmarked car, and two plainclothes cops observed the comings and goings of every tenant. Additional police cars had also been dispatched to patrol the surrounding vicinity.

Somewhat reassured, Charlie tread the well-worn path back to her closet, this time settling on the type of outfit Devin had asked for in the first place: a slinky black number with the price tags still on. The Lycra dress had been purchased months ago. She'd been swayed by the saleswoman's compliments after slipping into the simple black dress. Now she smoothed the material over her hips, dropped the sheer chiffon cover-up over her head, and muttered, "What the hell, he wanted wanton appeal, he's got it. Might as well be daring for once in my life."

She twirled around. The cover-up swirled midthigh. Before she could chicken out, she slid midnight-colored hose up her legs and stepped into the high-heeled pumps she'd put aside. Only then did she dare peek in the mirror.

The reflection was a stranger's. Using fingers less shaky than before, she feathered her hair into tiny swirls and returned to the dresser to add another layer of sienna to her lips. Devin had indicated he wanted a vamp—tonight he was getting a vamp. Adding the final dramatic touch, she outlined her eyes in kohl then tossed the pencil on the dresser.

"Charlie, are you almost ready?" Devin called. "Don't forget we have to be in Tarrytown in half an hour."

"I know. I know. I'll be right out." Charlie tugged the dress across her hips for the hundredth time, spritzed her favorite scent, Paris, in the hollow of her neck, and looked around for her evening purse.

"Charlie!" Devin's tone rose several octaves. "It's getting late. We've got reservations."

"I said I was coming."

Ignoring the tight feeling in her chest, she rummaged through the pile of clothing on her bed, located the small black evening bag, and looped the strap around her neck. She raced into the hallway and smack into Devin.

Devin's arms reached out to steady her. His sharp intake of breath, and the look he flashed her, told her she passed the test with flying colors.

"Sorry I took so long," Charlie babbled, ignoring tiny electric shocks coursing up her arms. "I couldn't decide what to wear." She fingered the diamond at her ear self-consciously.

"You look lovely. Just lovely." Devin's breath caressed her neck. "Mmmm. And your choice of perfume's right on the money. Paris, isn't it?

"Now how did you know that?" Hand on one hip she tapped a foot impatiently when he didn't respond right away. Sparkle back in her eyes, nerves under control, she couldn't imagine what had gotten into her in the first place. It wasn't as if she was having dinner with some stranger she'd picked up. She'd spent the last five days with Devin. And though the police might disagree, she could safely say, he hadn't turned into an ax murderer overnight. If anything he was still the kind, decent person she remembered. The person who'd made her feel worthwhile.

Not that they'd had much time to think about romance. In retrospect that was a good thing, wasn't it? She wouldn't have been able to cope with soul-searching confessions or even declarations of like. She'd had more than enough to deal with after getting that distressing message about Kasey, then being knocked unconscious. Through it all she'd leaned on Devin, trusting him to care for her. She just didn't dare trust him with her heart.

"You must be a connoisseur of women's fragrances, Mr. Spencer. May I ask how you gained your experience?" Charlie teased, nuzzling Devin's cheek.

Devin's lips probed her neck and returned to claim her mouth. An eternity later they surfaced for air.

"Now what were we talking about before you took such wicked advantage of me?" Devin panted, his eyes smoky with passion. He cupped her chin between his palms. "Ah yes, you accused me of being a connoisseur of women and implied I was something of a Lothario." He paused momentarily to kiss the tip of her nose. "Well, just to set the record straight, my dear, my agency handles a competitor's account—and as Harry, my partner, will tell you, if you want to remain successful in any business, you'd better be familiar with the competition. Now shall we?"

He helped her on with her coat and offered his arm. Charlie crooked a hand through the arm he held out, letting her eyes roam the length of him. He'd changed into chocolate slacks, a beige shirt, rust and cream herringbone jacket. Out of the breast pocket of the jacket peeked a silk handkerchief. She sighed, inhaling the ever-present citrus, loving the smell.

During the twenty-minute ride to Tarrytown, they conversed nonstop. And in the midst of one of Devin's hilarious anecdotes, Charlie touched his hand and reluctantly interrupted. "Dev, we're almost there. You need to turn right at the light."

Thrown by her use of his old nickname, Devin slammed on the brake. "Sorry." He flashed an apologetic smile.

"It's okay." Charlie's hand covered his on the steering wheel. "Now make a left. Shellfish Annie's is the third building on the right."

She'd been the one to choose Shellfish Annie's, knowing that the quaint eatery attracted lively, artsy types. Even if you were just there for drinks, watching the patrons could be entertaining.

Devin pulled into the crowded parking lot and turned his key over to an eager valet. Together he and Charlie walked up a flower strewn path leading to the restored nineteenth-century mansion.

"Wow," Devin said, stopping to admire the sprawling grounds lit by tiny white lights. He turned his attention to the main house, pointing out stained glass windows and a huge wraparound veranda. "This place is beautiful!" he exclaimed.

Seconds later they stood at the bottom of three steep little steps, drinking in the vista. Devin took Charlie's hand and drew her against him. "Is anyone looking?" he whispered.

She shot him a puzzled look and shook her head. "Why? Are you planning to steal the shrubbery?"

"No. Just the gorgeous lady in the foreground." He tilted her chin. "Actually I've been dying to do this for the last twenty minutes." He demonstrated what he'd been dying to do, literally taking her breath away. The kiss was filled with such longing that her heart thudded against her ribs and her knees threatened to buckle. Somewhere deep inside she'd come alive again.

"Uh-um!"

The noise got their attention. The kiss ended. Charlie looked up to see a woman, she assumed to be their hostess, remove a delicate hand covering her mouth. "May I interest you in dinner?"

The woman appeared to be in her late forties and wore a flowing granny-style dress with billowing sleeves. Brown laced-up boots peeked from beneath an ankle-length dress. A crown of fresh flowers sat on top a flowing blond mane. An ex-hippie, Charlie decided, even as their hostess's warm smile welcomed them.

"You most certainly may," Devin said in his most charming voice. "We've got reservations for two, and I believe we're right on time." He relinquished his hold on Charlie, freeing her to step from the circle of his arms, then quickly claimed her hand again.

In a lyrical voice their hostess confirmed, "Why, yes, as a matter of fact, you are. Now come, I'll take you to your table." Using the menus she held, she gestured for them to precede her. "Trust me. It's a lot cozier inside. We've got a fire going."

True to her word, inside was much warmer and every bit as cozy as they'd been promised. Bypassing rooms filled with diners, they followed their ethereal hostess to a small parlor and were seated at a table draped in lace and rose damask. Candles threw off a rosy hue, illuminating crystal vases holding a solitary rose. The crackling fire served a dual purpose, both setting the mood and casting dreamy patterns on the cream-colored ceiling. The room's only occupants, another couple, looked up briefly, then returned to gazing into each other's eyes.

"This dining room is called Cupid's Lair. Bet you can't

guess why?" their hostess said in the same musical voice. "Now where would you like to sit?"

Devin indicated a table on the far side of the room with a window overlooking the Hudson. "How about over there?"

"An excellent choice. Couldn't have picked a better one myself." She tapped Devin's shoulder with her menus and batted her eyelashes. "Please have a seat. Your waiter will be over shortly."

After she'd left, Charlie leaned across the table and took Devin's hand. "So what do you think? Was this the kind of place you had in mind?"

Devin's fingers laced through hers. In a deliberate movement, he turned her palm upward and slowly brought it to his lips. His eyes were smoky with desire. "Exactly what I had in mind. I couldn't have picked a better place to show off my date."

Charlie felt the heat invade her face and turned to look out the window. Feelings too new to consider or even explore had surfaced. She couldn't still be in love with Devin? Not after all this time, not after all they'd been through. She focused her attention on the banks of the Hudson, on the twinkling lights of the expensive homes. Devin's sigh, a touch whimsical, brought her back to the present.

"You sound like you've lost your best friend," Charlie joked, hoping to keep things light. Devin's grip on her hand tightened. He held her prisoner with his eyes.

"Actually it's a contented sigh. I was just thinking what a pretty part of the country this is, and what a mistake it was to leave. See what being with you does to me?"

Charlie's free hand clutched the rose-colored napkin. She smacked Devin's hand lightly and paraphrased the old song: "Regrets. You have a few?"

Devin's smile seemed a little off focus. "Much as I like San Diego, this area's awfully tempting. Besides, things have changed a lot on the West Coast. It's far from the laid-back place it used to be."

Charlie's laughter seemed just a touch cynical. "Come now, you'd never abandon your business." The Devin she knew would never walk away from a successful business and start all over. Hadn't he told her that he still planned to retire at age forty-five?

Devin's answer came as no surprise. "I suppose not, especially since I'm this close to achieving my goal." He made a gesture with thumb and index finger. "In a few years I'll be able to devote my time to kids with learning disabilities. You know that's always been my dream. Life in San Diego is hardly perfect. I work long hours, and I'm alone a lot. Comes a time when a man needs more. He needs someone to share that dream with."

Charlie had difficulty believing the latter. She could hardly picture Devin alone, much less lonely. Surely he had more than his fair share of ladies banging at his door. "What, no girlfriend?" she teased.

Devin seemed to be working on a response when a deep male voice interrupted. "Hi, I'm your waiter. May I interest you in drinks?"

Charlie looked up to see a young man, pretty as an Armani model, beaming at them. He poured water into their glasses, set down the pitcher, and reached for his pad.

Devin's mask slid firmly back in place. "Sounds good to me." He released Charlie's hand and flashed his drop-dead smile. "I'm the designated driver, but I suppose I can have one gin and tonic. How about you, Charlie?"

"I'll have the same."

"Drinks will be up in a jiffy." Their waiter departed.

"You were saying . . ." Charlie probed.

"I believe you were asking about my girlfriends."

"So I was." Charlie sipped her water and gazed at him over the rim of her glass. What she saw in his eyes unnerved her, but she was determined to keep cool.

Devin's fingertips drummed the crystal tumbler. Their gazes locked until at last he broke the silence. "There aren't any. Hasn't been for months."

Charlie expelled the breath she'd been holding. If he was telling the truth, that made things a lot less complicated. Not that she'd expected Devin to be a monk, but if they were to give their relationship another try, it did make things easier. Still, the thought of him being with other women caused an inexplicable twinge in her gut. It had nothing to do with jealousy, she was sure. How could anyone be jealous of a man they hadn't seen in eighteen years? She gulped her water and avoided looking him in the eye.

Devin's gentle voice intruded. "I had a girlfriend up until a few months ago. When I realized the relationship was heading nowhere, we broke up." He looked at Charlie as if expecting an interruption. She nodded and signaled for him to continue. "Call me gun shy, but my marriage ended after eight miserable years of trying to make it work. Now in retrospect I realize I married Lila for primarily one reason: She reminded me of you, though she was nothing like you on the inside. Unfortunately I found that out way too late, after I'd married her."

Charlie's fingers tightened around her glass. "Didn't you love Lila?"

While she held her breath, Devin contemplated the question.

"Initially I thought I did." He reached across the table to take her hand again. "Truth is, Charlie, you were one of the few people who understood me. I never stopped loving you."

Their waiter's return ended the conversation. "Two gin and tonics coming up," he announced, setting down their drinks. "Are you ready to order?"

They'd barely glanced at the menus.

Devin flashed another of his killer smiles. "Can you give us a few minutes?"

"Sure thing." The waiter turned away.

Conversation on hold, they made their selections. Charlie set down her menu, took a deep breath, and plunged in.

"Let me ask you something, Devin. If you never stopped loving me, how come you gave up on me so easily?"

Devin's fingers stroked her inner arm; his eyes caressed her face, focusing on the lower lip she nibbled on. "Be fair, Charlie," he said. "I already told you that your father intercepted every telephone call that summer. Even my letters were returned unanswered. It all seemed clear when I heard you'd married Tarik. Shortly after I got word of your baby. Imagine what I thought? Imagine how devastated you'd be, if you found out the person you loved had run off with your roommate? You were my best friend. I'd trusted you. I'd loved you, for crying out loud. You'd loved me, or so you'd said. We'd practically discovered sex together. I couldn't accept the fact that you were sleeping with Tarik and me at the same time. When it finally sank in, I was angry for a long, long time."

She knew he needed to hear that she'd remained faithful up until the night of her marriage, that she'd never stopped loving him, and that she'd hoped he'd come after her. Yet words remained lodged at the back of her throat. She squeezed Devin's hand. She wasn't ready to tell him about his daughter, but she did want him to know she still cared.

"Honey, you're dead wrong," she whispered. "I married Tarik because I believed you didn't want me. Remember, I hadn't heard from you all summer. I'd try calling. I'd dial the phone and lose my nerve when your parents answered—then I'd hang up without leaving a message. I didn't want you to think I was hounding you."

Devin gulped his drink and set down the empty glass.

Abruptly he stood up, came around to Charlie's side, and placed his hands on her shoulders. "Sweetheart, we've already wasted too much time. Tell me you're not particularly hungry?"

Heart pounding, breath coming in little spurts, Charlie stared into Devin's soulful gray eyes. She couldn't say yes if she wanted to. "Not really," she managed to get out.

"Then let's get the hell out of here. We've got a lot of lost time to make up for."

Devin plucked money from his billfold. He tossed down a fistful of bills and slid Charlie's chair out. Too impatient to wait while she gathered her purse, he took possession of her purse and hand simultaneously.

Almost halfway across the room, their waiter called after them, "Is it something I said?"

Turning, Devin flashed him a wicked smile. "No. It's something the lady just said."

Back in the apartment Devin helped Charlie off with her coat. His fingers lingered at the nape of her neck before turning her around to face him.

When he spoke, his voice was low and urgent, his eyes intense. "I love you, Charlie. What I need to know is, do you still love me?"

She wanted to tell him she did, that in fact she'd never stopped loving him, but something stopped her. A declaration of that kind could only complicate her life. She needed time to examine his sudden reappearance in her life—his motives. Right now she was happy, had a good-paying career, a beautiful apartment, and child she adored. If the ratings continued to soar, someday she'd even have her own show. Most would say she had it all.

Charlie hedged, then finally said, "I care about you a lot, Devin."

Devin's lips heated the side of her face. His whispered

retort sent a tiny shiver down her spine and up again.
"Now who's being evasive? That's not what I asked you.
Do you still love me?" He didn't give her time to answer
but covered her mouth with tiny kisses.

His kisses left her unable to concentrate, much less respond. Little jolts of electricity ricocheted through her
body, leaving her tingling all over. Rational thought disappeared.

When she came up for breath, she said the first thing
that popped into her head. "I've never stopped caring
about you, Devin."

Devin sighed his frustration. His index finger outlined
her lips. "I suppose I'll have to accept that answer for now.
I sensed you'd be hesitant about committing, so I'll have
to show you how deeply you're loved." She was lifted off
her feet and cradled in his arms.

Despite her fist beating a rapid tattoo against his chest,
he ignored her. A man with a mission, he headed down
the hallway and with the toe of his shoe pushed her bedroom door open. He set her down on the bed and wasted
no time joining her. Wrapping her in his arms, he drew
her close to his heart. She smelled the citrus of his cologne,
heard his rapid heartbeat, felt his torso contract and relax.
His hot kisses covered her mouth and cheeks. She knew
she'd died and gone to heaven.

Reality returned when his hands cupped her buttocks,
and she realized that the delicate coverup had been removed—the tight black dress hiked up. Now nothing stood
between his heated palms and her bare skin, except for
panty hose and a tiny strip of lace.

Devin's hands molded her buttocks. He pulled her even
closer. His desire pulsated against her core, and she heard
his labored whisper. "Honey," he rasped, "how I've missed
you. We've been apart much too long. I intend to make
up for all the times I've thought about you, fantasized that

you were lying next to me, and wished that we were to-gether."

Already his hand had crept up her thigh, paused briefly to caress her belly, and found a home at her breasts. Braless she was at his mercy, giving him easy access to nipples that had already been coaxed into taunt replicas of each other. When his mouth replaced his hands, and the straps of her dress slid down her arms, she moaned. He laved her nipples, crooning words that made no sense, though she was able to make out, "Ditch the dress, honey."

She'd barely had time to comply when Devin slipped off the bed, kicked off his shoes, and in swift motions dispensed with jacket, slacks, and shirt. Hands on both hips he watched her dispose of the rumpled dress.

Charlie's eyes remained riveted on Devin's wide chest. She longed to run her fingers through the curly hairs weaving tight little patterns around his pectorals. Daring to peek lower, she followed the path of fine hairs making their way down his abdomen. She stopped short, confronted by the elastic band of his briefs and didn't dare look lower. Instead she hooked a thumb through the band of her panty hose.

"Hey, that's my job," Devin said, waggling a finger at her. Before she could protest, he'd gotten down on one knee in front of her and placed a possessive hand on her stomach. "Surely you'll allow me the pleasure of relieving you of that contraption." He slipped a hand under her silken hose, peeling the filmy material and scrap of lace away.

She sat before him naked and hot, blushing as his eyes burnt a searing path across her body.

"Oh, Charlie," Devin said, breathing heavily. "You're even more beautiful than I remember. Why don't you stand up so I can see you. All of you."

Hungry gray eyes ate her up when she slid off the bed. She nibbled on her lower lip and avoided looking him in the eye. But even that was a mistake because she faced his arousal. How could she have forgotten how well endowed he was? Cheeks hotter than a firecracker, she looked away.

"God, darlin'," Devin rasped. "It's really been much too long." He remained in his worshiping position, kissed her toes, and slowly worked his way up her legs. Arms fastened around her stomach, he pressed his face into her softness, letting his tongue explore.

"Devin," Charlie gasped. "I'm not going to be good for much if you don't love me soon."

Against her flesh his answer was barely discernible. "Baby, I've been ready to love you from the moment I saw you on that cruise ship."

His hold around her waist tightened as he shifted to his feet. He lifted her up and set her to rest on his shoulders, legs straddling his neck, mound pressed against his face.

Charlie's moan was pure animal. Humans weren't supposed to soar over the world, to feel like they would die without immediate gratification. Some semblance of reality returned when she touched down on the ivory comforter again.

"What are you doing?" Charlie asked, watching him pick up the slacks he'd discarded.

"Looking for this." He held out a foil packet, palmed it, and returned to her side. "Will you do me the honor?"

"Only if you do me the honor." She accepted the package and quickly ripped it apart.

He came to join her, placing his lips on her breasts, until she could hardly concentrate, much less make her fingers work. His hands explored the hidden alcove between her legs, delving into her softness. In and out and in again. "Baby, I'm not going to be able to last much longer," he whispered. She slid the sheath up the length of him. "Let me love you."

Charlie's answer came in the form of raised knees and parted thighs. Devin's RSVP was a quick entry. In a matter of seconds, they matched each other move for move. A slow crescendo built. Reality lost its meaning. As the rhythm picked up, Charlie whirred out of control. She heard a voice in the distance shout, "Wait for me, honey," and knew it couldn't possibly be hers. Then ripples of pleasure wracked her tingling body. And she heard the same voice scream, "I love you, Devin!"

Thirteen

Charlie'd been back at work three whole days before she'd found time to log on to the Internet. Now today she'd arrived a half hour early for that purpose.

Happy to find her office vacant and no Ellis in sight, she tossed her pocketbook on the room's only couch and flung herself into a chair. She flicked the switch to set the computer in motion, signed on, waited for art to download and the main menu to pop up, then made her selection. Devin had extended his vacation and was meeting a business associate for drinks in Ossining.

A smile curved Charlie's lips when she read the message indicating she had mail. So that was what Ellis had been going on about. He'd become noticeably more competitive since the implementation of Hot 101's home page. Even tracking fan mail had become an obsession for him. Charlie gave herself a mental pat on the back, glad that she'd had the foresight to see the possibilities the web offered.

Hot 101's home page had been her idea, and so far it had been a raging success. During its introductory week, they'd had over five hundred hits. That meant more than five times that many people had listened to the broadcast and heard her announce the introduction of the new web site. Before closing, she'd provided their e-mail address. In just a few months, the Internet had become one of the most popular mediums for the audience to voice its preferences. Now it had become increasingly difficult to keep up with the commentary, and management toyed with hiring a part-timer for that purpose. That's what the meeting had been about.

Charlie clicked on her messages and chuckled out loud as she identified the screen name and read the first message. Kimba was at it again. In a brazen bid to get attention, the ex-*Playboy* bunny's message read: "Aging hussy wants Hot 101's sizzling talk show host to call. No need to forward picture or phone—you're already a legend." She'd given her e-mail address before signing off.

Kim was back in New Jersey and dying to share the latest gossip, no doubt. Charlie's fingers flew as she typed the response: "How about I call you later this evening?" She couldn't wait to hear Kim's colorful version of her cruise experience.

She chuckled loudly, letting her imagination take over. Had Ellis considered the cryptic message his? The two had separate passwords, but they'd agreed to share in the event one or the other was out of the office. That way the audience's banter never went unanswered. She wouldn't put it past Ellis to use the privacy of e-mail to come on to Kim. She'd have to ask her later. Still chuckling, Charlie scanned the remainder of her messages. Judging by the number, her fans must have missed her. She wondered why Ellis had insisted that she check, when so far she'd not encountered anything out of the ordinary, just the usual requests for unique topics.

About to log off, she sensed Ellis behind her. He'd taken a bath in his cologne again. When his fingers stroked the nape of her neck, she swung around and glared at him.

"Is there a reason to creep up on me like that?"

Ellis's syrupy smile served to irritate her even more than his words. "I didn't creep up on you, baby. You were just too engrossed in what you were doing." He tapped a finger against the monitor. "Did you notice your man's at it again?"

"What man?"

"Don't tell me you missed it?"

Annoyed because he was being evasive, Charlie stood up to face him. "Don't play games, Ellis. I haven't a clue what you're alluding to."

He took the seat she'd vacated and grabbed ahold of the mouse, clicking several times until he found the message. "There. See for yourself." He stood up and motioned for Charlie to sit.

With some trepidation she peered at the screen. The sender's name was not one she recognized, though the tone spoke for itself.

"Sweet thang," the posting began. "I've missed that sexy voice of yours before I go to sleep. I've been so lonely for your body, babe. That woman Karen did nothing for my libido. She was a poor substitute, didn't hold a candle to you. Her voice didn't remind me of starlit nights and chilled champagne. Hell, I couldn't imagine her lying next to me, holding me, loving me. Hear this, sweet thang, Daddy'll be calling you soon, just to make sure you're back."

"Go back a couple of messages," Ellis ordered as Charlie's stomach threatened to revolt. Following his instructions, she clicked the mouse several times. "Hold it."

Charlie stared at the screen, hoping to make sense of the crazy message and uncover the writer's identity. Though the message had been directed to her stand-in, Karen Hardy, she continued to read. *Sivad Man*, weird as the screen name was, didn't provide a clue.

"Bitch," it began. "You don't hold a candle to my sweet thang. I can tell, you're cold and conniving, not warm and welcoming like my baby. . . ."

"You're on in five," Reginald Barker bellowed, entering the room.

Charlie nodded but continued to read. Over her shoulder she tossed, "Just a sec, Reg."

It was more of the same hate-spewing garbage. She raced through the remainder of the message, logged off the computer, turned the monitor off, and listened with half an ear to Reginald's briefing.

Ellis's hand twirled the curls at her nape. "You shouldn't take any of it to heart, baby. The guy's nuts."

"Who's nuts?" Reginald asked, looking from one to the other.

Ellis provided an answer. "Charlie's got this psycho dude calling her."

Not realizing the seriousness of the situation, Reginald teased, "New boyfriend?"

"Old boyfriend," Charlie answered, thinking Reginald had seen Devin drop her off.

"You know that perverted man who's bothering you?"

"Don't be an ass, Ellis. Devin's not the guy who keeps pestering me, he's the guy I'm seeing. He's the most together, wonderful, down-to-earth person you'd ever meet."

"So lover-boy's named Devin."

"What's that to you?"

Ellis continued. "Let me see if I've got this right. Out of the blue an old boyfriend reappears in your life, and you welcome him back with open arms. You're not even suspicious?"

"Why would I be?" Charlie sputtered. She wasn't about to admit that she'd entertained doubts. Ellis had already drawn his own conclusions. "I've known Devin since I was a teenager." Charlie threw her hands in the air and stormed off. "I don't need this right now."

Ellis trailed her. He glimpsed Charlie's strained face and tried his best to sound contrite. "Sorry, I didn't mean to upset you."

"Well, you did."

"Guys," Reginald called behind them. "You have exactly two minutes to get your butts in your seats before we go live."

Somehow Charlie made it through the broadcast, even though every inbound call brought with it anxiety. Using the chatty, down-home style that had made her a success and garnered her bonuses, she gabbed with Ellis, keeping up her end of the repartee, refusing to let her imagination get the best of her. At the end of two hours, when she felt as if her head would split in two, she tossed off her earphones and rested her head on the console.

For the last few days, she'd been convinced the pervert was scared off—now he'd surfaced on the Internet of all places, a decidedly public forum. Who was she dealing with?

"Can I get you some aspirin?" Ellis asked, for once surprisingly intuitive.

"Thanks. That would be great."

After she'd swallowed half a glass of water and the pills Ellis brought her, she forced enthusiasm into her voice. "Well, shall we get started on the mail?"

"Do you really feel up to it? Wouldn't you much rather be at home in bed?"

He was right. She didn't feel up to it and would much rather be at home under the covers. But she didn't trust Ellis to wade through the fan mail Reginald had brought them. She wouldn't put it past him to conveniently lose hers.

"It's not going to kill me to spend a couple of more hours here," she said. "I'm sure the aspirin will kick in. In a few minutes I'll feel like an idiot for even thinking of leaving."

"If you say so."

Ellis had already preceded her down the hall. Charlie followed slowly, liking the idea of going home to bed more and more. But that wasn't even a viable option, since she didn't have her car and hadn't committed Devin's cellular number to memory.

By the time she'd waded through her fan mail and read the assortment of memos management distributed, her head pounded. She swiped a hand across her forehead, simultaneously glancing at her watch. Devin should be there any minute, thank goodness.

"Time to go home," Ellis confirmed, tossing some of the more sycophantic letters from his female fans into his briefcase then snapping the latches shut. "Come on, I'll walk you to your car."

She threw him a wary smile, glad to have an excuse not to accept his invitation. "I didn't drive," she said. "I'm waiting to be picked up."

Ellis arched an eyebrow. "Aaah, by your new man. Things must be pretty serious if your wheels are at home. I'd be careful though. I wouldn't trust him."

"Oh, shut up, Ellis," Charlie snapped. She crumpled a piece of paper, tossed it at his head, then turned back to the computer. The last thing she needed was a ride from Ellis. Alone in his car she'd be completely at his mercy. She looked up to see him still standing, staring at her. "Go on now. Go home," she urged, forcing a smile. "Devin should be calling from the lobby any minute."

Ellis smirked, brows at an odd angle. "Devin? What a name." He chuckled.

Charlie refused to take the bait. She focused her attention on the keyboard and ignored him.

"Sure you don't want a ride?" Ellis persisted.

Without looking up, Charlie waved. "Have a good evening, Ellis."

When she could no longer hear his footsteps down the hall, she concentrated on the monitor, scrolled through the messages, and found the pervert's.

As she read, she replayed what little she knew of her pursuer, concluding as the police had surmised, that he was a neighbor or someone she worked with. Most definitely he was someone she knew. Who else would have such in-depth knowledge of her comings and goings? Also statistics proved that the average Internet user was Caucasian, thirty-something, a white collar worker, and male. Except for being Caucasian, Devin filled the bill.

Charlie shook her head, dismissing the ridiculous notion. The Devin she used to know could barely kill a mosquito without flinching. Two tiny furrows emerged between her brows as she printed out the messages and shoved them into her pocketbook. She'd turn them over to O'Reilly and Phillips first thing tomorrow. Glancing at the phone, she wondered what was keeping Devin.

"I guess I have time to go to the bathroom," she said out loud, eyes still focused on the silent phone.

Leaving her pocketbook behind, she walked down the deserted hallway and into the pristine ladies' room that always reminded her of a hospital.

She'd completed her business and stood washing her hands, when she had the eerie feeling she was being watched. Dismissing the notion as ludicrous, she headed for the exit. She placed a hand on the doorknob and turned it to the right, only to find the door stuck. She jiggled the knob with all the energy she could muster, but the door did not budge. After minutes of fiddling with the handle, and screaming her lungs out, disheartened, she sank to the floor.

To steady her nerves, Charlie drank in deep gulps of air. The pressure in her diaphragm didn't seem to want to ease. Curling her knees tightly to her chest, she clasped her head between both palms, and said a silent prayer. How on earth had she managed to get locked in? Could the cleaning crew, assuming she'd gone home, mistakenly have locked the doors? Panic slowly began to build as she pictured Devin dialing her number and getting no answer. What would he think, that she had left? How long would he wait in the lobby before he went home? Would he even have the presence of mind to ask the guard to check her office? Bottom line, how long could he be expected to wait?

Trying her best to remain calm, to breathe slowly, Charlie pulled herself together. She'd try the door one last time. This time she placed one hand on the door, the other on the knob, twisting, pulling. The door did not yield. Using her fists like hammers, she pounded as hard as she could against the frame, screaming, "Help me, somebody! I'm locked in."

An eerie echo prevailed as her screams reverberated around her.

She pounded harder, putting her fears into each blow, her energy into escaping. "Is anyone out there? I'm locked in. Please help me!" she screamed.

Click, then a whirring sound, and the room filled with canned laughter. The laughter started out soft then grew in intensity, eventually becoming a roaring crescendo. *"Ha-ha-ha-ha-ha . . . ha-ha-ha-ha . . ."*

Shocked by the unexpected sound, Charlie shrieked. She covered her ears to shut out the laughter. As her hysteria built, so did the maniacal cackling. "Stop it," she shouted over the noise. "Stop." As quickly as the laughter began, it stopped. A whirring noise followed. Charlie began pounding the door, hollering to be let out. Over the noise the familiar voice of her captor was heard.

"You made me unhappy, sweet thang. I've loved you for far too long to let anyone stand in my way. Tonight I was looking forward to seeing you, talking to you, holding you . . . loving you." Then another crazed peal of laughter—a truly gruesome sound, echoing off the walls, filling her ears, her mind.

She was losing it, had to be. How did a few strange phone calls escalate to the point where she was trapped in a bathroom and forced to listen to a madman? Tears welled in her eyes. She let them fall. Continuing to drum her fists against the wood, she screamed, "Help me, somebody! Help me!"

Sobs racked Charlie's body as her energy slowly faded. Summoning her last bit of strength, she slammed her aching body against the door and was sent sprawling against the white tile floor. The door pushed open.

"Oh, my God, Charlie. Are you all right? What happened?" Devin threw down Charlie's pocketbook. He stooped to cradle her in his arms. "Baby, I've been so worried." He kissed away the tears. "We've been looking all over for you." He planted a kiss on the crown of her head and tucked her under his arm.

The guard's words eventually penetrated. "Ms. Canfield, can you tell us what happened?"

Charlie looked up to see one of the newly hired guards, who'd let her into the building that evening, lurking behind Devin.

Embarrassment the last thing on her mind, she accepted the handkerchief Devin proffered, blew her nose, then shook her head. "No. But you could help me find whoever locked me into the bathroom and forced me to listen to a sick message."

The guard came to kneel only feet away. "Who would have done that, Ms. Canfield? There's no one left in the building. The cleaning crew went home a half hour ago, and Mr. Greene was the last person to leave the building. If Mr. . . . ." He looked at Devin, waiting for him to fill in the blank.

"Spencer," Devin supplied.

". . . Spencer hadn't insisted we come up and look for you in your office, I would have assumed you'd gone home. I'd already left for my coffee break."

Devin's hands lingered around Charlie's waist when he helped her up. He kept his arm firmly in place and turned her to face the man.

"Who relieved you during your break? Can I speak to that person? He must have seen something, heard something?"

The guard's sheepish expression confirmed a problem. He looked at them through lowered lids. "There's really no one to talk to, other than me," he ventured. "See, I'm really not supposed to leave my post, but I was falling asleep. I work three jobs to keep food on my table, man. Know what it's like to have three kids to feed? Well, anyway, after Mr. Greene left, I thought it was safe to run to the coffee shop. It's right across the street, see. I was hardly gone five . . . well, maybe . . . ten minutes. I kept an eye on the place the whole time I was there. Trust me, no one came into the building. Considering no harm was done, you won't tell my boss, will you? I really need this job—my wife's pregnant again."

Devin pursed his lips, letting the guard stew. Finally he came around. "Well, seeing Ms. Canfield wasn't injured, I'll let it go this one time. We're going to have to report it though, so who knows what the cops will do. In future you might want to consider bringing a thermos of coffee with you"—he glared at the guard—"just in case that coffee shop ever beckons." Devin's arm tightened around Charlie's waist, his fingers stroked her side. "Is there a phone we can use to make that call?"

After they'd called the cops and spent another hour answering questions, Devin brought the Lexus around. He ushered Charlie into the passenger seat and said, "Time to go home, love—it's been one rough day."

Inside Charlie leaned her head on Devin's shoulder, closed her eyes, and breathed in the smell of citrus. Just being with Devin had helped regain equilibrium. His presence made her feel safe.

"Headache?" Devin wrapped a finger around a curl.

"A fierce one. I feel like someone's using my skull as a drum."

Almost feeling her pain, Devin stepped on the accelerator. The car shot forward. "I'll have to get you home quickly and put you to bed."

Massaging her aching temples, Charlie forced her eyes open. "Why me, Devin? What did I do to deserve this treatment?"

Devin's hand left the steering wheel for a brief moment to cover Charlie's. He knew that more than anything she needed his reassurance. His jaw clenched, but he kept his voice gentle. "You're in the public eye, my love—and as you once told me, fans come with the territory. You must know you're a very beautiful woman and, unfortunately, you've become some man's obsession."

Charlie changed the topic. She didn't want to hear that. The idea that someone's sick fantasy had gotten way out of control scared her. The fact that she was being stalked wasn't something she wanted to acknowledge, not right now anyway. "So how come you were late?"

Against her ear Devin's voice seemed smooth, too smooth. "Would you believe, flat tires."

"Oh, honey, I hope you weren't on the highway."

"As a matter of fact, it happened in the parking lot." Under his breath he mumbled, "Thank God, I wasn't."

The little furrows between Charlie's brows were even more pronounced. "You could have waited until tomorrow to change the tires and just used my car. Didn't I show you where I keep the spare keys."

"It was *your* car."

"My car! But I just had it serviced."

Devin debated telling her about the nightmare he'd been through. But she'd already had enough to contend with tonight—he didn't think she could handle more. Then again, if she found out from someone else, all hell would break loose. He'd be forced to explain why he'd kept it from her.

"This wasn't just some simple flat tire, Charlie," he began. Seconds ticked by as he struggled for words. "This was deliberate. Every one of your tires were slashed. I was late getting here because I called those jokers, O'Reilly and Phillips. Then I tried to find a mechanic and a place to buy new tires. Someone was out to prove a point, Charlie. First the flowerpot then this. There's a maniac on the loose—and I plan on getting him."

Fourteen

"Drink this, Charlie," Devin ordered. He pressed the cordial glass holding a transparent liquid into her hand. Charlie raised the glass, took a tentative sip, and set the glass down. She savored the peppermint-tasting liquid, ignored the slight burn at the back of her throat, and waited for the warmth to invade her stomach. "Feeling better?"

Devin joined her on the damask couch. He reached for her hand.

"A lot better now that I'm home." She squeezed his hand. "Thanks for getting me the Sambuca. I haven't had this stuff in so long."

"It's good, isn't it? It's been one of my favorite liqueurs ever since my first sip in Italy. Now tell me, how do you really feel?"

Charlie sipped the liquid slowly. She set her glass on the coffee table and hesitantly began. "Well, I have to admit this whole incident's left me pretty shaken up. It's quite the traumatic experience to be trapped in a bathroom and forced to listen to a madman rant. There were actually times I thought *I* was the crazy person."

Devin kissed the crown of her head. "Poor baby." His eyes were the color of gunpowder as he contemplated what he'd do given the chance. "I can't even imagine what you've been through. The guy's obviously certifiable. Who in their right mind would have a bathroom wired to accommodate speakers? The police think he may have used a tape recorder to get his message across? Just pray I don't get my hands on that maniac or I won't be responsible—"

Charlie's voice was reed thin when she interrupted. "Dev, you promised me." She tugged his hand. "Didn't you say in the car that you'd let the experts handle this, that this was a job for the police? You assured me you wouldn't do anything foolish."

"So I did," he said, more to convince her than anything. Deep down he knew he could never sit still while the cops poked around. He'd given those jokers Phillips and O'Reilly long enough to play sleuth. Where were they to-night when Charlie needed them most? He changed the topic. "I'm really worried about leaving you, love, especially after this. I'm going to have to go home to San Diego . . ."

"How soon?" Charlie's voice was barely a whisper.

"Probably in the next couple of days."

Charlie blinked back tears and smiled for his sake. "Dev, I want you to know I really appreciate everything you've done for me. I'll miss you."

"Whoa!" Devin said, cupping her chin in both hands and maneuvering her jaw until she faced him. "Are you trying to get rid of me so soon? I'm not disappearing out of your life, honey, just going home to help Harry close a piece of business. I'll only be gone a week."

Charlie's entire body sagged with relief. The lump in her chest shifted, leaving in its place a warm glow. He was coming back to her. "Oh, Devin," she said, snuggling into the haven his arms created. "I've been racking my brains, searching for reasons to make you stay."

How had she become so dependent on him in so short a space of time? But Devin wasn't any ordinary man, she reminded. He'd always made her feel safe. Safe and beautiful. Wasn't that why it had hurt so badly when he'd walked away?

Devin's arms tightened around her waist. He covered her face with kisses then eagerly sought her lips. When he finally released her, he asked, "Can your parents stay with you while I'm gone?"

Charlie nodded, knowing that Marilyn and John would be only too happy to visit. They'd always been there every step of the way. They'd supported her through her pregnancy, seen her through the ups and downs of a rocky marriage, and held her hand through a painful divorce. Even so, much as she loved them, they would never take Devin's place.

Devin rose from the couch, handed her the glass of Sambuca she'd abandoned, and threw words over his shoulder. "Oh, before I forget, Kasey called. I left a note in the kitchen."

He headed off in that direction and returned with a folded piece of paper. "Though she didn't say, I got the feeling she's with the young man she's seeing, Brian something or other. Could be the reason she said there's no need to return the call tonight." He made a face, waiting for the explosion.

Charlie surprised him. She glanced at the number he'd handed her. It wasn't Kasey's. Shaking her head, she envisioned her wayward child at some guy's place. Although she'd done her best to make sure Kasey knew the facts of life, she hoped birth control had become part of the regimen. Charlie folded the paper in two and placed it on the coffee table. "Did she sound okay to you?"

Devin's dimpled smile surfaced. He tilted Charlie's mouth upward with his fingers. "Stop being a worrywart, baby—from the way that child carried on, I'd say she's just fine. Her pocketbook might be suffering but not her health. This call was purely an SOS for money."

Horrified, Charlie gaped at Devin. It sounded just like Kasey to go on and on. But how did Devin know she needed money if Kasey hadn't asked? "She didn't. Dear Lord, tell me she didn't."

"No, she didn't. Surely Mama know's she's much too well brought up for that. I told her you'd call her." Placing a finger against Charlie's lips, he shushed her. "I didn't make any promises, just said you'd wire the money into her account if she was desperate."

"And you call that not making promises." Charlie jabbed her elbow into his gut. "That child spends money like it's going out of style. What she needs is a job, not you misleading her into thinking I'm going to bail her out again. If Kasey were your responsibility, you'd see what a little spendthrift she is."

Devin kissed her open palm. "Funny but I've come to think of her mother as mine. By virtue of that fact, I consider her daughter my responsibility." For a fleeting moment his lips covered hers, and a surge of warmth infused her body. He looked at her with those smoky gray eyes that spoke volumes, and asked, "Now you wouldn't happen to have any pictures of that beautiful child lying around, would you?"

No sooner had the words left his mouth, he could kick himself. How stupid of him to forget that the photos of Kasey had been mutilated. "Oh, Charlie, I'm so sorry," he added.

"Nothing to be sorry about." She slid off the couch and picked up the tumbler she'd set down. He didn't need to know there were photo albums in Kasey's closet that had survived. Her daughter's face would be a definite giveaway. Those sultry gray eyes practically shouted Devin. Only a fool wouldn't guess the child was his.

"God, look at the time," Charlie said between yawns. "I told Kim I'd phone her."

"It's past midnight," Devin reminded.

"I know, but Kim's a night owl, and you know how she gets. If I don't call, I'll never hear the end of it."

"Please don't be long." Devin headed for the bedroom, sensing she needed privacy. He flashed that smile of his and turned to add, "You've already had a rough night, baby. I can't wait to hold you in my arms and soothe away your aches and pains."

With Devin out of sight, Charlie dialed Kim's number.

On the second ring Kim greeted, "Hello." Her voice sounded dreamy, as if she were asleep.

"Kim?"

Recognizing Charlie's voice, Kim perked up immediately. "Hey, girlfriend, what's up?"

Charlie flopped onto the couch, immediately forgot her woes, and in her chattiest voice said, "So what did I miss?"

"Plenty, girlfriend, plenty. Remember that man I mentioned?" Kim's words flowed in torrents. "He wasn't just any old man, honey, husband material. You remember Jackson La Salle?"

Charlie didn't, as she told Kim.

"You sure now? He transferred from NYU. That's right, you wouldn't remember. You would have been gone by then. Anyway he shook that big ole 'fro in front of me, blocking my view of that anthropology professor, Bert something or other—the one I had a one-nighter with?" Though Charlie didn't have a clue who either men were, that didn't stop Kim. "Anyway though I knew Jackson had RSVP'd, I didn't recognize him till he came up to me at embarkation. Boy, he turned into one fine hunk of a man now. Real stud muffin material. He practically begged me to rescue him from Bessie Collins after you'd left. She'd latched on to him something fierce."

Kim's chitchat made Charlie feel a whole lot better. She chuckled, adding, "You mean Tarik got dumped. Wish I was there to see that. I had the distinct impression Bessie had her hooks into him good. Personally I thought they were a match made in heaven."

Kim's guffaw almost blew Charlie's eardrum. "Chile,

didn't you hear about Tarik? The captain kicked his butt off the ship shortly after you and Devin disembarked. That night he got into this fight in the dance club with some woman's husband. I don't have to tell you, he was drunk. From what I hear, they tore the place up—"

"Wait a minute," Charlie shouted, stopping Kim before she began another run-on sentence. "You mean Tarik was tossed off the ship? The story he's been giving me is pure bull?"

"Now that I can't comment on. Depends on what he's been telling you."

Charlie told Kim of Tarik's unexpected visit and what he'd said.

Her friend roared. Eventually, when Kim was able to speak, she added, "Honey, puh-lease don't believe him for a moment. He's an operator from the word go. The whole time he was on that cruise, he was hustling anything in a skirt, including me. If he hadn't been asked to leave, somebody woulda tossed him overboard."

They moved on to other topics, catching up, filling the blanks in on their respective life stories. When Charlie's eyeballs burned and her neck hurt, she brought closure to the conversation. She rotated her shoulders, hoping to ease the tight little knot forming between the blades. Tarik Connors made her so mad. How dare he play her for a fool, making up a story, then hitting her up for money? He'd outright lied. This time she would never forgive him.

Charlie stomped into the bedroom and began tugging off her clothes.

Devin's feet peeked out from under the covers. "Something wrong?" he asked, as Charlie's balled-up silk shirt whizzed by his head.

Too angry to answer, she struggled into the satin pajamas Devin had laid out and joined him under the covers. This time when Devin reached for her, his bare chest did not provide the usual comfort. It felt hard and bony.

"Want to tell me what's wrong?" Devin smoothed the top of her head and nibbled on her ear. When she didn't answer immediately, he probed, "Did Kim make you mad, by chance?"

"Nope, I'm fine." Charlie thumped the pillow with her fist.

"That's a bunch of bull, and you know it."

Charlie knew that if he kept probing, it would be only seconds before she exploded. In a flow of words, she repeated verbatim what Kim had told her, ending with, "So now you know what a liar he is."

Devin nodded, propping himself on his pillow. His fingers trailed Charlie's collarbone. "I wonder what his objective was, telling you that story?" he said after a second or two passed. "Have you considered that Tarik might be the person stalking you?"

Wide-eyed she looked at him. She'd be lying not to admit that the thought had crossed her mind on more than one occasion. But even now it seemed a ridiculous notion. Admittedly Tarik was manipulative, untrustworthy, and a liar, but did that make him a stalker? Besides, what reason would he have for making her life a living hell? He had to know by now that there wasn't a snowball's chance in hell of them reconciling.

Forcing her voice to sound normal, Charlie said, "Don't be ridiculous, Devin. Tarik's no angel, and there've been times I've questioned his sanity, but that hardly makes him psychotic."

"Think, Charlie," Devin said, reaching for the half-empty glass of water he'd left on the nightstand. "Isn't it somewhat peculiar that Tarik shows up on your doorstep the same day of the flowerpot episode? Could there be a remote possibility that after he was asked to leave that cruise ship, he followed us here? And having deduced that we might have slept together, he got angry. Angry enough to . . ." Devin drained the water in his glass.

"To try to hurt me," Charlie finished. It was too much to digest all at once, though what Devin said did make sense. "But why would he wait until now to be this vindictive, Devin? Tarik and I have been divorced for a long time."

"Now that's true," Devin said, setting down the empty glass. "But from what you've told me, you were a student and homemaker for many years. The few jobs you held weren't exactly high profile until you started hosting your show. How long has it been now?"

"Over two years," Charlie supplied.

"Bingo! And now you're one of the most successful women in the business—and Tarik wants you back."

Charlie thumped her pillow and adjusted its position to cushion her back. "That'll never happen."

"Says who? You maybe. But does Tarik believe that? Let's say he doesn't. Let's say he thinks that you still love him, that with a little bit of sweet-talking he can worm his way back into your life. Then ex-boyfriend, Devin Spencer, enters the picture, and that pushes him right over the edge. Remember, Tarik is one of the few people who knew about the kind of love you and I shared."

Charlie shuddered. God help her if Devin was right. "Is there water left in that glass?" she asked, suddenly needing a drink.

"No, but I'll be glad to get you some."

Devin swung long legs off the edge of the bed. At any other time Charlie would have ogled his half-naked body, zeroed in on his tight little butt in those skimpy black briefs. She would have wanted to run her fingers through the thick patch of chest hairs he'd grown while they'd been apart. But tonight Devin's theory weighed heavily on her mind, and she only halfheartedly acknowledged that his walk was sexy—a rolling gait, she'd once heard it called.

"Do you want ice?" Devin called from the outer regions.

"Not if the Evian's been in the refrigerator."

At that precise moment the phone rang. Charlie settled more comfortably under the covers. After the fourth ring she reached over and picked up the receiver.

She came on the line in time to hear Devin's sultry, "Hello," and was just about to let Devin know she was on, when the rough voice on the other end got her attention. Skipping the customary greeting, the caller grunted, "Spencer?"

"Yes."

She knew she should hang up. Eavesdropping had never been her style, but the stranger's voice had a familiar ring to it. She was curious. What if this was the mysterious Harry she'd heard so much about? What if Devin's partner had called to summon him home even earlier than planned? She needed to be prepared.

"I'm calling about my check," the gravelly voice continued.

Silence on the other end.

The caller's voice had an edge to it, his words now flowing in run-on sentences. "I appreciated your sending the money for the first job. But I need another check—soon. Getting into the apartment was a piece of cake. Nothing to it really. When I found out she wasn't goin' be around, I just used the key you gave me. If I say so myself, I did a beautiful job. You'd be proud of it. Now I hope you're goin' show me some real appreciation in the form of a little extra dough. Can we call it fifteen hundred even?"

"I'll pay you sixteen," Devin countered. "Consider it a bonus. My way of rewarding you for a job well done. Believe me, she's freaked out and still hasn't figured it's me. Now stay in touch in case your services are needed again. And I'll get that check to you tomorrow, first thing." Devin hung up, omitting the customary goodbye.

The dial tone resounding in Charlie's ear, she heard Devin call, "Sure you don't want ice? The Evian's not real cold."

Puzzling over the conversation, she forced herself to say, "Okay, maybe one cube."

What had the caller meant when he'd said Devin owed him money? He'd alluded to needing to be paid for work on an apartment. Immediately her wayward brain had jumped to one wild conclusion. This wasn't the only time this guy had called Devin for money. The first had been on the cruise ship when she'd overheard the one-sided conversation. Then Devin had said he was his assistant.

Why would an assistant do work on someone's apartment? Charlie tried to shrug away the nagging suspicion, but evil thoughts kept surfacing. Only Devin held the answers. Just how did she go about questioning him without letting on she'd been eavesdropping?

She was still pondering the question when Devin entered the room holding two glasses of water. He handed Charlie hers, set the other down on the nightstand, and climbed into bed.

"Who was that on the phone?" she asked, raising her glass to take a tentative sip. Over the rim their eyes held.

A beat or two later, Devin came back with, "No one important. Just one of the guys I do business with."

"The same one you met for drinks?"

"Yes."

Charlie's fingers reached for his ear. She didn't buy his answer. She stroked the velvet lobe then tugged. "So what did he want?"

Devin's attention now seemed focused on the remote control. He snapped the TV on full volume and shouted over the commentary, "Oh, I don't know. He was rambling on about something or the other. To tell the truth, I listened with half an ear."

Suddenly even the cool water Charlie sipped tasted lukewarm. She set down the glass, remembering that on the ship when she'd asked that question, he'd been equally as evasive. She couldn't come right out and call him a liar—

best to try another tack. "It must have been very important
for this person to call you this late. You're sure everything's
okay?"

Devin's focus shifted from the screen to Charlie's face.
"It's ten o'clock on the West Coast, hon. What's this, the
third degree?"

She'd been too obvious in her grilling, but his answer
was important to her, and she needed to know. It wasn't
a pleasant feeling thinking that the man you loved would
just as gladly kill you as make love to you. She wished she
could make sense of the whole crazy business. Devin had
been there for her from the moment she'd gotten that
crazy message on the ship. He'd offered support in every
possible way: He'd left the ship with her, made sure she
got home safely, and even remained in her home. Logically
she knew he wouldn't have broken into her apartment, or
pushed the pot off her patio, or locked her into the bathroom. Still, the conversation she'd overheard replayed itself. Distrust replaced trust. And the frightening thought
surfaced, What if he had an accomplice?

Fifteen

Throughout the night Charlie tossed and turned, finally managing a few fitful moments of sleep. She'd rebuffed Devin's overtures, pleading a headache. No way could she bring herself to make love to him. Come dawn, she crept from bed, leaving Devin asleep, and blissfully unaware of the havoc he'd created. She set about brewing coffee then decided that the crisp morning air would do her good, help clear her aching head and put her thoughts in order.

On the patio she braced against the coolness, crossing both arms, and taking a deep breath. The subtle scents of spring permeated the air, an indescribable smell, hard to explain, if you weren't a Northeasterner. Even more flowers had bloomed, turning the sizable patio into a kaleidoscope of colors. In celebration of her horticultural success, she stopped to pluck a daffodil. Flower in hand she leaned against the railing, letting her gaze drift downward.

Inconceivable that yesterday someone might have stood in that very same spot and deliberately hurled a flowerpot at her. She doubted a person could survive the fall, much less a fragile flowerpot. She shuddered to think what might have happened had it not been for Devin's intervention. That made the words she'd overheard even more confusing. Drumming her fingers against the railing, she played back a fragment of the conversation: ". . . she's freaked out and still hasn't figured it's me. . . ." Could the "she" Devin referred to, be her?

Shoving the thought to the back of her mind, Charlie jumped a mile high on spotting a man's silhouette in the doorway. She clutched the railing for support and gasped, "Oh, my God!"

"Sorry, hon, I didn't mean to scare you." Devin rushed to her side. His robe flapped open, revealing a wide expanse of bronze skin and the skimpy black briefs he'd worn to bed. Charlie's eyes scanned his face and slid downward to take in his sculptured body, noting the way his muscles flexed with the slightest movement. *Who is this man? Could he have changed so much after eighteen years? Why would he want to hurt me?*

In a swift motion, Devin pulled her into his arms, his hips pressing against her pelvis. When he dipped his head and sought her mouth, she turned her head slightly, letting his lips graze her cheek.

"My, we have attitude this morning?" Devin's arched eyebrows clearly revealed his feelings. "What's going on? First you refuse to sleep with me, now you push me away?" Even miffed, his voice was husky and filled with desire.

At any other time Charlie would have gone willingly into his arms, welcomed his embrace, his intoxicating kisses. But not today—not until she could make sense of the puzzling conversation she'd been privy to. She stepped out of his arms, summoning a half-hearted smile. "Would you like coffee?"

"Actually I'd like you." Devin reached for her again, this time pulling her up against him. He rubbed his stubbled cheek against her face until it tingled.

"Ouch!" Charlie said, relishing the smell of citrus and spice, but resisting the urge to hurl herself into his arms, to beg him to tell her it was a huge misunderstanding. That would also mean admitting that she'd been listening in on his conversation.

"What's wrong, baby?" Devin asked, tilting her chin to search her face.

Charlie summoned a watery smile. "I guess I'm not in a good mood. Too much trauma. Too little sleep."

"Oh, sweetheart." Devin drew her closer and wrapped his arms around her waist. She felt like a wooden doll, unyielding and unbending. He did his best to comfort her, whispering soothing words in her ear. "Oh, baby, I'm sorry. Perhaps we can get you in to see the doctor today, have him prescribe you something?"

Charlie made a face. "No. I hate doctors and I hate pills. Just give me a little time to recover. Now how about that coffee?"

Refraining from further comment, Devin followed her indoors. He wondered why she seemed out of sorts and should have insisted she see a doctor. Come to think of it, she'd been acting strange since last evening—noticeably so after he'd gotten that phone call. Could her odd behavior have something to do with that?

He focused on his own problems. Sometime he'd discuss the situation with Charlie but not now. He'd felt guilty breaking things off with his ex-girlfriend, Jennifer. Truth was, he'd never been in love with her, and she'd known that. He'd hoped to make amends by helping her find a comfortable apartment and ensuring she wanted for nothing. Hopefully in time she would get over him, and the threats and harassment would stop.

"Feel like breakfast?" Charlie asked, breaking into his reverie. She set a mug of steaming coffee before him.

Devin yawned. "Thanks, but it's way too early for me to eat." He jutted his chin, acknowledging the clock on the wall. "I haven't been up this early, since"—he snapped his fingers, remembering—"freshman year at college when you dragged me off hiking."

In spite of herself Charlie laughed. "We had a lot of

fun, didn't we? Remember the time you spotted that black bear and had me convinced it was Big Foot."

"Uum-hmm. It was the perfect excuse to have you leap into my arms."

Memories, long forgotten, surfaced. Back then had been an uncomplicated time, just the two of them against the world, or so it'd seemed. No game playing, just fun, and lots of good loving. Charlie felt the heat in her cheeks, the stirring in her loins. Even now she wanted him. To cover her confusion, she said the first thing that popped into her head. "Sure you're not hungry? It's a little after six, hardly the witching hour."

"Way too early for me. I'll join you for coffee though. Then we'll go back to bed." He wiggled his eyebrows. "Perhaps I can help put you to sleep."

Charlie's lips twitched. "What exactly did you have in mind?"

"Let me show you." Devin seized her by the waist and dipped her, pretending they were engaged in a complicated tango. His lips found hers, and his tongue slid into her waiting mouth, silencing any protest. Coming up for air, he moaned, "Baby, can't you feel how much I want you?" He guided her hand to make his point.

The shrill ringing of the doorbell made them both jump.

"Who could that be at this hour?" Charlie slid out of his grasp prepared to take the intruder's head off. Devin groaned. "Whoever it is, I'm going to kill them."

Charlie checked the peephole but could only make out the black leather-clad shoulders of a man. "I'm not sure who it is," she whispered.

Devin's hands grasped her shoulders, gently moving her from the spot. He took the place she'd vacated, slumping in order to get a better view. "I can't make out his face," he said, turning toward her, then back again. "Who is it?" he called.

Though silence prevailed on the other end, the body

stood rock solid, blocking the peephole. "Who is it?" Devin repeated, this time enunciating every word.

The man on the other side cleared his throat.

"If you don't speak up, I'm calling the police," Devin threatened.

"Man, what you want to do that for?" the visitor slurred.

"Tarik!" Charlie and Devin whispered in unison.

Charlie shouted through the closed door, "Okay, Tarik, there'd better be a good reason why you're here at this ungodly hour."

Raucous laughter broke out. "Do you want me to shout my reasons to the walls? Better open up, sweet face, unless you want your neighbors to hear your business."

She didn't like the fact that he'd threatened her but had to concede the point. The shouting back and forth had gone on far too long, and she couldn't blame her neighbors if they'd called the police, or at the very least building security. At that early hour even the nosiest tenant would hardly welcome a loud exchange in the hallway.

Yet how had Tarik gotten in? So much for having a doorman and undercover police casing the grounds. She looked at Devin, pleading with him to understand, then whispered, "I'm going to have to let him in."

Defeated, Devin shrugged his shoulders and stood aside. He watched Charlie lift the chain and slide the latches back. When Tarik lurched into the apartment, he discretely stepped out of his path. But even from that distance, he could smell the odor of booze and cigarettes surrounding him.

"How about a kiss, sweet thang?" Tarik said, reaching for Charlie.

Charlie stepped back and warded him off with her hands. "How about some coffee?"

"Nah, no coffee for me, though I will take a beer. So how ya doing?"

Charlie folded her arms. "Why are you here, Tarik?"

"That's no kind of greeting." A lopsided smile played across Tarik's face. He slid a pack of Dunhills from the pocket of his leather trench coat, jammed a cigarette into his mouth, and lit the tip with an expensive-looking lighter.

Charlie held her nose and fanned the air with her free hand. "Do you mind?"

Tarik ignored her. He took another toke of his cigarette and exhaled the largest smoke ring Charlie had ever seen. Then he plopped onto the couch and for the first time acknowledged Devin's existence.

Cigarette dangling from his fingers, he slurred, "Well, this is a real cozy scene. Looks to me like I might have interrupted something."

Devin's pupils were chips of ice. He held his bathrobe closed with one hand and fumbled for the robe's belt with the other. The time spent tying the sash, he used to gather his composure. It would take a lot to be civil. Through clenched teeth he managed to grind out, "Good morning, Tarik. Yes, you most certainly are interrupting something."

Tarik's gaze focused on Charlie. Under the intensity of that stare, her face heated up. What had she expected, Devin to deny that they were sleeping together?

Tarik's next words were designed to hurt. His slur seemed less noticeable now. "You let this gigolo move in with you?"

"What's it to you?" She was in his face, cheeks flaming, dander up. Over her shoulder she spat, "I asked you once and I'll ask you again. Why are you here, Tarik? What do you want?"

Tarik's cigarette ashes floated toward a nearby philodendron. He stubbed out the butt in the soil. Smiling the same lopsided smile as before, he said, as coolly as you please, "What if I told you I was in the neighborhood?"

"At this hour?"

"Something wrong with the hour? Wasn't like you weren't up?" He smirked.

"Stop it right now," Devin snapped, his temper flaring. "It's six thirty in the morning, man. Nobody comes visiting at this hour."

"Nobody?" Tarik eyed Devin then backed off when Devin's eyes flashed. Sticking another cigarette in the corner of his mouth, Tarik mumbled under his breath, "By the way I don't recall talking to you."

Noticing Devin's curled fists, Charlie quickly stepped between them. The last thing she needed were two grown men brawling in her living room—that would push her neighbors over the edge.

"Guys," she said, holding both hands palms up. "Cool it!" To Devin, "Would you mind waiting in the bedroom?"

Devin looked like she'd cut his legs out from under him. After a beat he acquiesced. "I'll be in soon, sweetie," Charlie promised in softer tones.

Tarik's cigarette smoke lingered heavily in the air. He'd made a home for himself on the couch and showed no signs of leaving. His eyes were hooded even as he smirked at Charlie.

"Damn, you're beautiful when you're angry," Tarik drawled.

"All right, Tarik," Charlie began. "Say what you have to say, then hit the road."

Tarik settled back on the couch and wrapped his leather trench coat around him. He crossed one leg over the other and struggled for words. When he spoke, most of the slur had disappeared. "It's like this. I booked into a nearby hotel just so I could talk to you. I knew you'd never voluntarily agree to meet me, so I hoped the element of surprise would—"

"All right, Tarik," Charlie interrupted. "Cut the bull and get to the point."

"Come over and sit next to me." Tarik patted the spot beside him. Charlie pretended not to see. It would be the worst mistake of her life to get comfortable. She'd never get rid of him then.

Slowly Tarik eased himself into an upright position. He tried taking her hand. "You've got two minutes," she said, her tone brooking no nonsense. She jammed both hands into the pockets of her robe and glared at him.

"Okay. Okay. I came to warn you."

Charlie narrowed her eyes. "Go on."

"Spencer's no good, Charlie. Did you know he just dumped his girlfriend of several years? He's on the rebound. He's not looking for a long-term relationship, more like a quick roll in the hay. Can't you see that? You're a divorced woman of a certain age. He's pegged you as an easy target. You know he's always been envious of everything I have. He's decided to use you to get to me."

"Envious of you?" Charlie sputtered. "Jealous?" She shook her head and laughed raucously. "Why would he be?"

Tarik's guttural laughter rose to join hers, the sound reverberating off the walls. "Devin Spencer's always been jealous of me, Charlie. My looks, the way I talk, everything. Remember, I was the one who always got the women—even you."

Charlie didn't remember any such thing, though what he said about her was true. If anything, Devin had been the one to attract women of all ages. She stared blankly at Tarik and waited for him to continue.

"He's always envied my success. He enjoys putting me down. I'd hazard a guess, he still carries a grudge because you chose me over him."

Charlie dismissed Tarik's ludicrous story with a flick of one hand. Her expression remained stony and unyielding. "Are you done?"

Tarik tried another approach. "What about your daughter—aren't you setting a bad example for her, letting

Spencer move in with you? How are you going to feel if Kasey thinks you're a slut?"

Charlie winced at the harsh label but managed to maintain her cool. Enunciating each word carefully, she walked to the door. "You're way out of line, Tarik. I think you'd better go. Our daughter's hardly a child anymore, and I think she can handle the truth about you." She held the door open, adding, "And just in case you forgot, you're no longer a part of my life."

Tarik remained rooted to the spot. He taunted, "Though you aren't much of a mother, Charlie, I still love you."

"Enough!" Charlie roared, not caring what neighbors heard. "Get out of my apartment this minute. I'm counting to ten, and if you're not gone, I'm calling the police." She started a slow countdown.

Outside, Tarik's response drifted in. "Be assured, baby, if I can't have you, no one will."

Devin tried his best to tune out the loud voices. Still, bits and pieces of the exchange floated his way. He knew Charlie was capable of handling Tarik, but he wished that she hadn't relegated him to the bedroom. He would have liked nothing better than to throttle Tarik Connors.

As loud portions of the conversation drifted his way, Devin heard Tarik's raised voice say, "What about your daughter—aren't you setting a bad example for her . . ." He clenched his jaw and bit down on his tongue. He could quite easily go out there and rip Tarik apart. Moments away from busting out of the room and rearranging his nemesis' face, he heard Tarik clearly say, "Though you aren't much of a mother, Charlie, I still love you."

That was what finally did it. Devin reacted emotionally rather than logically. He flung the door wide and charged to Charlie's aid. His steps slowed as he played back frag-

ments of the conversation, the tidbits he'd overheard.
Tarik had never once referred to Kasey as "his daughter"
or even "our daughter." Why would a father do that?

Sixteen

"It's another Friday night in the suburbs. Do you know where your loved ones are?" Ellis breathed heavily into the microphone, sounding like he'd just surfaced from the throes of an orgasm.

It was Charlie's turn. Smoothly she interjected with, "Tonight's sizzling topic is bound to make even the most secure of us wonder . . ."

They were off and running, Ellis adding, "When the cat is away, will the mouse play?"

Together. "You're on the air with your Hot 101 talk show hosts, Ellis and Charlie. Welcome to *He Said, She Said.*"

Again tonight's hot topic had been Charlie's idea. She'd been intrigued by a magazine article in which a freelance journalist, who'd interviewed five hundred suburban couples, stated that more than eighty percent cheated on their spouses. The journalist had aptly captioned the article, "Suburbia: A Hotbed for Cheating Spouses." The writer, also claiming to be a sexologist, had statistics to support his claim. Truth or fiction, Charlie knew the topic would be a winner. Sex sold—and illicit sex especially intrigued an audience.

Charlie took the first call, listening intently to a breathless young woman give a titillating account of a three-year affair with her personal trainer. The subject seemed to be of particular interest to Ellis, and she let him handle the questions, using the time to regroup.

Tomorrow would be the beginning of a lonely week. Devin would be on his way to San Diego, leaving her alone to deal with the pervert. She couldn't fault Devin—he had business to tend to, just like she did. He'd already devoted much of his time to baby-sitting her. All in all it just wasn't fair. So she'd let Devin assume that her parents would stay with her, when in fact she'd discouraged their visit. She'd coped before and could easily cope again. No need for further baby-sitting.

Charlie tuned back into the conversation, listening to another caller graphically describe her young lover's attributes. She claimed to be a new woman under his tutelage, and took it a step farther, saying that for the first time in years she'd been responsive.

Hearing the woman's elated tone, Charlie was struck by a sudden awareness. It had been years since she'd felt so alive, fulfilled, and ready to handle whatever life dealt her. Did good sex really do that to you? How would she survive when Devin was no longer a part of her days? Would tomorrow be the dress rehearsal for the rest of her life? What if he got on that plane for San Diego and never came back?

In the midst of her reverie, Charlie heard Ellis say, "Jeannette, you're on the air with Ellis and Charlie. What have you to add?"

Forced back to the present, Charlie focused on the caller's words. A chirpy female confessed to having a torrid affair with her next-door neighbor. What's more, she suspected her husband slept with her lover's wife.

"Well, that certainly puts new meaning to the words ménage à trois, or in this case would it be ménage à quatre?" Ellis cackled.

"Better referred to as swinging," Charlie added.

Call after call came in. Charlie made comments where

appropriate, but for the most part let Ellis carry the show. The topic had brought a lilt to his voice and the same sparkle to his eyes usually reserved for encounters with attractive women. As the second hour came to an end, she breathed a sigh of relief. Reginald signaled they had time for one last call.

"You're on the air," Charlie said, picking up on her production assistant's cue.

Silence on the other end.

Ellis, sounding more than a little irritated, urged, "Better speak up, and make your point—we're about to sign off."

There was a whirring noise, followed by canned laughter. The same laughter she'd heard the evening she'd been locked in the bathroom. Her chest tightened and feelings of light-headedness prevailed. Hitting the kill switch, she cut off the caller.

Devin sorted through the stack of compact discs Charlie kept by the CD player. He selected an old Marvin Gaye favorite, popped it into the stereo, then set the stack to the side. Closing his eyes, he allowed the singer's powerful lyrics to wash over him, letting the fantasies build. Convinced that only Marvin had the power to soothe, he hummed aloud and set about dimming lamps and lighting candles.

Now that the mood had been set, all that remained was a trip to the kitchen to check on the hors d'oeuvres. He was determined to make tonight special if it killed him. Even if that meant keeping the incident in the parking lot earlier that evening a secret. It had been one close call, and he'd been so shaken up he'd called the cops, even suffering the overbearing presence of Phillips and O'Reilly gracefully.

While the two plainclothes men hadn't exactly dismissed

his story, they'd seemed dubious. They'd poked around
the lot, and after a while, given an explanation that didn't
quite cut it. They'd made light of the attempt on his life,
citing kids with BB guns as the reason he'd been shot at.
Even he knew better than that. Someone had deliberately
aimed a gun and fired at him. Thank God, he'd had the
presence of mind to duck. The last shot whizzing by had
missed his ear by fractions, shattering the windshield of
the bright red Cherokee next to him.

When he'd questioned O'Reilly and Phillips about the
whereabouts of the plainclothes cops assigned to the building, he'd been informed that the surveillance team had
probably taken a break. He'd found it strange that both
men would go on a break at the same time but had wisely
kept his mouth shut. He was hardly Mr. Popular with either
man.

Devin removed the bottle of Dom from the refrigerator
just as Charlie's key jiggled the lock. He hurriedly retrieved
the tray of hors d'oeuvres from the oven and rushed to
greet her.

"Madam," he gushed, bowing low, as she swept through
the door.

Charlie played the game well. She selected an exotic
concoction from the tray he held out and tossed back,
"Ah, Jeeves, what do we have here?" Flashing him a smile,
designed to charm the shorts off even the most resisting
mortal, she bit into her pastry. No way would she allow
their last evening to be ruined with tales of a sicko who'd
surfaced again. She pushed the unpleasant thought to the
back of her mind and said, "Marvin to soothe the soul
and a delicious smell to boot. What have I done to deserve
this?" She took another bite. "Mmm."

Devin set down the tray and bottle and gathered her
close, arms lingering at her waist. He nuzzled her neck,
sending chills through her body. His whispered words
made her tremble. "Everything."

Charlie's lips curved into a half smile. Devin always knew the right things to say. She sniffed the air appreciatively and said, "My guess is you've got scented candles lit. Aren't you the romantic. Now tell me what have you been up to on your last day."

Devin's finger found her lips, shushing her. "You make my last day sound like doomsday. It's not like I'm disappearing for ever and ever. I'll be gone only a week."

Ancient memories surfaced, and Charlie blinked the moisture back. Her lips trembled as she struggled to make her smile full. Was it déjà vu, or hadn't he said something similar a long time ago? But back then it had been the prelude to an eighteen-year separation.

"I know what you're thinking," Devin mouthed, breaking into her thoughts, his tone suddenly serious.

"I doubt that."

"I'm coming back, baby. I'm coming back. There ain't no mountain high enough to keep me away," he sang, waltzing her around. "And I'll definitely be back for your birthday."

"Well, you'll never make it on *Soul Train*," Charlie said, swatting his hand and abruptly changing the subject. "Are you going to dance away the evening, or are there plans for that bubbly you've been chilling?"

Gray eyes sparkled as Devin cupped her chin between thumb and forefinger and blew gently against her eyelids. "Come," he said, taking her hand and leading her toward the couch. "You've had a long day. Have you eaten?"

Charlie nodded. She'd choked down a turkey sandwich only minutes before going on the air. After the night she'd had, a full meal sounded absolutely repulsive.

Seated on the couch, Devin poured the champagne and handed Charlie a flute. "To us," he said, clinking.

"To us," Charlie repeated less enthusiastically. Who knew if there would be an "us" after tomorrow? She wanted to believe he'd come back, to trust him with her heart. The conversations she'd overheard replayed in her mind, coupled with his disappearance before . . . What was a girl to think?

"Why so sad?" Devin probed.

"Am I?"

"Umm-hmm. You sound and look like you've lost your best friend."

Charlie took another sip of champagne, gathering her courage. "Is that a possibility?"

Devin took her glass and set it on the coffee table. Covering her hands with his, he slowly brought them to his lips. His eyes never left hers. "You've never forgiven me, have you?" He looked like she'd walked all over his heart. "Even though I told you that I wrote you several times, called you every moment, you still don't believe me. Wouldn't it be easier just to talk to your old man? It's been a number of years, but I'm sure he'll remember me. I was that persistent."

He must be a mind reader. She'd planned on broaching that very subject with her dad, delicate as it was. Even now, it seemed uncharacteristic of her father to be that forgetful or that devious. Either way he'd have to answer to her—explain his reasons.

"What will it take?" Devin asked, his lips brushing hers, "to make you trust me?"

Good question. Assurance that he would never leave her again seemed a selfish thing to say, especially since he'd worked long and hard to establish himself. She couldn't expect him to give up his career just to be with her. On the other hand, she'd gone through hell and back, finishing school, raising a child, and taking any job that would give her media experience. She had no plans to move, not unless that move came with a show, and no one in San Diego had made an offer. A commuting relationship couldn't even be considered. Much too much wear and tear on the soul—and low possibility of survival.

"I don't know," Charlie said, debating whether to tell him that it wasn't just the past that made her leery. Total honesty would mean admitting she'd been eavesdropping. How would that go over? Still, he'd be forced to provide straight answers to questions she needed to hear.

"My ebony princess," Devin said, massaging the nape of her neck. "I love you. Don't you know that? This isn't about lust or desire, although admittedly I can't look at you without wanting you. Baby, I've loved you for almost two decades. You stood by me through one of the roughest periods of my life. I've told you things about myself I never admitted to another living soul. And although I've mastered my dyslexia, there's not a day that's gone by that I didn't think about you, and miss you something crazy."

"You don't need me anymore, Devin. You're no longer the insecure boy I used to know."

"Oh, but I do. I need you even more, Charlie. These last few days have made me realize what it's like to have you back in my life. Made me realize what I was missing. You're someone I can talk to. You've always supported me, stood by me. I love you, Charlie."

The feeling was mutual, though she'd denied it—and over the years had even allowed herself to hate him a bit.

"I've never stopped loving you, Devin," she admitted, not looking him directly in the eye. "At times I'd felt that I'd never find another you."

Devin's arm snaked around her waist. "Then why are we wasting time with conversation? We should be making mad furious love right now, creating memories to have during the long lonely nights ahead." He brought her close against him and reached for the bottle of Dom Perignon. "Let's promise right now to show each other just how much love there is between us." He hooked an arm around her waist, and together they walked down the hallway.

In the bedroom Devin fingered the top button of Charlie's cream silk blouse. He blew against the hollow of her neck and whispered, "I want to memorize every luscious inch of you." He unbuttoned yet another button, his hand reaching between the open gap to caress the skin beneath. Charlie trembled as his mouth found her ear and he bit down gently on the lobe, working the remaining buttons. The shirt came off. The ankle-length skirt soon followed in its path. On his knees he peeled away her hose then kissed the exposed flesh.

Charlie thought she would literally melt in his arms and was one step away from attacking him, when he abruptly stood up and held her at arm's length, his breath coming in erratic bursts. "God, you're lovely."

Two scraps of lace kept her from feeling totally exposed. Her body heated up as his gaze stroked the length of her, and he lowered her bra straps and undid the clasp holding the tiny bit of fabric together. The garment fell, revealing nipples that had come to full attention. Devin's mouth quickly took the place of the absent fabric, warming her, driving her wild. He bit down on one bud then the other, letting his tongue go to work, laving her nipples and moistening the hollow between her breasts. She pressed into him, palms curved under each globe, offering herself up.

"Yes, I think I will," Devin groaned. His fingers manipulated her nipples and stroked the undersides of her breast.

She inhaled the smell of citrus, spice, and vanilla and tried desperately to ignore the hardness against her belly. God, she wanted him badly. His hands slipped below the elastic band of her panties, cupping her buttocks, pressing her against him. She could feel his need, his total desire for her. His hands continued their roaming, exploring secret crevices, slipping inside to find the moist spot between her thighs. Putty in his hands, incapable of logical thought, she groaned. How could she ever have suspected him?

"Shall we go to bed?" Devin rasped, already tugging her in that direction.

She couldn't formulate an answer, couldn't even protest when he swept her off her feet.

The muted light of flickering candles had turned her bedroom into wonderland. Gently Devin laid her on the bed and still fully clothed, straddled her. His arms supported his weight on both sides. "Undress me, love," he murmured.

Though already transported to a land of make-believe, Charlie hastened to comply. Soon Devin lay naked, cradled in her arms, his body wrapped around hers. Charlie savored his warmth, drank in the subtle scents of citrus and vanilla, and opened her mouth to let his tongue in. Doubt disappeared. She trusted him. How could she not?

Devin's fingers stroked her flesh, bringing her body alive, igniting little fires and sending her pulse racing.

"Baby, I don't want to wait much longer. I want you inside of me," Charlie begged.

He accepted the invitation, entered her swiftly and choked out, "I want to be there, baby."

The fires ignited soon turned into a raging bonfire. As sparks flew about her head, she felt her limbs buckle, reality fade, and an enormous feeling of pleasure wash over her. In the distance she heard Devin shout, "Wait for me, baby. Wait for me." She tried, but her body wouldn't obey. The heat had become an all-consuming burn. Limbs thrusting, she let go, half hearing Devin's declaration: "I want to marry you, sweetheart. I won't take no for an answer."

Charlie came to against his chest, her legs still wrapped around his torso. He held her, cradling her, whispering words that she thought she would never hear. "Marry me—say yes—please don't ever let us be apart again."

In her gut she knew it was the heat of the moment talking—he wasn't even making sense. She had a career to think about and couldn't ask him to give up his. Tomorrow, fully clothed and sane, they'd discuss his proposal. By then he might not even remember what he'd said.

"Can we talk about this another time?" Charlie asked, throwing cold water on her lover's enthusiasm.

Devin kissed her forehead and sighed. "If that's what you want, love. But I'm not about to change my mind in the light of day. And I'm not leaving for San Diego without an answer."

"I really would like a few days to think about it," she insisted, ignoring the little voice at the back of her mind that told her she shouldn't trust him.

Seventeen

"Would you like a refill?" the bartender asked, retrieving Charlie's empty Pellegrino bottle and pointing to her half-empty glass.

Charlie smiled at the blond young man in red suspenders and ratty old jeans. She shook her head as he placed an unopened bottle before her. "No, thanks. Looks like I've been stood up, so it's a safe bet I'll be leaving soon."

"This one's on the house."

She thanked him, glanced at her watch, then drummed her fingers against the cherry-wood bar. What could possibly be keeping Tarik? He was supposed to have met her here a half hour ago.

She'd decided to meet him because he'd called sober and making sense. The conversation, they'd agreed, would focus strictly on Kasey's financial needs.

Charlie knew that as each year passed, Kasey's college tuition would become more and more outrageous. Her and Tarik's combined incomes eliminated any possibility of scholarship monies. As it now stood, Tarik begrudgingly covered the half of Kasey's tuition Charlie insisted he pay. Books, pocket change, and other incidentals were Charlie's responsibility. She hoped that his initiating this meeting meant he'd finally come around.

Charlie drained her glass as Tarik swung through the revolving glass doors. She watched him scan the room, one hand buried deep in his trench coat, eyes lingering a tad longer than necessary at the back of the room. She followed his gaze, chuckling when she spotted the object of his interest. Apparently nothing had changed since they'd been apart. Tarik still preferred buxom light-skinned women with big legs. The zaftig creature he eyed was fifty pounds lighter but a dead ringer for Bessie Collins, the obnoxious classmate she'd had the misfortune to meet at the reunion. Thinking of Bessie immediately brought to mind the note from her brother. Devin had stuffed the envelope into his backpack, and that was the last she'd seen of it. She'd have to ask him about the note when he got back.

"Charlie," Tarik shouted, spotting her at last. She waved him over and watched him push his way through the crowd. Instinctively she swiveled her bar stool to avoid an enthusiastic embrace but wasn't quick enough to evade the wet kiss he planted. Tempted to wipe her lips dry, she decided against it. Why be confrontational? What purpose would that serve?

"You look beautiful," Tarik said, taking in Charlie's cherry red blazer, tan slacks, and jaunty beret pulled to the side.

Begrudgingly she acknowledged the compliment. "Thanks. It's nice of you to notice."

Tarik took the stool adjoining hers. He shrugged out of his coat and slapped his wallet on the bar. "What are you drinking, baby?"

"Water."

"So what's new?" He waved a twenty at the bartender to get his attention, then yelled, "Bourbon and Coke—and whatever the lady's drinking."

"Coming up." The bartender turned away to fulfill Tarik's request.

Charlie waited until their drinks were set down. "Okay,

Tarik, shoot," she said. "I've got a half hour to listen, then I have to go to work."

Tarik's hand reached out, fumbling for hers. He tried to entwine their fingers. Anticipating his intentions, Charlie quickly folded both hands in her lap. She smiled sweetly. "We're here to talk business, Tarik, not make love."

To cover his annoyance, Tarik quickly changed the topic. "Where's Spencer tonight?"

Charlie wondered what was behind the question. She'd made it clear, conversation about Devin was strictly off limits. She let the silence drag out before reluctantly offering, "He's in San Diego."

Tarik's eyebrows shot skyward. He smirked. "Lover-boy didn't waste much time running, did he? Is this a permanent move?"

"Look, I didn't come here to talk about Devin. You told me this was to be a discussion about Kasey's financial future. That's the only reason I agreed to come, so talk."

Tarik knocked back his drink. Ice clinked as he set his glass on the bar. "I knew you wouldn't come if I said it was about you and me. But I needed to warn you."

"About what?"

Tarik stalled. He signaled the bartender for a refill and waited till the drink was set down. Taking a big gulp, he spat out, "Spencer."

Exasperated, Charlie's palms slapped the bar. "What about him?"

Tarik took another swallow of booze. He tried reaching for Charlie's hand again, but she'd already linked fingers around her glass.

"You haven't been in contact with Spencer since—college—is that right?" Tarik probed.

Charlie nodded and waited for him to go on. Where was this leading?

"Charlie, Spencer isn't the same boy you knew. He's

grown up, and there are things about him you need to know. Like he's a real smooth operator and not to be trusted." Tarik drained his glass, letting his words sink in.

A muscle in Charlie's cheek twitched. Her voice was raspy when she said, "Why are you telling me this?"

"Because I couldn't stand by silently while you got conned. Spencer isn't the harmless nineteen-year-old you had a fling with. He's devious and conniving and may even be dangerous. Did he tell you that the woman he lived with filed suit against him?"

Despite Charlie's vow to remain cool, she reacted. "Suit?"

"As in lawsuit, Charlie. She's also petitioned the court for a restraining order to keep him away. She claims he's harassed her from the day she broke things off. Her name's Jennifer something or other. Spencer lived with her for years. Now she claims he's stalking her and threatening her life."

Charlie felt her throat go dry. This was unreal. Tarik was making the whole thing up, he had to be. "Where did you hear this?" she croaked.

Stalling again, Tarik signaled the bartender. "You forget Devin and I are in the same business. We know the same people. Gossip like this has a way of getting around."

It was a nightmare from which she would wake up, she was sure of it. Tarik couldn't possibly be talking about the same man she was considered marrying. Not her sweet, gentle Devin—the man she'd once trusted with her heart. She thought about the conversations she'd overheard, about how smooth he'd become. Deep down she knew there were plausible explanations.

"There aren't any secrets between me and Devin, Tarik," she lied. "He told me all about Jennifer, and it's not what you think."

Tarik belted his third drink. He used his finger to stir the remaining liquid then licked the tip dry. His face registered incredulity. "Spencer told you there was a restraining order against him?"

Charlie nodded. Love for her man had forced her to go along with the story. Or was it stupidity? Would she perjure herself if it came down to it?

"Then how did it go over when you told him our little secret? Did he go ballistic?"

Charlie refused to look him in the eye.

"You *did* tell him?"

She remained silent for a beat too long.

"You didn't." Tarik's ugly laughter soared above the patrons' patter. "Spencer still doesn't know about Kasey. What are you waiting for Charlie, *me* to tell him?"

She controlled the urge to slap the supercilious smile off his face, rub his nose in the remnants of bourbon. Why was he doing this to her now?

"I never thought you would sink this low," she whispered. "What is it you want from me?"

Tarik scraped his stool across the polished wooden floor, bringing himself closer. The sound had the same effect on her nerves as screeching chalk against blackboard. He was close enough for her to get a good whiff of bourbon. She drew back.

"Come now, sweet thang," Tarik baited, leering at her. "Surely there's no mystery about that. It's always been you."

The room was suffocatingly warm all of a sudden. Charlie grabbed her purse, hopped off the bar stool, and threw down a crisp ten-dollar bill. "I've got to go Tarik—no need to see me out."

Tarik's words followed as she wove her way through the predinner crowd. "I forgot to ask—you didn't by chance come across a gold identification bracelet?"

She ignored him.

* * *

"I'm coming home, Mother," Kasey announced.

Charlie's voice held a slightly hysterical note as she quizzed her daughter. "You're not driving by yourself?"

"No, Mother. Brian's doing the driving. He's very excited about meeting you, and we're both looking forward to your birthday."

A smile curved Charlie's lips as she listened to her child's gleeful babble. She'd walked into the apartment only moments ago, found the phone ringing, and ever since had been forced to listen to Kasey's patter.

Charlie shifted the receiver to rest between shoulder and collarbone then got in, "Honey, you seem to mention this Brian more and more. Are you two serious?"

There was a sigh of frustration on the other end, followed by a wailed, "Oh, Mother, now you know I don't like discussing my personal life. But if it answers your question, I like Brian a lot, but we're not thinking of eloping or living together. You know I like my space."

Charlie exhaled the breath she'd been holding. She'd tried to bring Kasey up the right way. And though her daughter had a pretty good head on her shoulders, she was what was known as an independent thinker, a free spirit in her own right. "Yes, dear, I know. Now when shall I expect you?"

"Well, that's the thing. We thought we'd leave on Thursday, the day before your birthday, but Brian's got this exam, so we're hoping to leave after dinner. I know you'll be at work, but I have my key, and I'll let myself in. Hey, Mom, are you still seeing that guy?"

"Is Brian staying with us?" Charlie asked, deliberately ignoring Kasey's question.

A short pause followed. "Well, I can't ask him to go to a hotel, not after he's driven me all this way."

"Good point," Charlie conceded. "I'll assume that you'll make him comfortable in the guest room. Drive safe

and I'll see you in a couple of days. Till then I'll be counting the moments."

Charlie hung up to Kasey's, "You're an old fogey, Mom,
but I love you anyway."

Smiling, Charlie dragged herself up the hallway. It had
been a long, exhausting day, one filled with rumors that
the station was sold. Though much of the gossip had
seemed farfetched, she replayed the more plausible bits
and pieces in her head. Was there some credence to the
rumors? What would it mean to her career? Shelving those
unpleasant thoughts for a moment, she focused on her
conversation with Kasey.

In the bedroom Charlie made a mental note to pack up
any personal items Devin had lying around. She chuckled,
imagining what Kasey would say if her fogey mother confessed to having sex. That brought to mind another issue.
Devin would be back in a couple of days—she'd have to
tell him about Kasey. It would be awful to have him look
into those sultry gray eyes and draw the obvious conclusion. He'd end up hating her for the deception. And she
couldn't in good conscience consider marrying him without telling him the truth.

The phone rang. Charlie glanced at her watch, registered the time, and made a wry face. Who could be calling
at this hour—Kim perhaps?

The moment she picked up, a man's seductive voice
greeted, "Hello, sweetheart, I'd hoped to catch you before
bed."

Devin's voice had the usual predictable effect. A tingle
made its way from scalp to toe. Light-headed for a moment, Charlie grabbed the bedpost for support, slumped
onto the mattress, took deep breaths, and waited for her
equilibrium to return.

"Charlie, are you with me?" Devin repeated. "I've got
a dinner appointment but I wanted to check in. Is every-

thing okay? Have your parents been good company? Tell
me you haven't heard from that nut again?"

Charlie kept her voice even. What was the point alarming Devin on the West Coast? What good would that do?
She dismissed the eerie thought that he might already
know about the call. Perhaps he'd placed it himself. It was
a ridiculous notion and didn't even make sense. What
would be Devin's motive? Why come after her after all
these years? He'd been with her when the flowerpot came
tumbling down. He couldn't be in two places at once,
could he? Not unless he had an accomplice, a little voice
said.

"Everything's fine," Charlie said, speaking too quickly.
"My parents are wonderful." The latter wasn't exactly a
lie—she'd had lunch with Marilyn and John earlier that
day. "How are things going out there?"

"Couldn't be better."

Charlie could tell by Devin's voice, he was in a good
mood. She listened to him go on about the contract he
and his business partner had finally signed, and about the
new business that Harry had single-handedly drummed
up.

After he'd wound down, Charlie asked, "So do you know
what flight you'll be taking?" She'd already started feeling
guilty for taking him away from his business.

"The earliest one I can get, baby. I've missed you like
crazy."

Charlie's voice lowered. "Me, too, hon. Uh, Devin," she
said, figuring to get it over with. "We'll need to discuss
sleeping arrangements."

"Nothing to discuss, woman. Where you sleep, I sleep."

"Not this time. I just got off the phone with Kasey—
she'll be home the same time you are."

There was a long drawn-out pause, followed by a sigh
of exasperation. "Now that presents a problem."

Charlie's voice squeaked, appealing to his decency.

"Would you mind terribly sleeping on the couch? It'll be for only a short time, and I swear I'll make it up to you, once Kasey goes back to school."

His chuckle, a low rumbling sound, sent goose bumps up her spine. "I'll mind very much. But I'll do it, or I'll go to a hotel in the evenings. Guess if I had an eighteen-year-old daughter, I'd be concerned about appearances. You're a wonderful mother, my love."

She wanted to tell him he *did* have an eighteen-year-old daughter but over the phone was hardly the place. News like that required timing and the right setting. She hung up the phone with Devin's "I love you, Charlie Canfield," echoing in her ear.

In the midst of plumping up her pillow, the phone rang again. Immediately she thought of Devin. There was a three-hour time difference on the West Coast—he'd often call again just to say how much he missed and loved her. Charlie's voice was hoarse when she answered.

"Hello"

The sound of static greeted.

"Hello," Charlie repeated, this time louder, convinced that the crackling came from Devin's cellular phone.

"You slut," the familiar voice snarled. "You—"

Stifling back a scream, Charlie slammed down the phone. She picked up seconds later and with shaking hands dialed the beeper Phillips and O'Reilly had given her. She waited for the tone then punched in her telephone number.

Five minutes later her phone rang.

"Officer Phillips here, Ms. Canfield. Everything all right?" Phillips sounded weary, as if he'd had a hard day.

Charlie, sobbing like a madwoman, tried to formulate words.

Phillips's voice gentled. "Breathe deeply, Ms. Canfield, and tell me what happened."

"He called——he called——and said hateful things," Charlie sniveled.

"Did he threaten you?"

"Not exactly."

"All right Ms. Canfield, I want you to take slow breaths. Then if you haven't done so already, I want you to grab a glass of wine. Is there someone with you?"

"No."

"Can you call someone?"

"My parents."

"Good. I'll make sure our patrol cars keep circling your block every fifteen minutes or so. Then first thing tomorrow I'll arrange to have a tracer placed on your phone. The next time that joker calls, you'll need to keep him talking, the longer the better——that way we can pick up his exact location."

Charlie thanked Phillips and hung up. Much as she hated to do it, she dialed her parents' number.

Eighteen

Kasey's key jiggled the lock. She entered the apartment and called out, "Anyone home?" Not that she'd expected her mother to answer, but her grandparents might—they'd promised to be there for her mother's party.

Hearing no response to her query, she did a small jig in the middle of the living room. At least she and Brian would have some time alone, long enough to at least raid the refrigerator. After that drive they were both starving.

Kasey'd left the front door slightly ajar, so that Brian, who was parking the car, could come in. There'd been no doorman in sight when they arrived. But in case Brian had a problem getting back into the building, she'd left a note on the podium to ring 10G.

Kasey tossed her bulging laundry bag onto the damask couch and raced off to inventory the refrigerator. It had always been her mother's habit to buy special treats when she came home. The kitchen would probably be filled with goodies.

She wasn't to be disappointed. The counters held a sack of crispy rolls, several bags of chips, assorted candy bars, and two different types of pie. Kasey stuck her head in the refrigerator, found a plate of cold cuts, a large tray of lasagna, and a sealed plastic container holding a Caesar salad.

"Hmm, yummie," she said, hearing footsteps behind

her. "Brian," she called and without taking her head from the refrigerator yelled, "You've got to come help me eat all this stuff."

It was the last thing she remembered before blackness consumed her.

Ten minutes later Brian Matthews poked his head into the open doorway. "Kasey, I'm back," he shouted. "Sorry I took so long. It took forever to park the car. The visitor's spots were all taken—I had to wait for someone to move out."

Receiving no answer, he entered the apartment, crossed the emerald rug, and called again: "Kasey, where are you? I'm starving, babe. Are you fixing sandwiches or something? It's been hours since we've eaten."

Kasey's laundry bag sat atop an expensive-looking couch. She had to be here. Perhaps she had not heard him. He headed off in the direction of where a kitchen might be, shouting, "Kasey, I'm here, where are you, babe?"

Before Brian could cross the threshold separating dining area from kitchen, he knew something was wrong. The soles of his boots clung to a coagulating substance on the tile floor, making it difficult to lift his feet. Looking down at his feet, he saw the dark liquid seeping beneath his boots. He bent over, dabbed at the liquid with his finger, and brought it to his nose. His stomach rolled, and his chest constricted as he confirmed his initial thought. Blood. God, he needed air. Grabbing a nearby chair to steady himself, he continued toward the kitchen. There the sight that greeted, caused him to gag. Not two feet away Kasey lay drenched in her own blood!

Brian's mouth opened. He screamed the cry of a wounded animal, a creature about to be slaughtered. Then following his instincts, he ran.

* * *

"Evening, Sam," Devin said, jiggling the key Charlie had given him. Sam grunted a reply and Devin, unconcerned, continued. "What's all that commotion in the parking lot?"

Charlie's doorman shrugged. "I think there's been an accident."

Devin tossed back the question. "What kind of accident? Is someone hurt?" He noticed the man's sweaty appearance and threw Sam a quizzical look.

When the doorman didn't answer, Devin set down his garment bag. "Well?"

The man swayed a little, then leaned heavily on his podium. He removed a handkerchief from his pocket and swiped at his brow. His words seemed fragmented when at last he answered. "A little while ago—some young kid came screaming down here—asked me to call 911—claims there was an accident."

Though something about Charlie's doorman definitely made his testosterone surface, Devin covered the distance between them. He placed a hand on his shoulder. "Hey, man, you okay? Can I get you some water or something?"

Sam's gloved hands gripped the podium tighter; he winced then laid his palms flat. His voice took on a surly note as he responded. "I don't think water's goin' to help the flu, but a shot of bourbon might." He jerked his thumb in the direction of Devin's briefcase. "You got anything in there to soothe the ache?"

"Sorry, can't help you with that," Devin said, moving off. He wasn't at all surprised that Charlie's doorman drank on the job. It could very well explain his strange behavior.

Just then an ambulance came careening into the parking lot, siren shrieking. Devin set down his bag and turned back to Sam. "Can you watch this for a minute?" Without waiting for a response he headed off.

In the few minutes he'd stopped to converse with Sam, the crowd outside had grown even larger. Ears alert, Devin hovered on the edge of one group. The bits and pieces he overheard bordered on the sensational. According to the gossip, a young woman had been stabbed, pistol whipped, and bludgeoned to death—simultaneously.

"She interrupted a robbery," one person said.

"No," another added, "it was a drug deal gone sour."

Curious, Devin turned to the heavyset woman next to him. "What's going on?"

Eyes as wide as saucers, jumbo-sized pink curlers bouncing, she happily filled him in. "A little while back, a teenage boy came running out of the building, screaming for help. We live on the first floor, so my husband was the first one to reach him." She pointed to a balding man with the stance of a prizefighter. " 'Twas my Micky that got Sam to call an ambulance."

"This happened in the building? Where's the kid now?"

"Back in 10G. He didn't want to leave his girlfriend . . ."

Devin gripped the plump woman's arm. "10G? Did you say 10G?"

The woman's teeth chattered—she tugged her arm away and folded it round an ample middle. "Y-yeah. Why are you so interested? Do you know the occupants?"

Devin didn't stop to answer. He was already halfway across the parking lot.

He entered the building at the same time two burly paramedics wheeled in a stretcher. Forgetting about his luggage, he squeezed into the elevator with the men. Sam, the doorman, was nowhere in sight.

"10G" he confirmed, punching the number.

"Yup," said the larger of the two. "Supposed to be a nasty situation up there."

Devin grimaced, though he'd already deduced it

couldn't possibly be Charlie. He'd narrowed it down to Charlie's daughter, Kasey. He tried pleading. "Look, man, I live in 10G—can you tell me what's happened?"

The bald paramedic, the one who'd remained silent so far, threw Devin a curious look. "Hey, aren't you the guy that called this in?"

Devin shook his head. "Called what in? I just got off a plane from San Diego."

The bell pealed, signaling the car's arrival on the tenth floor. Devin, still clueless, preceded the paramedics down the hallway. He walked through the open door and was greeted by an assortment of Charlie's neighbors. Chatter ceased.

"I'm Devin Spencer," he said, looking around. "I'm a friend of Charlotte Canfield's." He waved his key to reassure the group he belonged there. "What's going on? What's happened? Who's hurt?"

A man in a plaid flannel shirt and baggy jeans pointed in the vicinity of the kitchen. "The bedroom's in shambles, but the girl's in there."

"Who's in there?"

"The daughter."

Not Charlie, thank God. Either way, not good. Devin raced toward the kitchen, the paramedics steps ahead of him.

The sight on the floor caused him to avert his eyes momentarily. When he could bring himself to look again, he saw a young woman, who even with eyes closed, bore a startling resemblance to her mother. She lay immobile, not making a sound, blood still flowing from a head wound. Slumped over her was a young man.

"Did someone call the cops?" Devin asked, watching the paramedics go to work. After being assured the police were on their way, he placed a hand on the boy's shoulders. "What happened, son?"

The teenager's bloodshot eyes rimmed with tears. In a

husky voice he answered, "I'm still trying to figure it out. Kasey left me parking the car. She went to fix us some food. I wasn't even gone ten minutes, but when I came back, I found this." He gestured to Kasey's bloody form.

Devin glanced at the still body now being strapped into a stretcher. God, she did look like the teenage Charlie. "Is she alive?"

"Barely." It was the bald paramedic this time. He steered the gurney from the room.

Devin let out the breath he'd been holding. Thank God, Charlie's daughter was still alive. He took hold of the boy's arm and tugged him along. Together they followed the progress of the stretcher.

In the elevator he asked, "What's your name, son? Have you had a chance to call Kasey's mother?"

The boy shook his head. Between sobs he answered. "Brian—No—I didn't know how to get ahold of her."

This time Devin directed the question to the paramedics. "What hospital are you taking her to?"

"Croton General," the larger of the two supplied.

"Now listen carefully, Brian," Devin said. "I want you to get into your car and follow that ambulance. I'm going over to the radio station to get Kasey's mother. We'll be over to the hospital shortly."

Nineteen

"Devin! What a nice surprise. When did you get in?" Even as the words tumbled out of Charlie's mouth, she sensed something was wrong. She hadn't liked the tone of his voice when he'd greeted her. "Devin?"

"I got here less than an hour ago, honey. I'm in your lobby. Can you come down?"

Charlie glanced at Reginald Barker, acknowledging his signal with a nod. Ten minutes to show time. She was glad to have Devin back, but his presence downstairs presented a problem. How could she pick up and leave only minutes before broadcast?

All in all it had already been the day from hell, with management finally making the announcement Hot 101 was sold. Her boss had even implied that a lucrative merger with the competitor would yield a new set of radio personalities. Though he hadn't exactly mentioned downsizing, his statement had sure made her feel insecure about her job.

Charlie spoke quickly: "Sweetie, it's nice to have you back. I can't wait to see that handsome face of yours. One favor though, can you come up? I'm going on the air in a few minutes, and I'd really hate to miss the start of the broadcast."

Devin's voice sounded strained. "Charlie, this can't wait. You need to come down *now*. There's been an emergency.

You'll have to find someone to cover for you." Although he hated to break the news this way, every second counted. Charlie was needed at the hospital right away.

"What kind of emergency, Devin?" Charlie asked, massaging her throbbing temples. When Devin didn't answer right off, she ignored Reginald's frantic signals, assured Devin she would be right down, and hung up. Stopping only to grab her pocketbook, she flung words in the direction of Ellis and Reginald. "Sorry, guys, gotta go, there's a problem at home. You're on your own this evening."

The moment Charlie stepped off the elevator, and spotted Devin, she knew the situation was serious. He paced the lobby looking like he wanted to strangle someone. She hurled herself into his arms, buried her head in his chest, and let the familiar smell of citrus fill her nostrils. Against his shirt she asked, "What's wrong, sweetheart?"

Gently Devin put her away from him. He cupped her chin in his palm, stared deeply into her eyes, then brushed her lips with his. In a stranger's voice he said, "I'll tell you once we're in the car."

"Devin Spencer, I'm not taking another step until you tell me what's wrong."

He knew there would be no arguing with her. Holding her by the elbow, he led her toward a group of uncomfortable looking chairs. "Sit," he commanded, pointing to the nearest chair. After she'd settled, he crouched next to her, took her hand and brought the palm to his lips. "I don't quite know how to tell you this, Charlie, but there's been an accident. Your . . ."

Charlie's face crumpled. "My parents, are they all right?"

"Your parents are fine, Charlie."

The light of recognition dawned. "My baby? Please, not my baby."

Devin nodded in silent confirmation. "We need to get going, Charlie. You'll need to give me directions to Croton

General." In the car he filled her in on what little he knew. Listening to her sob, he made a vow to kill the bastard if he ever found him.

Brian Matthews waited at the hospital. He told them Kasey had been rushed into surgery, and as yet there'd been no update on her condition. Then a nurse led them to a waiting room to sit and wait. When one hour turned into two, Charlie's face welded into a mask of pain.

"Maybe you should call Tarik?" Devin ventured. "I'm sure he'd want to know about his daughter."

Charlie's bloodshot eyes focused on him. "What?"

Devin repeated himself. "Sweetheart, you might want to let Tarik know his kid's been hurt."

She'd fallen into one of the fiberglass chairs, her head cradled between both hands. "You're right, Dev. But I can't. I just can't. I'm just not up to dealing with Tarik."

Devin squeezed her shoulders then gently massaged her neck. "I know, babe. I understand. How about you give me his number, and I'll call him for you."

Digging through her bag, she handed over a leather address book, then said, "If you can't reach him at home, you may want to try beeping him."

Devin already had his cellular phone in one hand. He punched in Tarik's home number and waited for the connection. For what seemed an interminable amount of time, the phone rang and rang, then a recorder picked up. Devin left a message and the hospital's number. Next he tried Tarik's beeper. After punching in his cellular number, he hit the number sign, then put the phone away. Minutes later his phone rang. He brought the receiver to his ear and acknowledged Charlie's mimed plea. She was not available.

"Hello," Devin greeted, his voice grave. He'd already anticipated Tarik's reaction and was not looking forward to breaking the news.

"Who's this?" the slurred voice on the other end asked. Music and laughter could be heard in the background.

"Tarik, this is Devin. I need you to come—"

"Hey Spencer, what you doin' calling me?"

Devin shouted over the noise. "I'm at Croton General, Tarik. Your daughter's been hurt. Charlie thought you'd want to know."

"Kasey? What'd she do? Break a leg rollerblading or something? That kid's always up to something. Her mother should never have bought her those skates—"

"Tarik, it's nothing like that. It's pretty serious."

"What do you mean, serious?"

Devin told him.

"Man, oh, man. Who would have thought. And her mother claims the suburbs are safe—"

Devin cut him off. "Are you planning on coming out?"

"I'll see what I can do." The line disconnected.

As Devin hit the End button, he noticed Charlie heading for the far side of the room toward a man in a green scrub suit who'd just entered. Hurrying to her side, Devin heard her ask, "Doctor?"

"Dr. Pearlman," the man in green confirmed. He glanced at a clipboard in his hand then back at Charlie. "You must be Mrs. Conners?"

It seemed unnecessary to mention that she had resumed using her maiden name. Charlie nodded confirmation. "How's my baby? Tell me she's all right. When can I see her?"

Pearlman adjusted granny glasses and peered at Charlie over the rims. "Why don't we sit down, Mr. and Mrs. Connors."

Neither Charlie nor Devin corrected him. Devin kept a firm hold on Charlie's hand as they followed the doctor. He waited until Charlie was seated then perched on her armrest and linked a possessive arm around her shoulders. "Will Kasey be okay, doc?"

Dr. Pearlman hesitated for a moment and seemed to fumble for words. Finally he said, "Actually your daughter's resting comfortably now, though unfortunately she's lost quite a bit of blood and will need transfusions. Problem is, she's a fairly rare blood type. But you must know that. We'll need a match." He looked from one to the other, acknowledged their blank stares, and continued. "Time is of the essence."

Much as Charlie would like nothing better than to sever every vein in her body to keep her baby alive, she shot the doctor a bewildered look. Truth be known, she didn't have a clue what her blood type was, and she'd just given blood last week but had forgotten to ask.

"What about you, Dad?" Pearlman directed his question to Devin.

Much as Devin regretted having to say it, in fairness to Kasey he was forced to. "I'm not Kasey's dad, doc. We're hoping he'll be here in an hour or so."

Pearlman's face didn't reveal his thoughts, though his eyes flickered. "Good. Then Dad should be along shortly. That being the case, Mrs. Connors . . ."

"Actually it's Ms. Canfield."

The doctor cleared his throat. "That being the case, Ms. Canfield, we'll go ahead and set you up for tests. The whole process shouldn't take more than a few minutes—"

"If it helps, I'm B-positive, doc," the forgotten Brian interjected.

"Thanks for volunteering, son, but I'm afraid that's not going to work."

Pearlman tucked the clipboard under his arm and graced them with a compassionate look. "Mr. uh . . . Ms. Canfield . . . son," he said. "The entire medical team's rooting for Kasey. We'll pull out all the stops if we have to. Meanwhile think positive thoughts and say a prayer. I'll be sure to let you know if there are any changes in the young lady's condition." On his way out, he tossed another

kindly smile their way, then said, "Ms. Canfield, a nurse
will be in soon to bring you to our technician."

Once Dr. Pearlman had disappeared from sight, Charlie
plucked at the half-dead ivy in her reach. The plant looked
like she felt, wilted and beaten down. She stared vacantly
at the room and silently recited her prayers. Should she
tell Devin about his child now, or should she brazen it out,
hoping that either she or Tarik would turn out to be a
match?

After a while Devin, observing Charlie's ashen face,
asked, "Did you eat?"

"I had half a sandwich."

Conversation ceased at the sight of the buxom nurse
beckoning them. Heart pounding in her chest, Charlie
rose to the summons and linked her fingers through
Devin's. "Please God," she said, vocalizing her thoughts.
"Please don't tell me Kasey's taken a turn for the worse."

The nurse's reassuring smile caused Charlie's heart rate
to stabilize. In a voice designed to soothe, she said, "Mr.
and Ms. Canfield, I still don't have news of your daughter,
but I have every confidence in Dr. Pearlman, he's one of
the best. He's asked me to take Ms. Canfield to our technician."

Though she hadn't gotten Devin's status right, Charlie
didn't have the heart to correct her. Besides, Devin didn't
seem to mind.

Removing a set of keys from her pocketbook, Charlie
turned to Brian. "Thanks for taking such good care of my
daughter. You've had a long day, and I know you're tired,
so why don't you go back to the apartment and try to get
some sleep. I promise we'll call the moment we hear anything." Though she appreciated the boy's concern, she
found a stranger's presence unsettling.

The teenager seemed reluctant to go but eventually did
so with Devin's urging. Leaving Devin behind in the waiting room, Charlie, like a zombie from the movie, *Night of*

the Living Dead, followed the nurse down dreary gray hall-
ways. Testing took barely five minutes, and she returned
to the lounge and Devin.

Entering the stark waiting room, she found another couple seated. The ill-fated potted ivy seemed to be taking a
real beating this time. Wilted leaves were strewn across the
carpet. Devin rose to greet her then led her to a seat at the
far end of the room. After minutes ticked by without
conversation, he said, "Sure you don't want some coffee?
The nurse said the cafeteria might still be open, and if
that's not so, we can always raid the vending machines."
He offered a weak smile and squeezed her hand. "Try to
hang in there, honey. My gut tells me Kasey will pull
through."

"Have I told you lately how much I love you?" Charlie
croaked, giving him a lackluster smile. He kissed her, and
in a tiny voice, she accepted his offer. "I think I will take
you up on that coffee. At the very least, drinking it will
give me something to do."

Twenty minutes later they returned to the waiting room
to find Tarik strutting and pacing.

"Where were you?" he demanded, accosting them.

Tarik's speech seemed clear enough, but a strong smell
of bourbon emanated from the area surrounding him.
Charlie stepped back and gave Devin control of the conversation.

"Hi, Tarik," Devin said, slapping his nemesis on the
shoulder. "I'm surprised you got here so soon. What did
you do, fly?"

Tarik placed both hands on his hips and glared at them.
"I wouldn't have expected you to have time for fun and
games, when your daughter's had an accident, Charlie."

Observing Devin's pointed finger, Charlie's mouth
snapped shut. She watched her lover narrow his eyes and
use that same finger to jab Tarik in the chest. "Look,
chump," Devin said. "Your daughter's condition is critical,

and your ex-wife's been put through the ringer. No one needs aggravation right now. Aren't you even going to ask how your daughter is?"

Confronted by steel gray eyes, Tarik's gaze shifted. "The nurse told me Kasey's stable," he muttered.

"Stable, and desperately in need of a transfusion. You happen to know your blood type, man?"

"Yeah. Why?"

"Because there's a good likelihood your daughter might need you."

Tarik's eyes flickered.

The entrance of Dr. Pearlman caused them to table the discussion.

"Ms. Canfield," Pearlman said, waving his chart at them. "I've got the results—"

"I'm Mr. Connors," Tarik interrupted, crossing the room to intercept the doctor. "I'm Charlie's husband."

"Ex," Charlie was quick to supply.

The doctor's brows knitted together. He glanced at his clipboard and back at Charlie and Devin. "Ms. Canfield and . . . uh . . . Mr. . . . ."

"Yes," all three said in unison.

"I'm afraid I've got some bad news. You're A-positive. I'll need to talk to Dad."

Tarik had somehow managed to bring himself to the forefront. "Doctor," he said, extending a hand. "I'm the child's father, and I'll be happy to donate blood if you need it. I'm AB-positive."

Dr. Pearlman blinked behind his glasses. He cleared his throat, looked at Tarik then back at Charlie and Devin. In a rush of words, he said, "Ms. Canfield, may I have a word with you in private?"

Charlie's stomach lurched. How could the nightmare possibly get worse? What more could go wrong?

"Charlie," Devin said, shaking her gently. "Dr. Pearlman's speaking to you."

Coming out of her haze, Charlie blinked. "I'm sorry, doctor."

"Why don't we talk over here?" Pearlman led her through huge double doors. He lowered his voice and placed a sympathetic hand on her shoulder. Sounding slightly uncomfortable, he continued. "Ms. Canfield, if you don't know who Kasey's father is, I'm going to have to find a universal donor. We don't have much time."

Charlie nodded, gulped, and got out, "Oh—but, doctor, I do."

Pearlman coughed discreetly. "Can we get him then?"

The doctor's words still ringing in her ears, Charlie headed back the way she had come. She found Tarik and Devin pacing opposite ends of the room. They spotted her and bolted in her direction. Devin got there first.

Clinging to the hand he offered, she asked, "Devin, what blood type are you?"

"Type O, Rh-negative. Why? Doesn't Tarik want to give his child blood?" He glared in the direction of Charlie's ex.

Charlie let out a huge whoosh of air. Ignoring the latter part of the comment, she added in a whisper, "Will you donate some blood to Kasey?"

He didn't hesitate. "Of course."

Forgetting the doctor and the surly Tarik trailing them, she flung herself into Devin's arms. "Thank you, Lord."

Devin hugged her back. For the first time that night, Charlie noticed the glint of gold at his wrist. She dismissed the uneasy feeling at the base of her gut, wrapped her arms around his waist, and let the reassuring scent of citrus wash over her. There was a God after all. She'd lucked out.

"We had an angel looking out for us," she whispered, omitting to add, "in more ways than one." Turning back to Dr. Pearlman, she asked, "Will my child be okay after Devin gives blood?"

"If Mr. . . . uh . . ."

"Spencer."

Pearlman's words were measured. "Ms. Canfield, if Mr. Spencer is an acceptable donor, we can be cautiously optimistic. Kasey has a swollen brain, but she's young and in relatively good health." He addressed Devin. "In a moment someone will be out to take you back to the lab. Meanwhile we'll keep you both informed of Kasey's progress." He loped off before they could get out the next word.

A sixth sense told Devin something wasn't quite right. He replayed the conversation and felt the flush at the back of his neck creep up to settle in his cheeks. It had been a while since he'd had a biology class, but if memory served him well, Tarik's type AB blood coupled with Charlie's A could in no way have produced an O-negative child. He was O-negative. Kasey was O-negative. He shook his head, reluctant to draw the obvious conclusion. Tight-lipped he snapped at Charlie, "We need to talk."

Tarik suddenly seemed in a hurry to leave. In his rush to escape, he tripped over his words. "Since I'm obviously not needed here, and you two seem to have a good handle on things, I think I'll head back. I'd like a word with you, Spencer." He glanced at Charlie, blinked rapidly, and added, "In private."

The last thing Devin needed was a tête-à-tête with Tarik Connors, but he couldn't very well say no without starting a scene. "I'll be right outside Charlie," he said, tossing words in her direction. "If Pearlman needs me, come get me." He followed Tarik from the room.

In the hallway Tarik faced Devin. "Look, man," he began. "I'm sure Charlie didn't mean for you to find out this way."

Carefully hiding his feelings, Devin kept his voice even.

"I don't know what you're talking about, Connors. What was I not supposed to find out?"

Tarik placed a comforting arm around Devin. "We're old friends, right? We go back a lot of years. Promise me you won't get angry?"

Remaining silent, Devin nodded.

Back to form Tarik's voice held its usual boastful tones. "Come on, Spencer, you know I once told you that Charlie and I had a thing going, at the same time you and Charlie had your thing. See, it was like this. When she told me she was pregnant, I knew there was a strong possibility the baby was yours, but I married her anyway. I loved her, man. Still do."

Taking imperceptible gulps of air, Devin digested the news. Though his suspicions had been verbalized, he was numb. How after eighteen years did you handle the news that you were a parent? That the woman you loved had carried your child but never let on? No way would he acknowledge that Tarik's admission had rocked his world.

Devin forced a smile. His voice took on silken tones as he lied. "Thanks for the update, Connors. It's old news. Charlie told me all about my daughter a week ago. In fact, the very night she accepted my proposal."

Waving at the gaping Tarik, he retraced his steps.

Twenty

"Why didn't you tell me, Charlie?" Devin started in, the moment the door closed behind them. He'd convinced her to stay at a hotel close to the hospital, until a cleaning service could be called in to deal with the apartment. When there was no immediate answer, Devin tossed his duffel on the bed and glared at her.

Charlie attributed his uncharacteristic curtness to lack of sleep. Heck—after what they'd been through, she wasn't exactly Ms. Congeniality either. She yawned, waited for him to fill her in, and changed the topic when he continued to glower at her. "Did you get a chance to call Brian and my parents?"

"Yes, I did."

Devin tugged her hand, moving her toward a horrendously ugly brown plaid couch. He waited until she was seated, removed her shoes, then took possession of her feet. He began a brisk massage.

"Charlie," Devin ventured, her instep firmly clasped between his fingers. "Why would you have kept something so important from me?"

Refusing to look him in the eye, she jerked her feet away. "Speak plain English, Devin."

"How much plainer can I get? I'm talking about our daughter, Charlie. Yours and mine."

She was suddenly wide awake, brown eyes searching gray

for a hint of understanding. "H-h-how d-did you find out?"
As if she didn't know the answer. Her hand covered her
mouth, the next words coming through splayed fingers.
"Not Tarik." With jerky motions, she leapt from the couch.
"Devin, I'm so sorry. I hadn't meant for you to find out
this way. I planned on telling you soon."

"When?"

"I was waiting for the right time."

"Right time? When would that be?" Devin sprang up
and swung her around to face him. "You can't blame this
on Tarik, Charlie. For once he actually did us a favor. When
were you planning to tell me?"

She hung her head, unable to face the fire in his eyes.

"Charlie?"

"I hear you, Devin." Squeezing her eyes shut, she imagined the pain she'd put him through. How could she make
him understand that her deception hadn't been meant to
hurt but to protect? Kasey had needed the security of a
father, and feeling she had no options, she'd taken Tarik
up on his offer. Poor as that choice turned out to be.

She tried moving out of the trap Devin had created with
his hands, but his fingers were steel, holding her captive.
She was forced to face him, to look him squarely in the
eye. "I'd planned on telling you, Devin," she whispered,
"the day I agreed to marry you."

"Is that so?" He snickered. There wasn't a hint of mer-
riment in his tone. "Then why didn't you say yes before I
left for San Diego? You would have saved us so much pain."

He had a point, but so did she. Charlie answered him
as honestly as she could. "Because marrying you means
the world to me, and I wanted to be sure I was doing the
right thing for both of us."

"Have you made up your mind then?"

"Yes. And the answer is yes."

He'd dreamed about this moment for a long time, anticipated laughter, champagne, and loving—not tears

from a fiancée he wanted to strangle and news of a ready-made family. Though the idea of a daughter excited him, Tarik's revelation had come as a shock, and he'd been quick to internalize his feelings. Now all of that built up resentment was directed at Charlie. What he couldn't understand was why she'd kept his daughter a secret after divorcing Tarik.

Perhaps he wasn't being fair. He'd been the one to let Charlie walk out of his life. He'd acted like a dog, relying on her father to relay messages. Surely he could have figured something out when his letters were returned, "address unknown"? She'd taken up with Tarik only out of necessity. Who could blame her? Still, he'd lost eighteen years of his daughter's life, and that hurt badly.

"Why, Charlie? I still don't understand?"

"Please, Devin, don't do this to us," she said hoarsely. "I already know marrying Tarik was wrong."

When Devin was finally able to speak again, he said in a husky voice, "I suppose I'm as much to blame as you, baby. I should never have let you go."

Hearing the pain in his voice, Charlie rubbed her cheek against his hand. "Please let's not rehash it. We both made mistakes. I should have trusted you, but I didn't. Back then I was an insecure teenager dating the campus jock. I didn't hear from you that summer, and naturally I thought you'd abandoned me. Believe me, it doesn't come easy telling you your kid exists after eighteen-plus years. It's hardly one of those things you blurt out overnight. I needed to find the right words . . . the time . . . the place." She brought Devin's palm to her lips and blew on it. "Have I ever told you how much I love you, Devin Spencer. Never for one moment did I stop loving you. Please don't stay mad at me, not when we're both hurting. Let's try to forget the what if's and think positive thoughts. That beautiful child of ours needs us right now."

"You can't just expect me to forget about this," Devin growled. "I had a legal right to know. The right to be involved in my daughter's upbringing—to be a father to her."

"I know that, Devin. I know that," Charlie said wearily. "I admit I made the wrong choice."

"I'm just too damn angry to talk about this now," Devin said, stomping off. He unzipped the duffel, removed two tiny boxes wrapped in pink and gold, and threw them on the bed. "Before I forget. Happy birthday. Now if you'll excuse me, I need air. I'll be back in an hour."

Two hours later the door opened. Devin's expression was hard to read. Charlie slammed down the receiver and rushed to his side. "Where did you go, Devin?" She touched his sleeve then dropped her hand when she thought he wouldn't answer.

"For a walk then to the hospital."

"Oh? I called the hospital several times. They never mentioned you were there."

"I was there." He shrugged wearily and looked pointedly at the bed. "You never did open your presents."

Charlie summoned a weak smile. "Not after you practically threw them at me."

He returned her smile, but the usual dazzle had disappeared. "I did, didn't I. I'm sorry. Now I've ruined your birthday."

It was the catch in his voice that got her. She wrapped her arms around his waist and placed her cheek against his chest. "Devin, I really am sorry . . . sorry about keeping Kasey a secret, sorry about hurting you."

"I know that, sweetheart," he said, kissing the top of her head.

She stood in the circle of his arms, drawing strength from his warmth, letting the familiar smell of citrus wash over her. She could swear he'd been crying.

Eventually he said, "Well, aren't you going to open up your presents?"

All thumbs, she took forever to open the wrapping and at last held a black velvet box in her open palm. After a couple of tries, she managed to pry the lid open. "Oh, Devin, this is beautiful," she gasped, holding up the delicate gold bracelet from which a tiny charm dangled. The heart hanging on the end had purposely been split in two.

"Turn the charm over and read the inscription out loud," Devin urged.

"My heart is incomplete without you. Oh, Devin, that's so sweet."

"I mean it."

About to kiss Devin, he waggled his wrist at her again. This time he tripped over words in his excitement. "I know I said I wasn't exactly the gold bracelet type—but I couldn't resist—see, I have the other half." He turned, placing the second box in her palm. "Open your other gift."

How could he possibly give her anything else to top this? Cheeks flaming, Charlie tugged at the bow, glad that it gave way easily. She dispensed with the paper and found herself clutching another velvet box. She snapped the lid open and let out a loud whoosh of air. Words finally came. "Oh, my God, Devin. This is truly magnificent . . . and expensive . . . and too much."

"And perfect for you," he said, sliding the square-cut diamond on her finger. Holding on to her hand, he got down on one knee and in a raspy voice said, "Charlotte Canfield, I know I'm not perfect, but will you marry me?"

Unable to utter a sound, Charlie gazed into eyes reflecting such passion, she was forced to look away. How had she lived without Devin this long? "I'd love to," she said, then tentatively, "Is our daughter a part of the package?"

"Unequivocally, yes. I plan on proposing to her, too." Devin drew her close. "If she'll have me."

* * *

On an unseasonably warm spring day, Charlie entered Kasey's hospital room to find her daughter sitting up in bed. "Hi, pumpkin," she said bussing her forehead.

"Hi, yourself. Where's Devin?" Frowning, Kasey looked up from her jigsaw puzzle. Devin and her mother were usually inseparable.

Charlie smiled. Kasey still didn't have a clue as to Devin's true identity, but instinctively she'd adored him. "Devin's downstairs, sweetheart," Charlie said. "I believe he stopped off to get you something."

"A present, eh? You know, Mom, I really like him. He reminds me of someone. But I can't quite put my finger on who."

"I should hope you like him, he spoils you rotten. Besides, I would hate it if you disliked the man I plan on marrying."

Charlie wondered what Kasey would say if she told her that she and Devin were mirror images of each other, that the father she'd grown up with wasn't her father after all. She and Devin had decided they'd wait for the right moment. They'd wanted to be sure Kasey was physically and mentally ready to handle the truth.

Kasey'd already gone through a rough time. The moment she'd regained consciousness, she'd had to endure the overbearing presence of Phillips and O'Reilly. She'd been forced to answer a slew of questions and revisit every moment of that horrendous night. Though it had been rough going at times, not once had she resorted to histrionics.

The cops had concluded that Kasey's attacker was someone familiar with Charlie's comings and goings. Charlie still didn't want to give credence to the assumption that it was someone she knew. She'd heard that the police had questioned neighbors, friends, and Charlie's coworkers. But as yet there'd been no arrest made.

Now with Kasey out of intensive care, Charlie and Devin

had decided to tell her the truth. They'd practiced how to break the news then decided that rather than sounding rehearsed, they'd just speak from the heart.

"You know, Devin adores you," Charlie began, smoothing back the shorn head that had once been Kasey's pride and joy.

"It'll grow back, Mom," Kasey said, shifting out of her mother's grasp. "And yes I do know that he likes me. Now can you stop fussing, and let's talk about stuff—like when I'll be well enough to leave the hospital? What date you've set to get married? How will this affect my life? And when Brian'll be back from school?" Brian had returned to school only after Charlie'd insisted he did. She'd practically had to push him out the door.

"Strange you should ask that question," Devin said, entering in the midst of Kasey's chatter. He eased himself onto her bed so as not to upset the jigsaw puzzle and took her hand.

"These reminded me of a certain young lady." He presented her with a bouquet of daisies wrapped in cellophane. "They're fresh, delicate, and ever so fragile." He nuzzled the shorn head of hair.

"Can it, Spencer," Kasey said, thanking him, then accepting the flowers. "What's the occasion?"

Devin's dimples were prominent slashes. "Such insolence from one so young." He clutched his heart. "Now you've hurt my feelings. Do I have to have an ulterior motive for bringing you flowers—"

"All right, you two," Charlie interrupted. "Enough." She took a seat on the other side of Kasey and held her daughter's other hand. "Honey, we've got something important to tell you."

Kasey looked from one to the other. She could tell by their faces this wasn't going to be easy. She hated bad news. "My attacker was found? You want me to identify him?" she said in a wobbly voice.

Both heads swung from side to side, and Kasey smiled with relief. She wanted her attacker found—she just wasn't crazy about going to court and facing him.

"Okay, I give up," Kasey said, throwing both hands in the air. "Did I get kicked out of school? Come on, guys, just tell me." Her face fell as another idea surfaced. "Is Brian planning on dumping me?"

Her mother's amused smile served to reassure. "No, baby, that's not even a remote possibility."

"Then what is it? Come on, you all, don't keep me in suspense."

Over Kasey's shorn head, Devin and Charlie exchanged glances. The emotions Charlie saw in Devin's eyes gave her the confidence to carry on. Taking a deep breath, she continued.

"Baby, what we have to say is bound to come as a complete surprise—"

Kasey clapped her hands, cutting her mother off. "How cool, we're moving to San Diego. We'll be living on the West Coast."

Charlie held up a hand. "Let me finish. There's a good possibility we might, but that's not it." She omitted adding that only yesterday she and Devin had discussed that option. With the radio station sold, and her career temporarily on hold, it was indeed a consideration.

Kasey's face crumpled. "Then this really is serious."

"Yes, it is," Devin said, coming to Charlie's rescue. He slid off the bed, jammed a hand in his pocket, and stared down at mother and daughter. "Kasey," he began, "what if we were to tell you that your father—"

"Dad's not hurt, is he?"

"No, Tarik's not hurt."

Devin ignored Charlie's silent plea. He fumbled his words. "What if . . . your mom were to tell you . . . that your dad's not your dad."

Kasey's brow furrowed. "What'd you mean? Am I adopted?"

Seeing the anguish in her daughter's face, Charlie took over. "No, honey, you're not. What Devin's trying to say is that he and I loved each other a long time ago—so much so, that we had a daughter."

Kasey's hands flew to her throat. She made a choking sound. "What do you mean? I'm the daughter? I'm illegitimate?" She began to cry.

Devin handed Kasey his handkerchief and resumed the seat he'd vacated. Taking his daughter's hand, he crooned, "Is it really that terrible having me for a father?"

"N-o-o-o," Kasey wailed. "It's just such a shock. Now I understand why Dad—I mean Tarik—I mean—heck, I don't know what I mean—never wanted much to do with me."

"He's always loved you," Charlie said, for once coming to Tarik's defense. Not because Kasey'd been wrong in her assessment, but having been dealt such a terrible blow, and having just had a near brush with death, she needed some illusions.

"What's all this?" a voice boomed from the open doorway. Charlie looked up to see her parents hovering at the entrance. Rather than trying to explain, she summoned a smile and waved them in. They didn't need to be drawn into this situation.

Charlie's father clutched an overstuffed Pooh bear, which he held out to Kasey. "Why the tears?" he asked his granddaughter.

"She gets tired easily," Charlie quickly interjected.

Marilyn Canfield wore a canary-colored shirt and an equally bright smile. She kissed her daughter then drew her granddaughter close. "Feeling better, munchkin?" Her smile a mile wide, she held out her arms to Devin. "Hello, young man, we've heard an awful lot about you. It's been a while since we saw you last, but Charlie tells me your advertising business is doing well." She engulfed Devin in a bear hug. "Uuuum-uuuum-uum. I think you've gotten even better-looking with age, better smelling, too."

Charlie's lips twitched.

John, Charlie's father, was far more restrained in his greeting. He stuck out a hand. "John Canfield, young man."

Devin shook the hand he extended. "Nice to see you, Mr. Canfield."

"John—if you're planning on being part of the family. Funny how things turn out. Weren't you the young man who caused Charlie such heartache one summer? The one I used to hang up on."

"Dad!" Charlie's jaw hung open. Devin's story had been corroborated at last. She faced her father, a funny expression in place. "What's this about hanging up on Devin?"

John Canfield looked from one to the other and decided to come clean. "Heck, it was a long time ago, honey," he said sheepishly. "My memory is a bit foggy, but I do remember this young hot shot calling, making a pest of himself. He used to even write you letters. He drove me crazy. You were so sad that summer, and I blamed him for your unhappiness, so I told a white lie or two when he called. I'd simply say you weren't home. And I returned his letters, 'address unknown.' Even so, you still got married"—he lowered his voice so that Kasey, who was involved in conversation with her grandmother, couldn't hear—"to a man I detested."

"But you never said anything, Dad. You didn't even try stopping me," Charlie whispered.

"Would you have listened? Young people aren't that easily dissuaded. I was afraid you'd end up hating me if I'd put my foot down."

"You must have known I was pregnant. I felt I didn't have a choice."

A sharp rap on the doorsill got their attention. Officers O'Reilly and Phillips, trademark baseball caps on backward, poked their heads in. Phillips, not waiting to be invited, strutted across the room, O'Reilly steps behind him. "Hope we're not interrupting anything?"

O'Reilly, the more mellow of the two, stopped to caress Kasey's cheek. "How ya doing, youngster? Feeling better?" His pale blue eyes roamed Kasey's face.

Charlie, observing her child's heated cheeks, decided that Kasey was beginning to develop a crush on the officer. So much for Brian.

"We've got news," Phillips announced, thumbing through his notebook. "Can you come out to the hallway, Ms. Canfield?"

Tossing a puzzled glance Devin's way, Charlie followed both men out.

"We think we're on to something," Phillips began as soon as they were out of earshot. "We've dusted your apartment for fingerprints and come up with several sets."

Charlie held her breath. "Go on," she urged.

"In your closet naturally we found yours"—he jerked his chin in the direction of the room—"Spencer's, and another party we're not able to identify. Based on the time and way your apartment was entered, we've ruled out forced entry. We still feel the perpetrator is someone you know. Does anyone else in the building have your keys?"

Charlie thought for a moment then finally said, "Actually building management requires each tenant provide them a key. In the event of an emergency, say a fire or something, they'd have access."

O'Reilly looked up from the notes he'd been scribbling. "What about your alarm, Ms. Canfield? You did have a burglar alarm installed. Was it on, when you left home?"

Charlie threw them a blank look. She nibbled her lip. Eventually she'd gotten around to having the alarm installed, though in her rush to get to work she might have forgotten to turn the thing on. Would it really make that much difference, if as the cops suspected, it was an inside job? Both the building's management and condo association required tenants provide their codes. Charlie told them that.

"Okay, Ms. Canfield," Phillips said. "Something smells here. We'll be in touch with the management, and we'll be speaking with each person on that condo board . . . soon." He tilted his cap and beckoned to O'Reilly to come. "Stay safe, Ms. Canfield."

Charlie returned to the hospital room to find everyone in remarkably good spirits. They were huddled over Kasey, laughing and joking.

Entering she said, "All right, guys, what's going on? What's so funny?"

"Come over here, Mom," Kasey shouted, gray eyes full of mischief. "We're planning a party for when I get out of the hospital."

"Good girl." Charlie took a seat at her daughter's bedside and playfully chucked her under the chin. Devin came around to stand behind her, his hands resting on Charlie's shoulders.

"We pray that's soon," he added.

Marilyn Canfield put in her two cents. "Is the end of the week soon enough? We ran into Dr. Pearlman on the way in, and he said, barring the unexpected, that's a certainty."

"What great news." Charlie kissed the top of her daughter's head.

"And we were thinking," Devin added, "that since we never celebrated your birthday, this party could be a combination welcome home for Kasey, birthday celebration for you, and engagement party for us. How does that sound? Did you see Charlie's ring?" The last was said to the Canfields who beamed their pleasure.

Kasey bounced back and forth on the bed, scattering pieces of jigsaw puzzle everywhere. "Killer idea," she said, clapping her hands. "Now who should we invite?"

Twenty-one

"Ms. Canfield, you have visitors. Says they're Mr. and Mrs. Ellis Greene." Sam Davis sniffed loudly into the intercom. He adored Ms. Canfield, but she was having a party and hadn't invited him.

"Send them up, Sam."

Shouting into the crackling intercom, Charlie's doorman spoke again. "Are you having a party, Ms. Canfield?"

Charlie squelched the guilt the question evoked. Had Sam really expected an invitation? He seemed so hurt. Sounding apologetic, she spoke quickly, "Sorry, Sam. I should have told you I'm expecting a bunch of people. It's my engagement party. There'll be more guests coming by." She hung up before he could say another word.

Charlie's party was only a half hour old. Small groups sat chatting and munching while the lyrical tones of Sade played in the background. Reginald and an elderly woman made a feeble attempt to dance. Despite the absence of caterers, whom she'd thought would be an unwelcomed intrusion, it had all gone off without a hitch. She'd opted to keep the party cozy, inviting only those with whom she was close. What a shame that Kim, who'd had other plans, couldn't make it.

Looking around, Charlie made sure drinks had been proffered and hors d'oeuvres served. The credit all went to her parents, who'd eagerly agreed to play host. They'd even helped concoct the delicious spread she would serve. Now they were scurrying around, greeting people and overseeing the kitchen.

Completely satisfied that her guests' needs were met, Charlie smoothed the wrinkles out of the cream silk dress, wound the sparkling scarf that Devin had given her around one finger, and went in search of him. She stopped briefly to acknowledge the congratulations of neighbors and friends, holding out her left hand so that the ring could be suitably admired. After hearing the oohs, aahs, and comments about the size of the diamond, she moved on.

Outside a setting sun bathed the patio in rosy hues. Charlie drank in the cool spring air and at the same time spotted Devin holding court with Kasey and Brian. Devin held the ever present cellular phone in one hand. As she listened to Kasey's high-pitched giggles, Charlie thanked God that her daughter's life had been spared.

She considered herself one lucky lady. Given Kasey's initial feelings that she'd been deceived, things had turned out surprisingly all right. Kasey and Devin had bonded in a relatively short time. While the teenager still couldn't quite bring herself to call Devin Dad, she'd bounced back relatively quickly, and was even more high-spirited than before. Today she wore a hot pink minidress and matching hoop earrings. Charlie, in a rush of pride, admitted that she was truly the prettiest flower on her patio.

Thrusting herself into the laughing circle, Charlie offered her lips for Devin's kiss. "Okay, guys, why are you here?" She tapped Devin on the shoulder. "Are you setting a bad example? Shouldn't you be inside with our guests?"

"Oh, Mom, stop lecturing. It's such a glorious evening." Kasey sniffed the air. "Can't you just smell summer? Why not bring the party out here instead of having everyone hole up in that poky apartment of yours?"

For Charlie's sake Devin stifled his amusement. He waggled a finger and winked at his daughter. How had he managed to produce such an insolent child? "Now don't be rude. Your mother's apartment's hardly poky. In fact, judging by what the realtor says, some would say it's too big for them."

Difficult as it was for Charlie, the prudent thing had been to put the apartment up for sale. With Hot 101 sold, it seemed wise to explore career opportunities with the larger radio stations in the San Diego area. There was even a distinct possibility she might score her own show. It had not been an easy decision. Her roots were here, she loved the Westchester area, and loved her apartment. But what could a girl do? Commuting was clearly out of the question, and she was no longer assured of a job.

John Canfield stuck his head through an open window. He waved a pair of oven mitts to get their attention. "Hey, kids. Your doorman's looking for you—says he has a delivery."

"I'll be right there." Charlie wondered if Sam had a true need to come up, or this was simply a ruse to see what was going on. He did have a tendency to be nosy.

"Would you like me to handle this?" Devin asked, rising from the lounge chair he'd commandeered. He tossed his cellular to Kasey. "Here, hold this."

Though a bit peeved by Sam's intrusion, Charlie gave Devin an impish smile. She didn't need two testosterone-driven males flexing their muscles. Not today anyway. "No, thanks—I can handle Sam." She headed off.

Inside Charlie greeted the new arrivals, even tolerating Ellis's wet kiss and ignoring his whispered come-on. When she could extricate herself from his embrace, she said hello to his long-suffering wife then moved on. She scanned the room, noting the absence of O'Reilly and Phillips. The two undercover cops had promised to be there.

Flinging the front door wide, she greeted her doorman. "Hi, there." He was partially hidden behind a huge floral arrangement. "Are those for me?"

Over the top of long-stemmed roses, Sam handed her an envelope. Charlie thanked him and quickly read the contents. Guilt surfaced again as she made out his scribbled signature. "Oh, Sam," she said. "How nice of you. You shouldn't be spending all this money on me." She wondered how he'd managed to procure the arrangement on such short notice.

He stuck his head around a white wicker basket, holding what must easily be two dozen red roses, and smiled at her. His eyes seemed suspiciously bright. "You've always been so nice to me, m'am, I just wanted to give you something back in return. Can I come in for a moment, just till I can set these down?" Still clutching the massive arrangement, his eyes roamed the room. He lurched across the threshold, brushing by her.

Charlie wrinkled her nose as the smell of alcohol and tobacco threatened to engulf her.

"Have you been drinking, Sam?" she asked, noting his unsteady gait.

"I only had one drink, Ms. Canfield. You ain't goin' tell no one now?"

She knew it was wrong to promise. But he'd always been nice to her, always seemed to have her best interests at heart. "Why don't you set the flowers over there?" She pointed to a place on the coffee table, anxious to have him gone before the neighbors saw his inebriated state.

"I think this might be a better spot," Sam said, heading for the opposite end of the room where a small group gathered.

Out of the corner of her eye, Charlie saw Devin intercept his progress. Her fiancé's voice was surprisingly calm when he said, "Can I take that from you?"

Sam's answer came through clenched teeth. "Thanks, but I got it under control."

Even though each man had maintained their own space, Charlie sensed a showdown coming. She could tell that

Sam felt Devin had issued a challenge. His whole stance had changed. His body loomed, huge and menacing, threatening even. His eyes bulged. Clutching the huge arrangement, he spun around and glared at them over the greenery, shouting, "Don't none of you move. I've got a bomb in this thing." He held the flowers at arm's length, making his point.

Sam's loud shouts got the attention of Charlie's guests. People came running from the kitchen, stopping short when they realized that their lives were endangered. Charlie's mouth opened, but no words came out. At last she'd made the connection. Sam, the doorman—the man she'd thought a friend—was the lunatic she feared. He was the stalker.

All of a sudden everything seemed crystal clear: an intruder with a key, the flowerpot falling off her roof, someone knowledgeable of her comings and goings, an attempt on Kasey's life. She raised a hand to her mouth, stifling back the nausea. To think she'd suspected Tarik, Ellis, and even Devin.

O'Reilly and Phillips had it figured right after all. They'd called it an inside job. What she couldn't fathom was her doorman's motives. She'd never done anything to him.

Remembering the daughter she'd left outside, Charlie searched the room, looking for Kasey. Not spotting her, she breathed a sigh of relief. Now where were her parents? Her heart almost stopped when she realized that Marilyn and John were among those who'd come running from the kitchen.

Charlie's attention refocused on Devin. His hands were at half mast, and he'd taken a step back.

"Easy, man," he said to Sam, his voice surprisingly calm. "None of these people have done a thing to you. Why don't you let me fix you a drink, and we can talk about whatever's bothering you."

Sam pointed the arrangement in Devin's direction.

"This thing's set to go off in exactly twelve minutes. Don't even think of jumping me."

Charlie's heart rate tripled. In a fog she heard Devin attempt to reason.

"Heck, we can even forget this whole episode happened. Come on, man, I'm appealing to your decency. You're holding innocent people hostage and scaring the daylights out of them. These people haven't done a thing to you. Why would you want to hurt them?"

Devin took a step forward. "Why don't you just leave, Sam? Dump the flowers someplace where they can do no harm, and we'll forget this thing ever happened."

"Stay where you are," Sam shouted. His hand wobbled. "Don't come close."

Devin froze. Charlie froze with him.

"Sam," she said, when her tongue finally cooperated. "Sam, why are you doing this to us?"

In tones less aggressive than he'd used with Devin, Sam took his time answering. "You're not that dumb, Charlie. In fact you're very bright. You know exactly why I'm doing this. You've always known. I've loved you for let's see"—he began to count on his fingers—"eighteen-plus years. I've wanted you from the first day I met you. You sat next to me in journalism class, remember? I was the guy whose notes you'd borrow whenever you skipped out to meet him." Sam saw Charlie's puzzled frown. Desperation caused him to sputter. "D-d-don't tell me you d-d-don't remember Bessie Collins? I'm her twin brother, Sam. The guy you gave this to. He reached into his pocket and produced a small penknife. "You gave me this as a birthday present. You said you wanted to thank me for my help."

Chewing on her lower lip, Charlie struggled to remember who'd sat next to her in journalism class. It had been so long. A vague image of an overweight boy surfaced. He'd sat slouched over his desk, hanging on to her every word, though she'd barely said much to him.

"Don't tell me you don't remember me," Sam cried, his voice strident. The flowers wobbled ominously.

"Of course she remembers," Devin quickly interjected. "Heck, even I remember you. You were the nicest guy on campus. Everyone liked you." It was a blatant lie but said out of desperation. It seemed evident that Charlie's doorman was a sick man who needed stroking. He wasn't about to crush the man's already fragile ego and push him further over the edge.

"Liar," Sam screeched. "Liar." His face was beaded in sweat, his eyes wild. "All you jocks hated me. Thought you were somehow better, treated me like dirt." He spat on Charlie's emerald carpet. "She was the only one nice to me," he screamed, pointing at Charlie. "She was the only who seemed to care. Did you even miss me when I didn't come back sophomore year?"

Silence.

"Well, did you?"

"You never gave us an opportunity to know you, man," Devin said softly.

"You never tried getting to know me. I was a nobody. I didn't count," Sam shrieked.

Charlie clutched her Queen Anne chair for support as Sam's tirade continued.

"If I mattered that much, then why was it no one ever came to see me in the hospital? No one even cared."

"Why are you doing this, Sam? What do you hope to accomplish by killing innocent people and killing yourself—"

A loud rap on the front door interrupted Devin's question.

"Don't move," Sam threatened. "You," he said pointing to Charlie, "answer."

"Who's there?" Charlie managed to get out, her voice uncharacteristically squeaky.

Officer Phillips's booming voice filled the room. "Peter O'Reilly and Bob Phillips. We're here for your party."

Charlie's eyes found Devin's. His expression remained blank, though his eyes sent silent messages. "What do I do?" Charlie whispered to Sam.

"Stall them for a moment while I think." Finally, "Just say something. Anything."

Charlie tried to formulate her thoughts, wondering how she could get a coded message through without alerting her doorman. Sam gestured at her, urging her to answer.

"Hold on for a second, guys. I've got my hands full. I'll just set this . . . hot tamale down," she added, in a burst of words. "And I'll be with you in a moment."

"Was that okay?" she whispered to the sweating Sam.

"Fine. It'll buy us time. Okay, everybody, I want you all grouped together. We're having a party. We're supposed to be having fun. No funny stuff now." He patted his pocket. "And just in case one of you gets a brilliant idea to rush me, don't. I've got a gun. Now move."

Grim-faced, Charlie's guests hastened to comply.

"Not you," Sam said as Devin was about to move off. "I want you right next to me. You're goin' act like nothing unusual's happening. You," he said, pointing to one of Charlie's neighbors. "You in the blue shirt. You're goin' be the life of the party. You're goin sit right there." He pointed to the damask couch. "And you're goin' act like you're having a real good time. Don't one of you try anything funny now, or someone's gonna get hurt."

"Kasey, don't you think we should go inside?" Brian asked, his arm draped lightly around her shoulders. "You wouldn't want your mom mad at us, not today of all days. Not when it's her party."

"It's my party, too, in case you forgot. Come to think of it, where's my present?"

"I'm your present," Brian answered, turning her around to face him.

Kasey stood on tiptoe to brush Brian's lips. Her sigh was one of pure frustration. After being cooped up in the hospital for weeks, she hated the idea of being indoors. "I suppose you're right, we should go inside," she reluctantly admitted. "I'd hate to miss Mom's cake and Devin's public proposal." She jutted her jaw in the direction of the apartment, adding, "Hmm, it seems awfully quiet in there. Not like when we have parties." She made a face. "Boy, I hope we never get old."

Brian offered his hand, tugging Kasey along. "We'll pop in for a moment, grab something to drink, make nice-nice, then we're outta there."

They were almost at the patio door when Kasey heard her mother's doorman say, "Don't one of you try anything funny now, or someone's gonna get hurt."

"Wait a minute, Brian," she whispered. "Did you hear what I heard? Sam must have lost his mind. The ornery bastard wasn't even invited—what's he doing making threats?"

Her eyes clashed with Brian's, their thought's crisscrossing.

"Holy —" Brian signaled for Kasey to get behind him. He brought a finger to his lips. "Stay close. I'm going to peek inside and see if I can figure out what's going on." He stuck his head around the open doorway and with a stunned expression turned back to face Kasey. "Your doorman's holding everyone hostage. He claims to have a bomb in a floral arrangement. He's got everyone convinced he has a gun."

Anticipating Kasey's reaction, Brian forcibly held her back. "Babe, you're not going to help your parents any by going off. We've got to come up with a plan."

Kasey waved Devin's cellular at him. She'd already begun dialing. Despite the tension-filled moment, Brian kissed the top of her head. "You're amazing," he said, moving her behind a huge potted plant on the side of the building.

"A tamale?" O'Reilly repeated. "I hate Mexican food."

Phillips shrugged and eyed his partner. "I'm sure that's not all she's serving. Wonder what's taking Canfield so long?"

O'Reilly persisted, "I've never been to a party where tamale's were served. Is Canfield Spanish?"

Phillips groaned—sometimes O'Reilly could be so dense. "Now what kind of a stupid question is that? What's Canfield's nationality got to do with anything? He sniffed and placed an ear on the door. "Seems awfully quiet in there. Strange. No noise. Nothing."

"What's even stranger is that we just waltzed into the building. Isn't there supposed to be a doorman?"

"He's probably at the party. From what I hear, Canfield's no snob—if anything she's too friendly. Still, makes me uncomfortable there's no security." Phillips glanced at his watch. "Hope she hurries up. At the rate it's taking her, by the time we get let in, it'll be time to leave."

Both undercover cops had wheedled an invitation from Charlie. They'd viewed the party as the perfect opportunity to quiz unsuspecting friends and neighbors. Today they'd traded in their sweats and caps for chinos, collarless shirts, and jackets. Clutching brightly wrapped presents, they could easily be mistaken for yuppy puppies.

O'Reilly's cellular rang. He flipped up the antenna and barked, "Yeah— Sorry, can't hear ya. Speak louder." Frowning, he pressed his ear against the phone. "Kasey, where are ya, kid?"

"Let me have that." Phillips grabbed the cell phone away. He walked down the hallway, O'Reilly trailing him. "Hey, Kase, what's up? Why are we out in the hall . . . ?"

"Damn," he said. "We should have had that figured. . . .
We shoulda known she was sending us a message. You
called the precinct? Good. Now listen, I want you to stay
right where you are. You aren't going to do anyone any
good by barging in there—not in a hostage situation. Listen to me carefully. Call the precinct again, tell them where
we are, and tell them to make sure the bomb squad's on
their way. Have them send lots of backup."

Phillips ended the conversation then filled O'Reilly in.
"I feel like such a jerk," he said, slapping his forehead.
"Thank God the kid had the foresight to call. I totally
missed Canfield's clue. Now," he added, "the important
thing is to make sure no one gets hurt. Buddy, you and I
have been in far worse situations."

Both men withdrew guns from holsters. Phillips
dropped his weapon into his jacket pocket. He turned to
O'Reilly and ordered, "Now once Canfield opens that
door, I'll walk in, and you'll follow right behind me. Just
make sure I'm covered."

"Okay, walk slowly toward the door," Sam instructed
Charlie. "We've got six minutes left before this thing goes
off. I want lots of laughter now. Don't any of you make a
wrong move, or I'll blow her head off."

On wooden legs Charlie headed for the entrance. It was
the longest walk in history. Throwing open the front door,
she faced the officers and dutifully offered her cheek for
their kiss.

"Good of you to come, Bob and Pete," she chatted, teeth
chattering simultaneously. "And you've even brought presents, though I told you not to."

Phillips played it like he were an old boyfriend. He
hugged Charlie close and over her shoulder took in the
action. Judging by outward appearances, the party seemed
in full swing, though the scenario seemed rehearsed: the

laughter too forced, the conversation overly bright. Under the gaiety he sensed the tension. He entered the room, O'Reilly close on his heels.

"Won't you sit down?" Charlie motioned toward two vacant folding chairs she had rented.

"In a minute. These are for you." Phillips proffered both gifts.

His eyes scanned the room again, this time he spotted Canfield's parents and fiancé among the crowd. Neither looked particularly happy though lips had been stretched into the requisite smile. Phillips extended a hand to Devin. "So I heard congratulations are in order."

"Thanks."

He noted the tightness in Spencer's voice. The man sounded as if he were choking.

"Devin, can you get the gentlemen something to drink? There's alcohol in the kitchen," Charlie interjected.

"I'd be glad to help," Sam said, making his presence known. One hand remained tucked into the breast pocket of his jacket, the other carried the flowers.

Phillips thought quickly. How could he handle this? Canfield's doorman didn't have a clue they were undercover cops and as yet hadn't revealed his intent. Only two options could even be considered. They could follow the doorman into the kitchen, giving the hostages time to escape and jump Sam, or they could use the moment alone to come up with a plan.

"Why don't you just point us in the direction of the kitchen, and we'll make our own drinks," Phillips suggested.

The doorman actually looked relieved. "You sure?"

"Absolutely."

Nodding at the seated group, Phillips and O'Reilly headed for the kitchen.

Drinks in hand they returned to find Sam at the center of the crowd, his hand still jammed in his breast pocket.

He'd finally set down the flowers. "We haven't officially met," O'Reilly said, sidling up to Sam.

"Neither have we. I'm Bob Phillips," Phillips said, coming up on Sam's other side. "Looks like some party."

"Sam Davis," Sam offered and withdrew the gun from his pocket.

At that exact moment O'Reilly bumped into Sam, and Devin jostled him. Phillips's drink doused the doorman's jacket. The cop pressed his gun into Sam's side and yelled, "Everybody run. Get out of the building quick. Someone take that floral arrangement with you. Dump it in the parking lot. Bomb squad's on their way."

The sound of a shot shattered the silence. Pandemonium erupted as the shrieking crowd charged the exit. Devin carried the flowers.

Twenty-two

"Oh, God!" Charlie shrieked. "Devin, are you all right?"

She watched as Sam's body folded like an accordion onto her once pristine carpet, blood splattering everywhere.

"I'd be lying if I said I was fine," Devin eventually answered. "Wish I could say the same for him." He averted his eyes from Sam's writhing form.

Phillips and O'Reilly put away their guns and bent over the doorman, checking his pulse. The two exchanged glances. O'Reilly hissed a command at the few people that lingered. "Somebody better call an ambulance. Any volunteers?"

The wailing sounds of sirens penetrated the night. Phillips nudged the fallen doorman with his foot then turned away. "Backup's finally here—late but here. I best go talk to them." He headed for the front door and gestured for O'Reilly to stay put, adding, "Not that I particularly care, but he needs to be seen by a doctor, or you'll soon have a stiff on your hands."

"Mom," Kasey cried, bolting toward her mother, Brian steps behind. "Mommy, are you okay? what about Da—," she faltered. "Dev . . . Dad you aren't hurt, are you?" Fascinated yet horrified, Kasey looked at the circles of crimson quickly staining the carpet. "Do you think he'll live?"

The question never got answered. A neighbor stuck his

head through the open doorway. "I'm a doctor," he said. "Some guy went racing down the hallway, cell phone in hand, screaming for an ambulance. Is there something I can do?" Spotting Sam's inert body, he didn't wait for an invitation.

Shortly after the ambulance arrived, and Charlie's apartment was again flooded with people. Fighting the crowd, the paramedics loaded Sam onto a stretcher and hurriedly wheeled him away. He was barely breathing by then.

Once the hubbub had died down, Charlie stayed in the kitchen surrounded by neighbors and friends. She sipped a cup of mint tea that someone had handed her and rehashed the evening's events. It felt good to talk, good to put into words her feelings of despondency and fear. At some point Devin, who'd been in the living room with O'Reilly and Phillips, came to find her.

Primarily for the benefit of the onlookers, he forced a smile. Exhaustion had taken over, and even smiling must be painful. He draped an arm around Charlie's shoulders and kissed her cheek.

"Thank God, it's finally over with," he said, caressing her trembling shoulders. "To think it was your own doorman of all people. Though I must admit the man always galled me. He actually made the hairs on my neck rise . . . guess I must have a second sense or something." His fingers roamed the curls at the nape of her neck.

"You never did like him," Charlie said, touching his cheek.

"That's true, but Tarik was always my prime suspect. Think about it? He was on the cruise ship when we were on. He could have bribed a waiter to deliver that envelope. He could very easily have made those phone calls. And he had access to the Internet. He was also in the area the first time your apartment got broken into."

Charlie interrupted. "And I thought it might be Ellis

Greene. Though I couldn't quite figure how he could call
the station when he was sitting right beside me."

Devin yawned, his hands expertly kneaded Charlie's
back. "And the cops thought it was me. Phillips just got
done telling me that I was the main suspect, that they'd
expected to arrest me before the end of the week. It
seemed strange I had reappeared in your life after a long
absence. Don't forget my fingerprints were all over that
closet. Those two were even convinced that I'd attacked
Kasey. Guess they'd figured me for some kind of animal,
bludgeoning my own daughter."

"I can't believe they suspected you." Marilyn Canfield
sounded genuinely outraged. She handed Devin a cup of
tea. "If you don't like that, I can make you something
stronger."

Devin sipped on the mint-flavored drink then set down
the cup. "Are you about ready?" he asked Charlie. They'd
booked a hotel room for the night, deciding that staying
at the apartment would prove far too traumatic.

"Definitely." She motioned to the living room, where
O'Reilly, Phillips, and a handful of detectives remained.
"Are those guys planning on leaving anytime soon? Think
they'll lock up?"

Devin rolled his eyes. "Wouldn't much matter if they
didn't. The whole neighborhood's crawling with cops. The
last thing you need worry about is anyone breaking in. I
think they're waiting to hear about Sam's background
check. So am I, for that matter. Wonder if the bastard has
a criminal record?"

"It's been confirmed he's certifiable. Hard to believe he
helped himself to your neighbor's floral delivery, just so
he could have an excuse to come by. If he survives, I hope
they lock him up and throw away the key." John Canfield
encircled his granddaughter in his arms. "Especially after
what he did to Kasey." He kissed the top of her head.

Marilyn Canfield's sigh summed up their feelings. It had

been a rough night for all. Her face registered exhaustion, but she smiled anyway. "He certainly put us through enough. I find it amazing, Devin, that you guessed the bomb was a hoax." Wearily she changed the topic. "Kids, why don't we call it a night? John and I have a big house, plenty of space for everyone. Come on, y'all." Her gesture included Brian and Devin.

Devin, though grateful for the offer, diplomatically declined. "Thanks, Mrs. Canfield, but why not take Kasey and Brian with you. I'm sure they could use a good night's sleep. Charlie and I made plans to stay at Ross Liljenquist's place. We need to get a couple of things straight between us. We'll most likely remain until the apartment gets cleaned up."

He took Charlie's hand and led her from the room. "Let's touch base tomorrow. Breakfast is on me."

In their hotel room Devin clutched his chest, feigning pain. "I'm crushed," he said. "You've made all my insecurities resurface. I can't believe you thought I would hurt you." He tilted Charlie's lips up to accept his kiss.

Earlier, in a burst of honesty, Charlie'd expressed both joy and relief when Devin's innocence had been declared. Able to breathe again, she admitted, "Well, the thought did kind of cross my mind that you might be in some way responsible."

He scowled, playfully swatting her bottom. "Mind telling me how you came to that conclusion?"

Charlie hesitated a moment then decided to come clean. "I'd overheard a conversation on the ship between you and some man. Weeks later the same man called you at my apartment, and I sort of listened in on the conversation."

"Sort of?" Devin's smile took the sting out of his words.

"I couldn't help myself. Both times he called looking

for money, urged you to pay up. I thought maybe you'd turned into a deadbeat. When I overheard him talking about the job he'd done on the apartment—well, I didn't know what to think—especially coming right after the break-in at my apartment."

"And when you asked me about it, I sort of blew you off. Oh, Charlie, I could have saved you so much heartache if I'd just been up front." Devin hugged her. "I'd hired this man to renovate my ex-girlfriend's apartment. I didn't want her to know I was behind it, so I'd worked something out with the building's management to make it appear that they were the ones renovating the place."

"Jennifer's apartment?" Charlie repeated, giving him a puzzled frown. "Why would you do something like that?"

"Guilt, I guess. She'd grown used to a comfortable life-style. We'd been together for a while. The breakup was a major shock to her. Since Jennifer doesn't make a lot of money, I felt the least I could do was ensure she lived in relative comfort."

"Oh, Devin, why didn't you just tell me what you were doing?"

Devin laced his fingers through hers and pulled her down to sit with him on the bed. No longer the supercool charmer, he smiled tentatively. His voice sounding more like the vulnerable boy she remembered, he continued. "I didn't think you'd understand. I'd reappeared in your life after a long absence. We were just starting to get to know each other again. I couldn't just spring it on you that I was paying someone to fix up an ex-girlfriend's apartment. What would you have thought?"

Charlie squeezed his fingers. "That you were very sweet. But, Devin, why was the man so persistent? Didn't you pay him?"

He shot her a startled look, then reassured by her smile, plunged on. "Of course I paid him. He was just one of these persistent little buggers who'd finish a job and expect to have check in hand before the last nail was in place. When he called my office and found out I was on a cruise, he panicked—thought he wouldn't get paid. Somehow he managed to con my secretary into telling him the name of the cruise line. Then he called their executive offices and obtained the ship's satellite number. When he called me, you and I were just starting to work things out. I was reluctant to involve you in my problems. Truth is, I didn't know if you'd understand why I was doing what I was doing."

Charlie wrapped her arms around Devin's waist and pressed her face into his chest. "You should have trusted me," she said, breathing in the refreshing smell of citrus.

He chuckled and kissed her forehead. "Yeah. Like you trusted me."

A week later Devin, Charlie, and Kasey were seated on the patio, sipping iced tea.

"God, it feels good to be finally free of that man," Charlie said, admiring her little garden and the amazing transformation that it had undergone. Pots of colorful impatiens and begonias had replaced spring blooms, and budding rosebushes filled previously empty corners.

"What I don't understand"—Devin took Charlie's hand and brought her fingers to his lips—"is why a man as sick as Sam Davis was ever allowed out of the hospital. Even the records show that as a teenager he'd been diagnosed a paranoid schizophrenic. The man spent sixteen years in a sanatorium, for crying out loud. He was treated for irrational mood swings but remained unresponsive to medication. Then some hot-shot doctor comes along, decides he's cured, and presto he's free."

"It's kind of sad though," Charlie added. "He must have led a lonely life. Bessie basically gave up on him. The cops said they hadn't been in touch in years, not until Sam

learned about the Mount Merrimack reunion on the Internet. Since he couldn't afford to go, he pleaded with
her to give me those messages. The first one she handed
to a waiter, the other . . . well, you know the story. Bessie
hadn't a clue what they contained."

"Oh, Mom," Kasey wailed, "why are we rehashing this
sorry story? I don't feel one bit sad for that mean man.
I'm glad he died on the way to the hospital. If you ask me,
Bob Phillips did the world a favor when he accidentally
shot that sleazeball."

"Now, Kasey, let's not speak ill of the dead," Devin said,
rising and bringing Charlie up with him. He lifted her off
the chair, lowered her onto his lap, resumed his seat, and
kissed the top of her head.

After Charlie settled, Devin continued. "You know
what's even sadder? Here's a really bright guy, at least that's
what his college transcripts say. He'd been labeled a genius—wanted to be an engineer. A real whiz at electronics.
That's how he knew how to hook up the device in the
bathroom that damn near scared you to death. He surfed
the Internet, calling himself Sivad Man, Davis spelled backward. He'd changed his last name. Anyway, because of an
illness, he ends up serving no useful purpose to society.
Even in this so-called enlightened age, Sam's medical condition prevented him from holding down a good job. It's
tragic really—employers don't want to touch anyone with
emotional problems. What I still find difficult to believe is
that he's been keeping track of you ever since college."
Devin's voice sounded whimsical. "Wonder what made
him nosedive over the edge?"

Charlie sipped her iced tea. "The cops claim he'd actually erected a shrine to me in his apartment. It held
newspaper clippings, photos, and scraps of memora-
bilia—anything about me he could get his hands on. He'd
created this idea in his mind that he and I had something
going. That it was only a matter of time before our rela-

tionship got off the ground. He'd hoped the cruise would do it. When Bessie turned him down, and he realized he would not have the money to go, he grew angry. That anger became focused on you and me when he called Bessie and learned you were on board."

"Must we talk about this?" Kasey wailed. She checked her watch, set down the half-empty glass of iced tea, and said, "I gotta get going. I've got a date with Peter."

Devin's scowl didn't seem to scare his daughter. "This wouldn't be Peter O'Reilly?" he asked.

Kasey was already halfway across the patio when she answered, "Yup. See you."

"Isn't he too old . . . ?"

Charlie rolled her eyes. "I warned you, you'd have your hands full."

Devin chuckled and bent his head to claim her lips. "Wouldn't have it any other way." When he finally allowed her to surface for air, he added, "Now are you convinced I'm over Jennifer?"

Devin had told Charlie all about his ex-girlfriend and the problems he'd had after they'd broken up. Jennifer had refused to let go, and had gotten ugly after he'd asked her to move out. Though Devin had helped her find the apartment, and secretly financed the renovation, that hadn't been good enough. She'd rewarded his largesse by spreading ugly rumors.

The gossip had somehow reached Tarik, who'd deliberately twisted the story to suit his own purpose. There'd never been a restraining order against Devin. Other than a few painfully ugly scenes, Jennifer had never filed suit against Devin. Tarik had made up the whole sordid business.

"So," Devin asked, "how did it go over when you told Tarik you were leaving town?"

Charlie wrinkled her nose, remembering how the scene had played out. "He wasn't too happy. But from what he told me, he might be moving out-of-state as well. One can only hope he doesn't choose San Diego." The last was said tongue-in-cheek.

Charlie caught the startled expression on Devin's face and quickly reassured him. "My love, I don't think he's going to be able to afford the West Coast. He was laid off from his job, or so he says. My guess is, he was probably fired. I imagine he saw it coming—hence the investment schemes he kept cooking up. Anyway I think he's looking to relocate to Florida or the Carolinas. Someplace where the cost of living's less steep, and rental property's affordable."

"What about Ellis—how did he react when you told him you were leaving? You more or less handed him the show."

Charlie chortled. She truly enjoyed telling this particular story. "When I gave my notice, the producers decided that Ellis couldn't carry the show on his own. They also didn't want to risk another Karen Hardy situation. You do know she's suing the station for placing her in a compromising situation. And she's suing Ellis for sexual harassment. Management doesn't want to deal with the bad press. It's certainly not going to help the station, so they paid Ellis a handsome sum and accepted his resignation."

"Then everything worked out in the end, Ms. Canfield," Devin said, shifting his seat and turning Charlie around to face him. He stared into those huge brown eyes before pulling her up against his chest. "My life's finally perfect now that I've got you, baby. Really we should count our blessings. The apartment's sold. I'm starting to get to know my daughter, and you and I are on our way to San Diego."

"Ah. Ah, Mr. Spencer, not so fast." Charlie waggled a finger at him. "You promised me a wonderful wedding complete with reception and exotic honeymoon. It's time to pay up."

Devin's dimples were prominent slashes. His gray eyes sparkled when he answered, "I aim to please, my love.

How does Cupid's Lair sound for the wedding and reception? The honeymoon, let's see . . ."

"A cruise," both said at the same time. "Aboard *The Machination*."

Epilogue

"Mr. and Mrs. Spencer, I'm here to show you to your penthouse." The cruise line's pretty social hostess shook their hands, then led Charlie and Devin down a long hallway. Without looking around, she spoke again. "Is this your first time with us?" Getting no immediate response, she looked over her shoulder.

The couple lagged several feet behind. The man had a lip-lock on the woman like there was no tomorrow. The hostess cleared her throat. "Excuse me," she said. Cheeks flaming, she stifled a giggle.

Devin caught the woman's amused look as he surfaced from the kiss. He'd been unable to keep his hands off Charlie even for a few seconds.

"Sorry, we're coming." Reluctantly he let Charlie go.

Two more winding corridors later, their hostess stopped before the penthouse door. A discreet brass sign indicated AMBROSIA. Appearing anxious to leave them, she handed over their key then asked, "Would you like me to come in with you and show you how everything works? TV, VCR, Jacuzzi tub . . ."

"That won't be necessary," Devin said too quickly, hoping the woman would just go. She'd been nice enough, but now he wanted to be alone with Charlie.

"Well, if you need anything, just ring your cabin steward. And if you have a special request, our guest relations manager will be happy to help you. Luggage should be delivered shortly."

Charlie tugged on Devin's hand and smiled sweetly at their hostess. "Thanks, you've been very kind." Sotto voce she added, "Are we supposed to tip her?"

Devin gave an almost imperceptible shake of his head. He'd already unlocked the door and was halfway in. "Thanks for bringing us here." Over his shoulder he added, "I'm sure we won't be needing a thing. In fact I'm very sure. I've got everything I need right here." In the doorway he kissed Charlie then closed the door on his hostess's open mouth.

Charlie hovered on the threshold, drinking in the scene. "Oh, my God, Devin, this is breathtaking," she gasped, gazing at the opulent penthouse, the abundance of burgundy leather and rich brass sconces, and the oversized floral arrangement with the cream-colored card stuck in the center. "This suite must have cost you a fortune" She stared at pieces that just had to be genuine antiques.

Side-stepping the question, Devin said smoothly, "Glad it meets your approval, madam." He bowed low, making a reverent gesture with his hand. "Like I've always told you, I aim to please. Now just to fill you in, this here's the owner's suite." He affected a southern accent. "He's a collector, in case you couldn't guess." He blocked her path, denying her further access. "Now don't you dare take another step, not if we're going to start this honeymoon off right." With that he swept her into his arms, lifting her across the threshold.

Outside on the balcony Devin deposited Charlie onto a wooden lounge chair, and plucked from a silver bucket a chilled bottle of Perrier Jouet. He popped the cork, poured the contents into two glasses, and handed Charlie hers. "To us," he said, raising his flute then clinking glasses. "May we enjoy a long and happy life together." He took the seat adjoining hers.

Charlie sipped on the bubbly while looking out on the port of Miami. The ocean was so blue, it literally took her breath away. A distinct smell of salt and sun lingered in the air. Small boats bobbed on the crests of frothy waves. Close to shore jet skis whizzed by, carrying minuscule passengers, and across the bay tiny islands were home to the rich and famous, or so she'd been told.

Looking Devin directly in the eye, she raised her glass, adding, "One tiny correction. May we enjoy a long, happy, and fruitful life." She clinked their glasses.

"Uh, uh. Does that mean babies?" Devin seemed startled.

"It's something we haven't talked about."

She was right—they hadn't discussed additions to their little family. He was curious to hear Charlie's response.

"How do you feel about having a baby in your late thirties?" He sucked in his breath, awaiting her answer.

Charlie chose her words carefully. She wanted to be sure she said the right thing. In all their talks, Devin had never expressed a preference one way or the other. "Well, I do feel guilty that you missed seeing Kasey grow up." She reached for his hand, the balls of her fingers caressing his knuckles. "But I'm not sure I want a baby right off. I mean, we'll need to get settled. Considering I'm starting a new job and all, I'd like to wait at least a year. But the answer is a most definite yes. I'd love to have your baby."

After considering several job offers, Charlie'd accepted a position as talk show host at a small radio station on the outskirts of San Diego. Granted, her broadcast would be at an off hour, but at least she'd gotten her own show.

Feelings of excitement bubbled within Devin. He expelled the breath he'd been holding with a loud whoosh of air. "Jeez, baby, that feels so good to hear. Even at my advanced age, I think I'd like being a father . . . again," he added.

"Then what are we waiting for?" Charlie set down her

glass and stood up. "Don't you think we need to practice?" She crooked a finger and with a seductive wiggle, headed inside.

The lovemaking that followed was slow, sweet, and filled with promise. Afterward they lay in each other's arms, listening to the ship's whistle, and the passengers shouted excitement.

"I love you, Mrs. Spencer," Devin whispered, holding Charlie close and nibbling on her ear.

Charlie sighed contentedly, buried her head in Devin's chest, and let the scent of citrus wash over her. "Not as much as I love you, Mr. Spencer."

Dear Reader:

I hope that you enjoyed reading Remembrance as much as I loved writing it. I must admit that when I ended this novel Devin and Charlie had captured bits of my heart. If you feel the same way, please write to me in care of Kensington/Arabesque.

Thanks for your support and do look out for my next novel scheduled for release sometime next year.

Marcia King Gamble

Biography

Marcia King-Gamble was born on the island of St. Vincent in the West Indies. At age fifteen she relocated to the United States, and has since lived in New York, New Jersey, and Seattle. Currently she resides in Florida. Marcia is a graduate of Elmira College and holds a Bachelor's degree in psychology and theater. Currently she is pursuing a Master's degree in communications. Although Marcia started off as an international flight attendant, she has since held several management positions within the travel industry. Her speciality is quality assurance and guest services. Business and leisure travel have afforded her the opportunity to see the world and experience diversity in its true sense. She currently holds an executive position with a major cruise line.

When she is not working, writing, or globe-trotting, Marcia serves on the executive board of the Society of Consumer Affairs Professionals in Business. She is president of the Florida chapter and has a byline in their newsletter. Quite recently Marcia received an honorable mention from the judges of the "Love In Uniform" contest for her completed manuscript, Jumpshot.

Despite Marcia's many commitments she makes time for step aerobics and fund-raising.

Look for these upcoming Arabesque titles:

May 1998

LOVE EVERLASTING by Anna Larence
TWIST OF FATE by Loure Bussey
ROSES ARE RED by Sonia Seerani
BOUQUET, An Arabesque
Mother's Day Collection

June 1998

MIRROR IMAGE by Shirley Hailstock
WORTH WAITING FOR by Roberta Gayle
HIDDEN BLESSINGS by Jacquelin Thomas
MAN OF THE HOUSE, An Arabesque
Father's Day Collection

July 1998

HEAVEN SENT by Rochelle Alers
LYRICS OF LOVE by Francine Craft
BLUE VELVET by Monica Jackson
EVERLASTING LOVE by Kayla Perrin

BOOK YOUR PLACE ON OUR WEBSITE AND MAKE THE READING CONNECTION!

We've created a customized website just for our very special readers, where you can get the inside scoop on everything that's going on with Zebra, Pinnacle and Kensington books.

When you come online, you'll have the exciting opportunity to:

- View covers of upcoming books
- Read sample chapters
- Learn about our future publishing schedule (listed by publication month *and author*)
- Find out when your favorite authors will be visiting a city near you
- Search for and order backlist books from our online catalog
- Check out author bios and background information
- Send e-mail to your favorite authors
- Meet the Kensington staff online
- Join us in weekly chats with authors, readers and other guests
- Get writing guidelines
- AND MUCH MORE!

**Visit our website at
http://www.pinnaclebooks.com**

ENJOY THESE ARABESQUE FAVORITES!

FOREVER AFTER   (0-7860-0211-5, $4.99)
by Bette Ford

BODY AND SOUL   (0-7860-0160-7, $4.99)
by Felicia Mason

BETWEEN THE LINES   (0-7860-0267-0, $4.99)
by Angela Benson

Available wherever paperbacks are sold, or order direct from the Publisher. Send cover price plus 50¢ per copy for mailing and handling to Kensington Publishing Corp., Consumer Orders, or call (toll free) 888-345-BOOK, to place your order using Mastercard or Visa. Residents of New York and Tennessee must include sales tax. DO NOT SEND CASH.

SENSUAL AND HEARTWARMING
ARABESQUE ROMANCES FEATURE
AFRICAN-AMERICAN CHARACTERS!

BEGUILED (0046, $4.99)
by Eboni Snoe

After Raquel agrees to impersonate a missing heiress for just one night, a daring abduction makes her the captive of seductive Nate Bowman. Across the exotic Caribbean seas to the perilous wilds of Central America . . . and into the savage heart of desire, Nate and Raquel play a dangerous game. But soon the masquerade will be over. And will they then lose the one thing that matters most . . . their love?

WHISPERS OF LOVE (0055, $4.99)
by Shirley Hailstock

Robyn Richards had to fake her own death, change her identity, and forever forsake her husband, Grant, after testifying against a crime syndicate. But, five years later, the daughter born after her disappearance is in need of help only Grant can give. Can Robyn maintain her disguise from the ever present threat of the syndicate—and can she keep herself from falling in love all over again?

HAPPILY EVER AFTER (0064, $4.99)
by Rochelle Alers

In a week's time, Lauren Taylor fell madly in love with famed author Cal Samuels and impulsively agreed to be his wife. But when she abruptly left him, it was for reasons she dared not express. Five years later, Cal is back, and the flames of desire are as hot as ever, but, can they start over again and make it work this time?